MW01205014

Dirty Little
SECRETS

To: Susan,
I hope you enjoy the
Story. Thanks for
your support.

[signature]

DIRTY LITTLE
SECRETS

JOHN P. CHAMPLIN

TATE PUBLISHING *& Enterprises*

Published by Tate Publishing & Enterprises, LLC
127 E. Trade Center Terrace | Mustang, Oklahoma 73064 USA
1.888.361.9473 | www.tatepublishing.com

Tate Publishing is committed to excellence in the publishing industry. The company reflects the philosophy established by the founders, based on Psalms 68:11,
"The Lord gave the word and great was the company of those who published it."

Book design copyright © 2007 by Tate Publishing, LLC. All rights reserved.
Cover design by Jennifer L. Fisher
Interior design by Lynly D. Taylor

Published in the United States of America

ISBN: 978-1-6024735-8-4
1. Crime   2. Adventure

07.07.25

This book is dedicated to my mother, D. Ruth Burr Champlin, her brothers and sister. The Burr's had a very strong faith in God, Family and Education. They touched many young minds through teaching. I thank them for providing me a very basic set of priorities for living life evidenced by their daily walk. With much love and respect I thank each one.

Table of Contents

Preface

My name is Philadelphia (Phil) Alan Storm. Once discharged from the U.S. Navy I found myself with a pocket full of money and no direction. After failing to complete the police officer candidate program I lucked into a job that fit me perfectly. Being a private investigator allows me to work alone. That fits my personality. It exposes me to a wide variety of people for short periods of time, which minimizes long-term relationships.

That quirk in my character allows me to be successful in my professional life but somewhat of a failure as an individual. I make friends easily but when it comes to relationships I struggle. I consider life like a Banana Peel. I can walk around it if I keep each step in perspective and during those times I soar with Eagles. Or I can place my foot on the banana peel and slip perfectly. I have slipped more times than I like to admit but being able to soften my fall by knowing the worth of soaring once again keeps me in the game.

1

This story begins in the spring of 1945. With my Navy career behind me, a bankroll thanks to my Navy separation pay, I set out to discover what my future held. As I stepped off of the bus in Manhattan I was hit in the face with the most beautiful day I could remember. There was a breeze blowing, the sun was rising and there wasn't a cloud in the sky. Looking up into the sun as it bounced off of the Manhattan landscape gave the morning a blush colored tone.

Before we go forward let me provide you some background on Phil Storm. I was born Philadelphia (yes just like the city) Alan Storm, on February 29, 1920 in Manhattan, New York. Yes, I am a leap year baby. When my mother became pregnant she knew I would be a Nobel Prize winning child. I know that because she gave me a first name that required a first grade student to spell at a fifth grade level. I was fortunate that everyone but my mother called me Phil. A first grader could spell Phil. My middle name is the first name of my absentee father. This was my mother's way of ensuring I would always remember something about my father.

As a young man I was fascinated with police officers. What fascinated me was their uncanny ability to take scraps of information, sometimes microscopic in size, and locate a lawbreaker! I wasn't classified as a lawbreaker but being with friends at the wrong time did bring police officers to our home.

Having police officers visit my home was uncomfortable but what was worse was when my mother would call me from my bedroom, "Philadelphia come explain yourself to this police officer?" She just wouldn't call me Phil.

With high school behind me I searched for the perfect job but in the end all I found was a variety of dead end jobs. Then on November 7, 1941 I knew who my next employer would be. I enlisted in the U. S. Navy. While growing up I had watched ships enter and leave the New

York Harbor. I would try to guess where each ship was going and what it would be like seeing the world as a crewmember.

Two weeks after enlisting in the Navy I was off to Recruit Training at the Naval Recruit Training Center at Great Lakes, Illinois, just outside Chicago. All of the recruits boarded a train at Grand Central Station. I had never been anywhere except the various boroughs that made up the City. This was going to be my first opportunity to see other cities and states. I was excited with the thought of seeing the world.

When we boarded the train we were assigned a specific train car and seat. I had a window seat. For the first several hours my nose was attached to it absorbing everything that could be seen. I didn't know any of the other recruits so I was pleased with my window seat. There were two men seated beside me. I did determine they were from Brooklyn and they knew each other.

As the darkness began to replace the light our train car became quiet. The night was like magic to me. At first I could see the moon, stars and the lights from passing towns. Then the moon and stars disappeared as the sky was covered with clouds. I had never seen anything so black. In the City if clouds covered the stars and moon there was always light from buildings and streetlights. The only noise was the clattering of the train's wheels against the tracks. I couldn't allow myself to dose off. I felt insecure and alone in the darkness.

I did fall asleep because my dark world changed into a cloudless day. The first thing I noticed when I awoke was the young man seated beside me. He was carving designs in his wooden seat with a pocketknife.

By the time we arrived in Chicago he had very little seat left. He had also carved most of his friend's seat. I was afraid their seats would give way under their weight.

When we arrived in Chicago we were placed on buses for the trip to the Recruit Training Center.

Upon completing recruit training I received orders assigning me to the aircraft carrier, USS Franklin (CV-13). It was moored at the U.S. Naval Base, Alameda, California.

Once I had reported aboard the Franklin I was assigned to "G" Division. The men assigned to "G" Division handled the ordinance stored aboard the ship. When the various bombs, rockets, missiles or flares were to be moved to the Flight deck or Hanger deck "G" Division positioned them. Then the AirWing would spot them and load them on their aircraft.

The work was demanding and very physical. I enjoyed moving the ordinance to the flight deck. It gave me an opportunity to see the day and get a breath of fresh air. This particular job would not offer me many civilian opportunities other than ensuring that I would be in great physical condition.

Then on March 19, 1945 the thing that every sailor dreads happened. My crew was on the flight deck behind the Island (the superstructure where the ship is controlled).

A single Japanese airplane was spotted heading for our ship. That one Japanese airplane managed to drop two armor-piercing bombs. They penetrated the flight deck and exploded on the hangar deck. The hangar deck was covered with ordnance. The explosion that followed was devastating.

When the smoke cleared it was determined that 724 sailors were killed and 265 wounded. It was a horrible sight. There were dead or seriously wounded men everywhere.

Once the fires were under control and it was determined that the ship was going to remain afloat the Commanding Officer turned the ship's communication system on. Then he said, "All of us that have survived the Franklin's day of disaster have a common kinship forever more. It will be known as 'The Franklin Feeling.'

"It is that feeling that kept our ship afloat and saved our lives this day. As long as you are alive you will never be alone. If tragedy ever strikes you will know you are walking through it with your Franklin kinsmen." Always remember 'The Franklin Feeling.'

The reason I wasn't hurt or killed was because I was on the flight deck.

When The Franklin made port it's crew were relieved of duty and sent stateside. Each man was given the option of discharge or reassignment to stateside duty.

I chose to be discharged. I received my discharge on April 15, 1945. I was on my way home. The War and the Navy were behind me. Today I know what freedom is. It is my right to make choices. Many men and women gave their lives so I can enjoy freedom. I will never take freedom for granted nor forget the American's that provided it.

It was ten a.m. when I arrived at my mother's apartment. With a knock on her door the thoughts of yesterday returned. Prior to my enlistment in the Navy I lived at home but once I had graduated from high school I found it difficult to live by my mother's rules. That caused problems between us. During those days I could sense our living together had to come to an end. My current situation is rather the same. I am again knocking on her door asking for a place to live. As she opened the door those thoughts left my mind as she gave me a hug and a kiss. It was good to see her. Once we had visited for a few hours mother went to bed. She works the night shift cleaning office buildings.

I found living with my mother different than before. I appreciated her letting me stay. I knew it shouldn't last any longer than necessary. We both needed our own space. Finding a job was my top priority.

One day while reading the classified ads I came across an ad that read, "New York City is looking for police officers." As I read the headlines the item that stood out was the word "Officer." I quickly remembered how well Naval Officers were treated. So I decided to apply.

When I arrived at the address I found a sign that read, "Police Officer Candidates stop here for instructions." At the desk was a young lady. She looked familiar. Then I heard her say, "Phil Storm?" I said, "Yes." "Gayle Simpson?" She said, "Yes. I haven't seen you since high school. What have you been doing?"

I told her I had joined the Navy the day Pearl Harbor was attacked and I had just been discharged.

While we were talking three men walked up behind me. Gayle said, "Phil, I have to return to work but do you ever attend any of the USO functions?" "No." "I volunteer there three nights a week. I will be their tonight by seven, why don't you come by so we can talk." "All right. I'll see you tonight." She then handed me an application to complete.

Once I had completed the application I returned it to Gayle. She then instructed me to go to room 223 and wait.

In ten minutes a man approached me and asked me to follow him. We walked into a room with a desk and two chairs. The man asked me to be seated as he identified himself as a police-training officer. He then began asking me questions. Where did I grow up, what school did I attend and then he spent about twenty minutes asking me about my Navy experiences. I told him of my assignment aboard the USS Franklin and the day she took two direct hits from a Japanese bomber. He looked at me and said, "Sir I am very proud of you."

I was accepted into the police officer candidate program. That was exciting but I was more excited about seeing Gayle again. Here is a girl that was "Miss Everything" in high school. We didn't run in the same circles not even close. If she hadn't recognized me and spoke I wouldn't have said anything to her. I remember she was chosen as the girl "Most Likely to Succeed." I was chosen the "Luckiest boy to graduate." We were worlds apart.

I arrived at the USO at seven p.m. It didn't take me long to locate Gayle. She approached me with a soda in her hand. We walked to a table and sat down. She began asking me questions about my life since high school. Since the Navy was my only highlight I told her of my travels and about the Franklin being bombed. She hung on every word. She was still as beautiful as ever. Then I told her about the "Franklin Feeling." She asked me to explain it. So I did. Once I had finished she placed her arm around me and hugged me. I thought I was going to pass out.

Then I asked her to tell me about her life. She began by telling me she had enrolled in college after high school. When the War began she left school and returned to the City and took a job in her Uncle's Accounting Firm. Then a few months ago her uncle died, his business began to have financial problems and she left the Firm.

She currently is enrolled at New York University as a part time student and is working for the Police Department. That brought us both up to date.

The USO became very busy. She indicated she had to return to her volunteer duties but before she left she told me that she and some friends were going to Coney Island tomorrow. She asked me to join them. She provided me the place and time to meet. At first I told her I couldn't join them. Then she said, "It will be fun spending the day together." That comment closed the deal. I told her I would go.

The day at Coney Island was great. Gayle seemed to enjoy being with me. As we walked from ride to ride she held my hand. I was on top of the world. I could get use to holding her hand on a steady basis. When the day was over and we had returned to Manhattan I asked her if she would like to go to a movie sometime?

She gave me a puzzling look. Then she dropped the bomb. "I am unofficially engaged to Nathan Berry. He is a lieutenant in the Army Air Corps. It is unofficial because he hasn't given me a ring yet." I said, "That's great. I remember him. He's a great guy." With a large lump in my throat and a knife in my heart I told her it had been a great day and I thanked her for inviting me. We then parted company. I should have known some things never change. She and I still do not run in the same circles. I will remember today. It will be the day I almost made it to the upper class.

When I reported for the police officer training it reminded me of the Navy. We were taken to a large room and told to line up in alphabetical order by the first letter of our last name.

A training officer came into the room. He introduced himself and said, "The City of New York and the United States government are proud of each of you. As a representative of the State of New York I want to thank each one of you for your service to our great Nation." The sixty men in this class are all veterans.

One of the first things I noticed about the police training was the amount of classroom studies. The classroom studies were very difficult for me. The physical part of the training was easy. I was finding it difficult to keep up with the written assignments. So four weeks into the training I dropped out.

Leaving the police academy was much harder on me than I had anticipated. I wandered the streets of the City for the next three weeks. I was very aware that my Navy savings were running low. Christmas would be here soon and I didn't have a job.

I could tell my leaving the police candidate program troubled my mother also. It hurt me as I watched her leave for work each night. Her work hours were from eleven p.m. until seven a.m. I would set my alarm clock so I would be out of the apartment prior to her arriving home from work.

My daily schedule became walking to the neighborhood Newsstand to purchase a newspaper and then to the local pool hall to read the classifieds. While reading the classifieds one day I came across an ad that read: "Investigator Wanted." As I looked at that ad I said, "That looks like something interesting." The more time I spent thinking about the ad the more I wanted that job.

I decided to apply for it. When I arrived at the address I immediately began to feel sick. I didn't have any experience as an investigator. With that thought still fresh in my mind the door opened and a young woman asked me to enter. She gave me an application to complete. It had the same old questions.

I completed the application and returned it to the young lady. She took it and disappeared into another room.

She was young and attractive. She had a look of happiness in her large brown eyes.

In a few minutes she returned and asked me to follow her. I would have followed her anywhere. We walked into a room where a man was seated behind a desk.

After sitting in front of him for what seemed like an eternity he asked? "Why did you apply for this job? Show me your investigator experience?"

I looked at him and said, "I know I can do you a good job."

"You know you can do a good job? You have no investigation experience and you haven't even asked me to explain the type of investigations I accomplish? Don't you wonder about an investigator's job assignments? I felt like an idiot.

So I looked him in the eye and said, "Sir what type of investigations are you involved in? Will you explain an investigator's job duties?"

He looked at me with a half smile and said, "Most of my investigations delve into people's most private issues. These are the items that they don't want anyone to know about. At least fifty-percent of the individuals I am involved with do not like me nor do they welcome me. The other fifty-percent pays my salary.

"The best investigators are women but because of the hours required of this work and the places I send investigators I can't make myself hire women. In my opinion women have an inbreed sense of how to discover the most personal information about a person and how to convince that person to talk about it without making them angry. Do you think you could do that?"

I looked him straight in the eye and said, "Yes I can."

"Do you have any problem working whatever schedule the case calls for?"

"I will work whatever it takes."

"My name is Russell Alberson but everyone calls me Abe. I'm going to hire you because of your police academy training and because you are a veteran."

Abe looked at my application and said, "Phil, I want to tell you my golden rule. Case information is to be kept secret. You tell no one but me. I will then decide if anyone else has a need to know. I repeat, you never tell or trust case information to anyone but me. Understood?"

I said, "I understand."

He continued, "You will have women offer you anything if they think you have information they want. Men will do the same but not as often. You must always remember that while you work for me it is required that you follow my rules. In time you will see the importance in that. Phil, if you disobey my rules there is a price to pay and that experience will not be good for either one of us. The last item I have to share with you is that clients and employees are people you never get personally involved with."

I began working with Abe the next day. Working with Abe was great. He gave me every opportunity to learn the business. From my perspective Abe and I were perfect partners. I always remembered he was the boss.

I learned that the pretty young lady that provided me with my application was Jamie. Abe called her his right arm; she ran the office. She knew exactly how to handle Abe. I didn't have any interaction with her. Abe assigned my work and if I had questions he answered them. I would say hello to her when I entered the office and good bye when leaving.

Now that I had a job it was time to find my own home. I withdrew the remainder of my Navy separation pay and began looking for a place to live. What I found wasn't much but it was mine. It was a four-room flat in the Bronx. Only three rooms were furnished: the kitchen, living room and one bedroom. The bathroom set next to the unfurnished room.

My life as a civilian was taking shape. I finally had a job with a future and my own place. I liked Abe and he seemed to like me.

Then came the day that changed my life forever. For the first time I would face the death of a close friend. I was going to call on skills I wasn't sure I possessed. I had been on surveillance all night following a man who was having an affair with his wife's sister. I had remained on stakeout until this man had left his mistress's house.

It was three thirty a.m. when I arrived at home. I fell in bed immediately. I was sleeping soundly when my telephone began ringing. I remember rolling over and looking at the telephone thinking about not answering it, but it would not quit ringing.

When I answered the telephone I was about to tell the person, "I'm not interested" when I recognized the voice. It was Jamie. She said, "Phil something terrible has happened. Abe is dead."

I couldn't believe what I had heard. I said, "Will you repeat what you just said?"

"Phil, Abe is dead."

I held the telephone to my ear but I couldn't think of a thing to say. "Where are you Jamie?"

"I'm at the office."

I'm on my way. As I dressed I felt like a heel. I hadn't even asked what had happened to Abe. Abe dead! What happened? Why?

2

When I arrived at the office there was two police officers standing by Jamie's desk speaking with her. She looked hallow. As I approached her one of the police officers asked, "Who are you?"

I said, "I am Abe's partner." That was better than telling him I was Abe's hired hand.

The police officer said, "Come with me we need to discuss this situation."

"Give me a minute to speak with Jamie."

"You need to be quick we don't have all day." I looked at him and thought what an uncaring bonehead he is. Of course this is just another case to him. He didn't know Abe. His impersonal behavior told me he would wait as long as I wanted him to.

I approached Jamie and asked, "What happened?"

"Come with me."

I followed her to Abe's office. I looked in and became weak in the knees. Abe was just sitting there. Jamie said, "The coroner has not arrived." Abe looked like he was asleep. I looked at Jamie. She is a very pretty young lady but her beauty was being overshadowed by what she had found in Abe's office. There was no smile or look of confidence. I saw a scared and helpless young lady; I felt sorry for her. Once I had seen Abe's body I wasn't as confident as I had been earlier. This situation had my head spinning. My very first thought after arriving at the office was sadness.

Then my emotion tuned to self-pity. How could Abe do this to Jamie and me? How dare him do this to us! For the first time I had to reach down inside of me and realize I am a Franklin survivor; I do not walk alone. I came through that disaster I will survive this one also.

I asked Jamie again, "What happened?"

"When I arrived at the office I saw him in his office. I stepped in to say good morning and he was dead.

The coroner arrived. He performed an on site examination. I asked him, "What is your initial finding?"

"It looks like a death from natural causes. I will know more once I have preformed the autopsy." I thought as healthy as Abe appeared, what could have happened?

I should talk with the police officers but I found myself wanting to continue talking with Jamie. Since Abe's office was empty I asked her to join me there. "Was Abe working on anything other than the Burgess case?"

"No. That is the only case we have. Phil, look at this note. It has what looks like someone's initials and a meeting time?"

Jamie handed me the note. It said, "SLCR meeting Tuesday morning, eleven thirty a.m."

"What do you know about this note?"

She said, "Nothing."

"Since it is nine thirty Tuesday morning this meeting will not take place. Jamie, I need to speak with the police officers." She returned to her desk.

I left Abe's office and returned to where the police officers were standing. They asked me about our clients and the nature of the case Abe was working at the time of his death. I told the officers that currently we only had one client. Abe was handling the case during the day and I was handling the investigation at night. The case is a routine case of infidelity. A married man is having an affair with his wife's sister. The officers asked me to provide them our client's name. I told them that was confidential; they accepted my answer and left.

Jamie was still sitting at her desk. I walked over to her and said, "Lady, go home. Now that the police have left I will contact the coroner and determine when Abe's body will be released."

As she was about to leave I asked, "Do you know anything about Abe's next of kin?"

She looked at me and said, "Abe told me if anything happened to him it would be up to me to handle his final arrangements." Then she began to cry.

"Just go home."

Once Jamie had left I called the coroner's office to see when Abe's body would be released. The lady that answered the telephone said, "I would have to call tomorrow for that information?" I thanked her and ended the call.

As I sat in Abe's swivel chair spinning around I realized except for work related items Abe was a total stranger. I didn't know where he lived, where he banked, whom he owed or his next of kin.

I felt totally overwhelmed. Without being able to locate a next of kin it will be up to me to plan and pay for his funeral. That thought made me want to go home and place my head under my pillow. Maybe that isn't a bad idea. This whole situation may be a bad dream. It feels as if a week has passed since Jamie called me versus a few hours. Since it was after three a.m. when I went to bed I am dead on my feet. All my unanswered questions regarding Abe can wait until tomorrow. Yes tomorrow will be the day Abe and I become better acquainted.

As I was driving home I thought about the note on Abe's desk. "*SLCR* meeting, Tuesday morning, eleven thirty a.m." I wondered if *SLCR* would call back? I was assuming it was the initials of a person. I was going to need a client. Today's events reminded me of a saying my mother would use: "Don't worry about tomorrow, today has enough worry's of its own." I am going to rest today.

When I awoke Wednesday morning I felt well rested. It didn't take me long to realize why. I had slept through the remainder of Tuesday and until ten a.m. Wednesday.

I immediately dialed the office number. On the second ring Jamie answered the telephone. I said, "Jamie, I just woke up."

"That's fine but today has been a very lonesome day."

I asked her if there had been any calls?

"Only one and it was odd. A woman called wanting to speak with Abe. When I told her Abe had died she just hung up. She didn't leave a telephone number, name or any other information." That comment didn't make any sense to me either.

"Jamie, I remember Abe telling me that he had been married. Do you know if Abe stayed in contact with his ex-wife?"

"I never heard him speak of her. She has never called the office since I have worked here. I do remember seeing a telephone number for a Kitty Alberson on the office Rolodex. It was there when I began working for Abe five years ago."

"Call that telephone number and see if it is a working number. When we finish our conversation I am going to call the coroner's office before I came into the office."

I phoned the coroner's office. The coroner came on the line and said, "I find that Mr. Alberson's death was due to a heart attack. I am releasing the body today. Once you contact a funeral home have them call prior to picking up the body." I thanked him and ended the call.

I decided to contact a funeral home and make Abe's arrangements since there isn't any rush arriving at the office. I took my telephone directory and located a funeral home in the Bronx. A man answered the telephone. He asked, "How may I help you."

I said, "I need a body moved from the city morgue and prepared for burial."

"We would be happy to take care of the matter. What is the name of the person at the morgue?"

"Mr. Russell Alberson."

"Someone will need to come to our office and complete the necessary paperwork. Once that is completed we will take care of everything." I asked the man if I could do that now? He said, "Yes." "I will be there in a few minutes."

As I was driving to the funeral home I felt so inept. I had no idea how to handle Abe's funeral nor whom to contact regarding a church or pastor. When I arrived at the funeral home a man took me to a small office where I was given some forms to complete. One of the questions on the form was who would be responsible for the burial expenses? Like I knew what tomorrow held I indicated I would be responsible.

Once the paperwork was completed the man asked about the service? I said, "I have no idea; I wasn't familiar with Mr. Alberson's personal life." The man recommended that I allow him to contact a pastor and arrange a graveside service. I told him that would be great and provided him the office telephone number. With the arrangements underway I left the funeral home.

As I was driving to the office I decided to stop for lunch. While eating I thought, here I am straight from a funeral home to a restaurant! My appetite went away. I paid for my half-eaten meal and left.

It was three p.m. before I arrived at the office. Jamie was in Abe's office looking through the things on his desk. She had found two bills that were unpaid and a notice that the office rent was going to increase ten dollars a month the first of December.

Jamie told me she had called the telephone number of Abe's ex-wife. It was a working number but no one answered it. I asked her to continue calling the number during the day.

Jamie's telephone began ringing. She answered it and said, "Phil, it is the funeral home." I picked up the line. It was the man from the funeral home. He indicated he had contacted a pastor that would be available next Monday if that day is satisfactory. I indicated that Monday is fine. The man then said, "The funeral can begin at ten a.m. or two p.m. which time would be acceptable?" I looked at Jamie and said, "The funeral, what time? Ten a.m. or two p.m.?

"Ten."

I told the man, "Ten a.m."

"The Pastor will meet you at the cemetery a few minutes before ten a.m." I am glad that is set.

I asked Jamie, "Did Abe keep any personal documents such as a life insurance policy in the office?"

"Abe told me that if something happened to him to go to his house and retrieve a small box that he keeps under his bed. I have a key to Abe's house in my desk."

I said, "I need to go to Abe's house and retrieve that box."

When I arrived at Abe's house I was impressed with how well groomed the outside was. I felt uncomfortable entering his house. I was a stranger intruding into his life. As I stepped inside it was like being home. The house was a mess. The only difference between his place and mine was Abe purchased meals then brought them home to eat. I always ate out where there were other people. I didn't like eating alone. Even if I was the only one in my booth there were other people around.

In the living room there was a small table with about a three-inch stack of mail, a pillow and blanket was on the sofa. Beside the sofa were several empty glasses. The trashcan was full of carry out containers.

I walked into his bedroom and felt under his bed. I pulled out a black wooden box and opened it. In it was a bank savings book showing a balance of $524.95 and an envelope with New York Life Insurance on the front of it. I opened the envelope and found an insurance policy in the amount of $1,500.00. There was a document naming Kitty L. Alberson, beneficiary. There were some other papers and pictures of Abe and a lady; I am sure it is his ex-wife.

I tucked the box under my arm and began walking through the house looking to see if there was anything lying around that Abe would not want strangers to see. Of course it is a stranger that is looking around.

After walking through the house for several minutes I decided to take his mail to the office and open it there.

It was six thirty p.m. when I left Abe's house. I decided to stop at our favorite watering hole. Abe always took me to Tennyson's Club. The regular group was there. This place and its owner tickle me. He is an odd duck. He owns a Bar but calls it a Club. The only thing odder than that is when the owner decides to walk around the club reading poetry by Alfred Lord Tennyson.

He can quote the poem, "Charge of the Light Brigade" and "Crossing the Bar." If I hadn't experienced one of those occasions I wouldn't have known who Tennyson was.

Most of the regular customers had heard about Abe's death. I had a couple of drinks but it didn't feel right without Abe. I decided to go home.

On the drive home I began to think about my future. I know I am a good follower but do I have what it takes to run a business. I have to try. I owe it to Abe for giving me a chance.

As I lay in bed Abe's ex-wife came into my thoughts. Abe had mentioned an ex-wife once but never any details. I didn't know how long they had been married but I did know they split up five years ago. The reason I knew that is because that is how long Jamie has worked for Abe. Abe's wife was his secretary prior to their divorce. I drifted off to sleep.

As I looked at Thursday morning it glistened. It seemed to come alive with a hint of silver. Where the buildings hide the sunlight there was a mixture of black and white reflections forming small pockets of silver. It was a nice looking day. I entered the office at seven thirty a.m. Since that was the earliest I had ever arrived at the office I had to unlock the door. Abe allowed Jamie to set her own hours. I found myself walking into Abe's office. I knew it was my office but it was too soon to advertise it. I found it difficult to move anything.

I placed the box with Abe's personal papers in it on the desk. Today was going to be a better day. With Abe's savings account book and his insurance policy I knew he had money.

When Jamie arrives I will have her continue trying to contact Abe's ex-wife. I want to make sure she is aware of his death as well as knowing she is the beneficiary listed on his life insurance policy. Hopefully she will assist with the funeral expenses?

I began opening the mail that I had taken from Abe's house. It was unpaid bills. There were two utility bills and a house payment. A house payment! The house payment document provided the name and address of the finance company holding the loan on Abe's house. I wondered, what should be done with his house? If I can find his ex-wife maybe she could assist in locating other relatives.

At seven fifty-five a.m. Jamie came walking into the office. She had her normal smile and look of confidence back. I was glad she looked upbeat.

She told me that she had called Abe's ex-wife's telephone number several times yesterday but no one answered. I greeted her and asked her to continue calling the number during the day.

I filled my cup with coffee and returned to my office. As I sat there a thought hit me. I returned to Jamie's desk and asked for her telephone directory. I carried it into my office and opened it to the letter A. As I looked down the page I saw it: K. L. Alberson. I returned to Jamie's desk and asked her to show me the telephone number we had for Abe's ex-wife. It matched the number in the telephone directory. Now I had her telephone number and address.

As I sat thinking I wondered if *SLCR would* call again?

Thursday went flying by. I went though every drawer in Abe's office. I felt the need to become more familiar with the office and its contents. Jamie called the telephone number of Abe's ex-wife several times during the day without any contact. At five p.m. Jamie left for the day. I remained at the office but I wasn't sure why? I didn't have anything business related to accomplish. There still wasn't any information regarding who or what *SLCR* stood for.

As I sat in Abe's chair I picked up the telephone and dialed K. L. Alberson's telephone number. It was five forty-five p.m. The telephone rang. Then to my surprise I heard a woman's voice. I identified myself and asked her if she knew Russell Alberson? She said, "Yes I know him. He and I were married several years ago. We are currently divorced."

I asked, "Madam, are you aware Mr. Alberson has passed way?" Her voice was noticeably shaken. She was not aware of his death. I informed her that he had a fatal heart attack. I provided her the time and location of his funeral. She thanked me for contacting her and indicated she would attend the funeral service. Once I ended the call I felt better. At least Abe would have one family member at his funeral. I decided to leave for the day.

As Jamie was walking in the door I approached her and said, "I was able to contact Abe's ex-wife last evening and she will be attending his funeral."

Once Jamie had taken her coat off I said, "I haven't been in the office this many days in a row since I began working with Abe. What is the normal office schedule? What happens on Friday? She said, "Nothing much until I receive my paycheck!

Then she began to laugh and cry at the same time. I asked? "What's wrong?"

"Abe would have me come into his office each Friday and he would hand me my paycheck and say, "It's been another good week. Thanks. He did that every week for five years."

I thought, I don't know the amount Jamie is paid? I said, "Jamie here is your chance to tell a big lie regarding how much you are paid."

"I am paid $40.00 a week." I asked her, "Where did Abe keep his business check ledger? She said, "It is that large black spiral book in his middle desk drawer."

I opened the drawer and there it was. "I don't think I can write you a check. My signature will have to be on file with the bank before I can write checks." That thought led to the question, "Who handles Abe's business account?"

Jamie said, "Miss Emerald takes care of the business account."

"Have you talked with her since Abe's death?"

"No."

I asked her to call Miss Emerald and make sure she is aware of Abe's death.

Jamie called Miss Emerald and confirmed she was aware of Abe's death. Jamie informed her of the time and location of his funeral service. She indicated she would attend his funeral. She also indicated that she would bring the company's financial records and a signature card by the office prior to the funeral. Then she would make time afterwards to review them with me.

While Jamie and Miss Emerald were talking I opened my billfold and counted the money in it. I had $44.00. When Jamie ended her telephone call I asked her to come into my office. I handed her $40.00. "Can you afford to do this?"

I said, "Yes."

After I had paid Jamie I thought about Miss Emerald and her pay.

I returned to Jamie's desk and asked if she knew how Miss Emerald received her pay? Abe normally mailed her a check. I asked Jamie if she knew the amount Miss Emerald was paid? She said, "No." I then asked Jamie to call her and see if she could wait until Monday to receive her pay.

In a few minutes Jamie returned to my office and said, "Miss Emerald said she could wait until Monday to receive her pay." I thought if there is enough money in the account I will pay her and me.

The remained of Friday quietly pasted.

Saturday and Sunday were wonderful days of rest.

3

Monday morning came and I had a sick feeling. This will be the first time I have faced losing someone close. I had only known Abe for a brief amount of time but we had grown to respect and enjoy each other.

I thought back to that day on the USS Franklin when the Japanese airplane dropped his bombs. Many men were killed. I guess because of the number of men killed; the confusion and numbness I never let myself grieve over that situation.

Many of the men were considered dead because they were never found. The rest of the men were buried at sea. One by one a few words were said over them and then into the deep blue sea they went.

I arrived at the office at seven fifty-five a.m. Jamie was already there. She looked great. The black dress she was wearing was perfect. She is a beautiful lady.

I said, "Jamie, we will meet Abe's ex-wife today."

She looked at me and said, "Abe and Kitty."

Jamie and I met the pastor at the cemetery. He introduced himself as Brother Samuel Williams. He was about five feet ten inches tall, full head of white hair, about two hundred pounds and out of shape. He hadn't seen his toes in awhile. When he spoke he left you completely at ease. He had a demeanor that told you everything was going to be all right.

An older lady was approaching Jamie. Jamie saw her and said, "Good Morning Miss Emerald." She greeted Jamie. Then Jamie introduced her to me.

As I looked at Miss Emerald I could tell she had been Miss Emerald for at least fifty years. She looked like a bookkeeper. She was slightly over weight for her height. She had long hair and wore it in a bun on the top of her head. She didn't wear any makeup and her shoes would best be described as comfortable, not stylish. I liked her.

As we stood in silence I saw that Abe's coffin had arrived. I told the pastor we needed to wait until Mr. Alberson's former wife arrived.

At ten a.m. a very slim lady dressed in black approached the group. I approached her and asked, "Are you Mrs. Alberson?"

"Yes." I introduced her to Jamie, Miss Emerald and the pastor.

The service lasted about fifteen minutes. I paid the pastor and thanked him for a wonderful service. I then asked Mrs. Alberson if she had time to come to my office and discuss some items I had found in Abe's house? She indicated she could. All of the ladies walked quietly to my car.

When we arrived at the office I asked Mrs. Alberson to wait with Jamie for a few minutes. I could tell by the look on Jamie's face that she was going to enjoy that time.

I invited Miss Emerald into my office. I asked her how much Abe was paying her. "He pays me $55.00 a week." I thought to myself, Abe paid his help big money. I opened the business check register and wrote her a check.

Then she handed me a signature card and said, "I will take this card to the bank and file it, then I will cash this check and we will have all of our financial matters up to date. For your information the business account has a balance of three hundred fifty dollars with all bills paid."

"Madam I am pleased to meet you and I am looking forward to working with you in the future." With that said Miss Emerald left my office.

I asked Mrs. Alberson to join me. I reached in the lower drawer of my desk and placed the box that I had found under Abe's bed on my desk. "Have you ever seen this box?"

She smiled at me, "Yes. Abe always kept important papers in it."

"That is exactly what is in it now." I took the savings account book and the insurance policy out and handed them to her. "The insurance policy names you as the beneficiary." She was surprised.

"You will need to contact the insurance company and provide them all needed information. Once you do that the money is yours. She indicated that she understood and she would contact them.

"Please call me Kitty."

I said, "Please call me Phil."

I asked her, "Do you have the time to accompany me to the Bronx First National Bank. We need to determine if your signature is still valid for withdrawals from Abe's saving account?"

"Yes."

Jamie walked to the open door of my office like a little girl, who didn't want to be left out and stood there. I said, "Kitty how long were you and Abe married?"

"Four years." She looked at me then at Jamie as she continued. "We met on December 20, 1935 and were married February 15, 1936. Abe was the greatest husband any girl could have until he took a specific case. That case was the beginning of the end for our marriage." She had a tear in her eye and she said, "that is all in the past, let's leave it there."

I laid Abe's house payment statement in front of Kitty. "Also if you have time we need to determine if your name is on the deed. If it is that will make the decision on the house easy. You can sell it or live in it." Kitty said, "I feel so bad for Abe. I can't enjoy the thought of the insurance money nor house right now."

Kitty and I left the office and drove to the First National Bank. She presented the saving's book to a teller and asked to close the account. To our surprise she was told it would take just a few minutes. In a minute the teller asked Kitty if she wanted a check or cash? She indicated she would prefer cash. The teller told her it would take three business days before she can withdraw the cash. Kitty looked at me. I said, "That would be fine."

As we were returning to my car she said, "I will pay for Abe's funeral. I will bring the money to your office Thursday afternoon." I was relieved. I told her that the funeral expense was $315.00.

Then we drove to the Mortgage Company that holds the loan on Abe's house.

Once we arrived at the Mortgage Company I asked to speak to someone regarding a deed on one of their loans. We were seated with a mortgage officer. I told him that Mr. Alberson had past away and Mrs. Alberson wanted to make sure the deed on their home was in both of their names. I handed him the payment statement. He took the statement and indicated he would be right back. Upon his return he looked at Kitty and said, "Madam the deed is in both names. All is in order." I thanked him and we left the bank.

As we walked to my car Kitty staggered. I took her by the arm and said, "Are you alright?"

She stood there for several seconds then said, "I guess Abe's death is just now being realized. This day has been overwhelming." I helped her into my car and asked her if I could drive her home? She said, "If you have time that would be very nice. I don't want to cause you any trouble?"

"It is no trouble."

As we approached her house she said, "I want to thank you for everything that you have done for both Abe and I. It is very nice of you." I thanked her and returned to the office.

When I arrived at the office I told Jamie it is time to end Monday. She cleaned the coffeepot then put her coat on and left the office.

After she left I went for a walk. I didn't have Abe to lean on anymore so I needed to take what he has taught me and move on. I will learn as I go. I have the responsibility of Jamie, Miss Emerald and myself. After walking a few blocks I returned to the office. I turned on the lights and positioned myself in my chair. I retrieved the bottle of scotch from Abe's desk and poured a healthy shot in my coffee cup. As the taste of the scotch rolled down my throat the day and the events of the past few days began to melt away.

As I sat in the dim lit room I thought back on Abe. He was a husky man with a laugh that would shake the office walls when he would let it go. He was easy going. Jamie had commented several times about how he always seemed so relaxed and composed. I remembered after the funeral that Miss Emerald had said, "Mr. Alberson was a good man." It appears that this calm and composed man was a walking time bomb that quietly went off as he sat in his office.

4

My head jerking woke me. I looked at my watch and to my amazement it is two thirty a.m. I stood and looked around; I was still at the office. What am I doing to myself? I need to go home.

As I entered my place the telephone was ringing. Who could be calling me at three a.m.? As I raised the receiver I heard, "Is this Mr. Storm?"

"Yes I'm Phil Storm who is this?"

I heard a man's voice say, "Mr. Storm my name is Oscar Williams."

I briefly thought to myself, it is three o'clock in the morning and someone by the name of Oscar is calling me. Just my luck a man by the name of Oscar is calling me, not a Nancy or Sally. I caught myself talking to myself instead of Oscar. Oscar hasn't convinced me he is worth speaking with. I asked, "What's on your mind?"

Oscar said apologetically, "My employer, Mr. Robert Coleman would like to meet with you at nine a.m. this morning."

You do realize it is three a.m.?"

"I apologize for the three a.m. call sir but I have been calling you every thirty minutes since six p.m. It is most important that Mr. Coleman meet with you today."

I had to admit falling asleep at the office did make me unavailable. May be I will not place Oscar on my bad list just yet. I knew my words were a bit thick and slurred but I understood Oscar's question.

May I tell Mr. Coleman that you will meet with him at nine a.m. today?

"Can you provide me any information regarding why Mr. Coleman wants to meet with me?"

"No Mr. Storm. Mr. Coleman only indicated it is quite important to him."

Where am I to meet with Mr. Coleman?

"At his home." Oh! My first house call; isn't this cozy? I asked Oscar for Mr. Coleman's address. He provided it. I will be there by nine a.m. I spent the next few minutes picturing Oscar. He had a very high pitched voice and the speed of his speech indicated that he was a nervous wreck.

I sat on my bed and reviewed Oscar's call. I noticed Mr. Coleman's address. He lived in Scarsdale. Scarsdale speaks of money and notoriety in the same breath. I did not recognize the Coleman name. I looked at my clock and to my frustration it was three thirty a.m. I am very tired and somewhat inebriated. Since Scarsdale isn't a bad drive from my flat in the Bronx I set my alarm for seven a.m. and slipped off to sleep.

The loudness of my alarm clock began its unpleasant noise at what seemed to be only minutes after I had set it. I had a momentary thought that I was dead. No one could feel as bad as I do and still be alive. Of course if I am dead it is a case of suicide. You can't incarcerate a bottle of scotch but you can the hand that held it.

This will be a long morning. Having a hangover and attempting to roll out of bed showed me what a stumblebum I am. I nearly fell head-first into the shower. With great difficulty I managed a shower. I needed coffee for the headache and eye drops to dim my bright red eyes.

As the coffee perked I pondered my meeting with Oscar's Mr. Coleman. I have never heard of Mr. Robert Coleman so how does he know me?

Because of his location I decided to wear a clean shirt and add a tie. I was even going to button the top bottom on my shirt and make the tie look proper. Man, am I impressed with Mr. Coleman's address. I thought Mr. Coleman's power over Oscar indicated that he is not going to take no for an answer. So I will probably have a client. I am positive Mr. Coleman went to bed last night knowing that Oscar would schedule his meeting at the hour he had indicated.

As I sat drinking my coffee I looked around the kitchen for something to eat. As usual all I could find was some bread. I placed two slices in the toaster. After the toast and more coffee I was ready to meet Mr. Coleman.

Just before I began my drive to the Coleman home I called Jamie to inform her of my nine a.m. meeting, regarding a possible client. "I indicated I would see her after the meeting."

I arrived at the entrance to the Coleman home at eight forty-five a.m. I was proud of myself for arriving early. As I stopped at the entrance I could see a funny little man in a security guard uniform. He was sixty-five years old or older. He was a small man. He was probably five feet, six inches tall and weighed a hundred pounds.

He told me to proceed to the parking area. So the rich do not have parking places, or parking lots only parking areas. I began driving toward the parking area. Both sides of the road were lined with trees and shrubs. When I arrived at the parking area I pulled into a parking space.

I thought, being hired by a man this wealthy and being successful with his case could establish me as a private investigator worthy enough to represent other wealthy families. Of course, I must be hired first.

As I stepped out of my car a man driving a small motorized vehicle was coming towards me. The man stopped the vehicle and said, "I will take you to the house." This man didn't look like he belonged here. He looked rough. I would have bet a week's pay that if I could have patted him down I would have found a gun. He was dressed in a suit that was right out of a Humphrey Bogart movie.

The distance from my car to the house was a good two tenths of a mile.

The house was breath taking.

My driver whom I have so gracefully named Bogey rang the door-bell. In a few seconds a man opened the door. I knew immediately that this man is the butler. He looked like a butler so until I am told differently he is the butler. Mr. Butler told me to follow him.

Bogey drove away. I don't think Bogey could be trusted inside the house. He would probably steal the china. Who knows he maybe harmless and live with his mother in Queens? But I wouldn't waste much time looking for him there. Enough about Bogey.

Mr. Butler took me to a large open room. He told me to have a seat as he walked out of the room. I knew this room was the Parlor. Every grandiose home has a parlor. As I looked at the size of the room it was easy to see that it would hold thirty to forty people.

In a few minutes Mr. Butler returned. He again asked me to follow him. That reminded me of Groucho Marx's saying, "Walk this way." I wanted to waddle a little but I didn't. I tried to wipe the dumb look off of my face before I met Mr. Coleman. Mr. Butler escorted me into another very large room.

I immediately knew this room had to be the Study. There was a large bookshelf with rows of books and a desk that faced several large chairs. I noticed three pictures on the wall as I entered the room. From looking at them I imagine they are three generations of Coleman men. Mr. Butler pointed to a chair in front of the desk and asked me to sit. I thanked him.

As I was waiting for Mr. Coleman I began feeling very uncomfortable. I began sensing a cold sweat all over. I began telling myself I am feeling this way because of my surroundings. It isn't everyday I find myself in a mansion. I needed to remember that Mr. Coleman puts his pants on one leg at a time just like me.

Without a sound a man walked into the room. I stood. He introduced himself as Robert Coleman. I introduced myself as Phil Storm. We shook hands and he asked me to sit.

He had a good strong handshake. I like that in a man. Mr. Coleman was at least six feet, one inches tall and probably two hundred twenty pounds. He was in good physical shape. He had a full head of hair and a nicely trimmed mustache. He was a handsome man. When you looked him in the eye you saw certainty, wisdom and control. I liked this man.

Mr. Coleman gave me the once over. He seemed to have a need to pace. He said, "I know you are wondering why you are here and I will explain that soon but first I need to take care of some house cleaning items." I thought to myself how does house-cleaning fit into our conversation?

It was apparent to Mr. Coleman that he had confused me. He continued, "What I mean is we need to cover some ground rules before we discuss the specific reason for your visit."

Mr. Coleman walked over to a telephone and dialed a number. Since it was only a four-digit number I knew he had dialed another telephone number within the house. I heard him say, "Come in and bring the documents."

As he turned to face me a door at the other end of the room opened and another man entered. Mr. Coleman said, "Let me introduce Paul Winford." I stood and shook his hand. Another good hand shake. Paul Winford was also a tall man. He was just as tall as Coleman but not as heavy, maybe one hundred and eighty pounds. He had blonde hair and was very tan. He looked at least ten years younger than Mr. Coleman did. I wondered, in late fall how does he stay so tan. I liked this man also.

Mr. Coleman continued, "Paul is my personal attorney." I thought to myself, *Even though he is an attorney his look made me want to trust him.*

When he spoke he had a voice that commanded your attention. Mr. Coleman said, "I have asked Paul to provide you a document to read. If you have any questions Paul will answer them. Once you have read the document please sign and date it."

I read the document. The document indicated that once I signed and dated it I would not be able to discuss any issues Mr. Coleman confided in me with anyone except him.

Paul looked at me and reiterated, "This means any and all information provided by Mr. Coleman from this moment on is confidential. Failure to abide by this agreement will place you in a very uncomfortable situation."

"I understand."

I then looked at Mr. Coleman and asked, "Are you going to ask me to break the law?"

Paul spoke before Mr. Coleman had a chance to. "No. We just expect you to follow the before mentioned guidelines in receiving and handling information. As long as those guidelines are followed there will be no problems."

I asked Mr. Coleman a question and before he could draw a breath Paul answers the question. I guess that is what a personal attorney does?

I thought to myself, I'm going to have to be careful. I am not a seasoned PI. I have learned some things from Abe but now I will have to stay on my toes. I signed and dated the document. Mr. Coleman told Paul to provide me a copy.

Once Paul left the room Mr. Coleman began pacing again. He walked around the room looking here and there without a word. He returned to his desk and began taking documents out of the top drawer. While he was removing the items Paul returned and provided me with a copy of the document I had signed and dated. The first words out of Mr. Coleman's mouth was, "Phil, what do you know about me?" I looked at him and thought I probably should know something about him but I didn't.

"I didn't know anything about you." He smiled and said, "That is fine."

"How did you find me?"

"I didn't find you. I found your boss."

"I want you to call me Robert." I thanked him.

"Now I am going to provide the details of why you are here. It all started with a telephone call from Paul. He had received a call from one of my accountants. This accountant was seeing an unusual movement of money from one of my daughter's accounts. I asked him to monitor the account and determine if the unusual withdrawals continued. He was seeing withdrawals in the amount of $9, 950.00. This seemed highly unusual."

"Paul reviewed the situation and his first thoughts were the amount of money being withdrawn. It was just below the $10,000.00 limit allowed per individual American citizen traveling abroad without having to declare it on their customs form. This daughter had been traveling between New York, Paris and Rome during the timeframe of the withdrawals.

"Paul had recommended that I hire someone unknown to my family to look into this matter. That is why I have contacted you, Phil. I need this matter reviewed and a conclusion reached as soon as possible. I need it to be accomplished thoroughly, correctly and quietly. It may be nothing but it could be a number of things. I do not plan to discuss my thoughts until you have had an opportunity to look into the matter."

Robert began handing me pictures. As I looked at each picture he said, "The identity of each person is written on the back." The first picture was Sally Lancaster Coleman Robinson. The second picture was of her husband, Edward Curtis Robinson. He then handed me more pictures. Those pictures appeared to be other family members. Each picture had a name and relationship on it.

Once I had reviewed the pictures Robert handed me a piece of paper with the home address of the Robinson's, a business address for Mr. Robinson and a list of charities that Mrs. Robinson is involved with.

He said, "I want you to be able to recognize all of my family members but I did not want you to have any contact with them unless it is absolutely necessary."

"Any financial information you need should come from Paul."

Robert reiterated that confidentiality is the top priority. He then gave me an envelope and indicated he was paying half of my fee now and the remainder when my work was completed. He indicated if I have to travel that money will be in addition to my fee."

I sat there looking at Robert and asked, "What do you want me to do? Why my firm? What have I missed?"

He looked at me and said, "Read the name on this picture. I took it from him and turned it over." It read Sally Lancaster Coleman Robinson. I sat there still at a loss.

Then it hit me! *SLCR*. Those were the initials Abe had written on the note in his office. Mrs. Robinson had contacted Abe but the rest of the information died with Abe.

I looked at Robert.

"So you do know my daughter had contacted your firm."

"I found a note on Abe's desk with the initials *SLCR* on it indicating they were to meet the Tuesday he died. He didn't meet with her and he had not provided me any information regarding her."

Robert said, "She is a very private person. You will find her difficult to deal with."

"So you think this money issue is what she was going to discuss with Abe?"

"I'm not sure but if she contacts your office do whatever is necessary to gain her confidence."

Robert repeated, "If she calls gain her confidence and assist her no matter the issue."

"I will be happy to assist her."

"So the money in question was withdrawn from your daughter's bank account prior to each of her trips overseas?"

"Yes."

"I don't understand what you want me to do?"

"I want you to follow my daughter and determine whom she is meeting and why she is having the meetings. The reason she contacted your firm my not have anything to do with the earlier issue but it may. So follow her and let me know your findings."

"Do you have any other questions?"

"I want to be clear. Do you want me to wait until I hear from her before I begin following her?"

"No. You can begin that immediately."

"How will I determine if these withdrawals continue?"

"You will contact Paul. Do not try to gain the information without Paul's involvement?"

I was beginning to realize Robert wasn't going to provide me any information unless I could prove a need to know. "I will begin surveillance of your daughter immediately." Robert thanked me and ended our meeting.

I left the house with questions buzzing in my head. Why was Mr. Coleman so closed mouth? He hired me before he told me what he wanted me to do. He didn't want to provide me his opinion of what was taking place. How unusual this meeting was. He could have provided his thoughts. That would have given me a place to begin but no not a word.

I thought, how tough can it be to follow a wealthy lady? Determining whom she is meeting and why will be a little more challenging. I won't blend in with her crowd. As long as she meets in a public place I will be fine. Normally in situations where money is moving from one person to another there is a lover or an extortionist that becomes aware of the affair. I hope this case will be that easy.

As I walked out the front door Bogey was waiting for me. The smile on his face was one of curiosity. Without a word he drove me to my car. When we arrived at my car he looked at me and said, "Have a good day." I thanked him and drove off.

As I was driving to the office I realized the envelope that contained the first half of my fee remains unopened in my pocket. I decided not to open it until I arrived at the office. Jamie and I could celebrate that together. I felt this was going to be an easy case with a big payday.

5

It was five minutes after twelve p.m. when I arrived at the office. Jamie was seated at her desk eating lunch. I asked her to join me for a minute. As she entered I said, "Jamie I know what *SLCR* stands for. It is the initials of Sally Lancaster Coleman Robinson. She is one of the daughters of our newest client."

He has hired us to look into a matter involving Mrs. Robinson. He confirmed that she had contacted Abe. "Jamie we have our first client!"

She smiled as she said, "I knew you could do it."

I removed the envelope from my pocket and said, "Jamie, this envelope contains the first half of our fee. I haven't opened it yet because I wanted to share the moment with you." I removed the check and looked at it. Then I looked at Jamie and said, "This has to be a mistake." She took the check out of my hand.

"Three thousand dollars! This is half of the fee?"

"That is what the man indicated." We stood looking at each other for several seconds.

Before Jamie returned to her lunch I said, "Once you finish your lunch I need you to see what information you can gather on Mr. Robert Wayne Dunsworth Coleman and his family." What a name! This man is at least third generation money.

As Jamie was returning to her desk I remembered the family pictures Mr. Coleman had provided me. I had left the pictures in my car. I walked to my car and retrieved the photographs. I thought if Jamie is going to be gathering information on the Coleman family having their names would be helpful.

When I returned to the office I placed the pictures on her desk while informing her that the name of each person was on the back of their photograph. As she looked at each picture she said, "Thanks for showing me these photographs it makes me feel I am your partner." She then wrote down each name.

After meeting Mr. Coleman I knew he would expect detailed information. "Documenting is one of my weakest characteristics. I turned

Mrs. Robinson's picture over and looked at her address. Her home was not far from her parent's home."

I turned toward Jamie and said, "I am going to locate the Robinson home."

When I arrived at the Robinson's house I could see there was a problem. All of the homes were on several acres of land and each one had their own security entrance. This meant my parking place had to be out of the view of the security guard but with a view of the entrance.

After driving around the area I located a place to park. It's only draw back is the distance between it and the Robinson's entrance. If I expect to see who is in the cars coming into and leaving the Robinson's home I will have to purchase a pair of binoculars. With the binoculars and family photographs I will be able to identify the person in each car as well as obtaining their license tag number.

I planned to be in position at the Robinson's home by seven a.m. each morning. Since I didn't know if Mrs. Robinson had a daily routine or schedule I wanted to be in position early enough to catch the morning traffic entering and leaving the house. Mr. Coleman had provided charities Mrs. Robinson was involved in but it didn't indicate dates or times of the events.

I decided to call Jamie and see if everything is quiet. If it is, I well drive to a store and purchase my binoculars before going home for the day.

When Jamie answered the telephone she said, "Phil, you need to return to the office. There is someone here that wants to speak with you."

"Who is it?"

"It is Mrs. Robinson."

"Jamie, It will take me twenty minutes to arrive. See if she is willing to wait?" Jamie said, "Yes. She will wait."

I couldn't believe her timing. As I am preparing to begin surveillance for her father she appears.

As I was driving to the office I began thinking about how important secrecy was to Mr. Coleman. I was not to discuss his case with anyone but him. When I take Mrs. Robinson's case how much of what she confides in me should I pass along to Mr. Coleman? I was getting a headache.

Before I could take that thought any further I arrived at the office. It was four fifteen p.m.

I entered the office and introduced myself to Mrs. Robinson. She gave me a Marine handshake. She looked to be in her mid-thirties. She was a knock out. I found it hard to look her in the eye. Her eyes were the bluest eyes I had ever looked into.

I asked her to be seated and tell me how I could assist her. She said, "Before I discuss my issue I need your assurance that you will not discuss our conversations with anyone."

"I am a Private Investigator. I do not reveal information entrusted to me in confidence to anyone other than the client." I realized that statement may be untrue in her case but she needed to hear it.

I did inform her that I would not withhold information from the police if by doing so I would be breaking the law. I will not spend time in jail for anyone. She said, "I understand."

"Are you as good an investigator as Mr. Alberson?"

"I doubt it. I haven't been in the business as long as Abe was but he was a good teacher. I understand Mr. Alberson's creed of ethics. Secrecy was at the top of his list.

She stood and looked at me for several seconds then returned to her seat. It was as if she was deciding whether to hire me or not.

"Someone is following me. I have noticed it for the last two weeks. I don't know how long it has been going on."

"Do you have any idea why someone would be following you? Do you have any idea who it could be?"

"I do not know who or why? But it must be someone my father has hired. He is always getting into my business. If I didn't like his money so much I would tell him to get out and stay out of my life. But daddy rules."

I could hear a real dislike for her father as she said, "Daddy rules." She sounded like a spoiled child who had just been grounded by her daddy.

"How do you know you are being followed?"

"Two weeks ago when I was leaving my home I had stopped at our entrance and looked both ways. There was no traffic but as soon as I pulled onto the road a car was instantly behind me. It was a Black Ford Coupe. It looked like a new one.

"As I drove to a friend's home the Black Ford remained behind me. When I left my friend's home and began driving into Manhattan the same car was behind me. I made several stops in the City and each time

I returned to my car and began driving I could see the Black Ford in my rearview mirror. When I parked in front of a restaurant on Forty Second Street the Black Ford drove past me.

"I entered the restaurant to meet a friend for lunch; my friend was already seated. I approached her and spoke then I excused myself and walked to the ladies room.

"When I exited the ladies room I asked a restaurant employee if there was a rear door that would lead out of the restaurant and return me to Forty Second Street? He indicated there was. He then escorted me to the rear door and told me if I entered the alley then turned left I could enter a shop whose front door would open on to Forty Second Street. When I walked out onto Forty Second Street and looked down the block, sure enough I spotted the Black Ford with a man behind the wheel. I returned to the restaurant and had lunch with my friend.

"When I left the restaurant I made several stops. Each time I returned to my car it wasn't long before the same Black Ford was behind me. I know someone is following me and my father is involved."

I asked her, "What would you like me to do?"

"I want you to determine who is following me and why." I looked at her and saw a lady that was frustrated not scared. I said, "Provide me your address and I will look into your issue. I drive a black Ford but it isn't new."

"If you take my case I will provide you an automobile."

"Do you think that is necessary?

"Yes I do. One black Ford following me is enough. I have a yellow Chevrolet that has never been driven. I thought, *Me driving a yellow car?* "I will place a specialty tag on my front bumper just below the license tag. When you see a black Ford with a specialty tag you will know that I am behind you. If you don't see the specialty tag, just continue your day. I will be behind the Black Ford that is following you. I explained that I would be too noticeable in a yellow car. If I was following the Black Ford it wouldn't take him long to realize he is being followed by a yellow car." She agreed and I was glad.

Mrs. Robinson said, "I do not want you to come to my home nor are you to call me at my home. I will meet you in your office each Monday morning at ten a.m. If I should need to meet more frequent I will call your office and make an appointment."

She repeated, "I have no idea who or why I am being followed." "I will determine who is following you and why." Then just like her father she handed me an envelope and told me this would be her first payment for my service. I opened the envelope and found it contained a check for five hundred dollars. I told her this amount of money up front isn't necessary. She insisted that I take the check. I thanked her and indicated that I would begin her case tomorrow. "Your case will be my top priority." This is the same thing I told her father and for the first time both statements are true.

When she left I walked out to Jamie and told her that Mrs. Robinson would be in my office each Monday at ten a.m.

Jamie gave me a confused look and said, "You are working for her and her father?"

"Yes. Mr. Coleman hoped his daughter would contact me and if she did he wanted me to make her case my number one priority."

"So you are getting paid twice for the same job?"

"Yes. At least I think when I solve Mrs. Robinson's case it will solve Mr. Coleman's case." I briefly explained both cases to Jamie. "Jamie, Mrs. Robinson can not become aware that her father is also our client."

I handed Jamie Mrs. Robinson's check and asked her to see it finds its way to Miss Emerald.

I told Jamie my surveillance at the Robinson's home will begin tomorrow morning. I will contact you as opportunities permit. I reminded her that she was my partner and I depended on her doing her part.

I returned to my office with my thoughts still on Mr. Coleman and Mrs. Robinson. Mrs. Robinson believes her father has hired whoever is following her. Her father wants to know why she is being followed and whom she is meeting.

I wonder if Mr. Coleman did hire the man that is following her? My thoughts were interrupted as Jamie entered my office. "Kitty Alberson is on the telephone." I took the call.

Kitty wanted to let me know that she had received a check from Abe's insurance company. She also indicated that she was going to sell Abe's house. She asked me if I would accompany her to Abe's house when she boxes up his personal items. I told her if she could provide me a day's advance notice I would accompany her. She thanked me and indicated that she would be in touch.

As that call ended I approached Jamie and told her I was leaving for the day. Then I asked, "Are you married?" She said, "No."

"I have a business reason for asking that question. If I have an emergency while on surveillance can I call you at home?" Without any hesitation she provided me her home telephone number. I thanked her.

I reiterated, "I will only use it in an emergency."

"Call me whenever you want to." I wish she hadn't been so inviting. I left the office.

I needed to locate a store that sold those funny and stupid license plates.

When I entered the store the large number and variety of tags was surprising. In looking through them I found the perfect one. It read, "Hire Me." I purchased it and left the store.

On leaving the store I looked at the front bumper of my car. Someone will have to drill two holes in my license tag before I could mount this tag. I drove to an automobile repair shop and asked if they would drill the holes. They not only drilled the holes they installed the tag.

I felt like a weird-o with that tag on the front of my car. I knew it would standout but it would standout less than driving a yellow Chevy. I could just see me driving down the road in a bright yellow car. All I could imagine was a car full of funny young men loving their car and themselves. A real man does not buy anything yellow.

After having the tag installed I drove to dinner.

After dinner I made a list of items I would need while on surveillance. I would need binoculars, a writing tablet and a pencil. I returned to my car and drove to a store to purchase binoculars. With the binoculars in hand I was off to the five and ten to purchase a pad. Then it was time to go home.

As I prepared for bed I thought? If Mrs. Robinson has been followed for two weeks why hasn't anyone contacted her? Who could this person be and whom is he working for?

6

I am on top of the world this morning. I have money, two new clients and a chance to become established in the investigation business. I had my coffee and then gathered my surveillance supplies. I nearly forgot my rogue gallery. The pictures of my new family will be valuable assets beginning today.

After leaving my place I drove directly to Mrs. Robinson's house. I drove slowly in front of the entrance. I could see the security guard but that was the extent of the activity.

I then parked in my predetermined spot. It gave me a good view of cars entering and leaving the Robinson's house. It was seven a.m.

I wish I had purchased a morning newspaper. I'll remember the newspaper tomorrow morning. As I sat there completely bored I began writing my first notes. "I arrived at the client's home at seven a.m."

Without a newspaper or traffic from the Robinson house I retrieved the envelope containing the Coleman family's pictures. I decided to become more acquainted with the faces of this family. I began with Mrs. Robinson's picture. She is as attractive in person as her picture. Frequently pictures are touched up and the picture is more attractive than the person but not in Mrs. Robinson's case. When she entered my office I was momentarily lost as I looked into her sapphire blue eyes. She had ebony hair and wore a crimson lipstick that made her face radiate. She had a slim figure with long legs. The way she carried herself high-lighted all of her.

Then I came to daughter Lisa Ann Coleman. She had a look of youth. She was probably the youngest of the children. She was also a very pretty young lady. She had dark hair and eyes. She looked perky or maybe cocky. For a young person she looked in charge of her life.

Daughter Mary Dawson Coleman had the ebony hair and blue eyes. She was a younger model of Mrs. Robinson. It was uncanny how much she looked like her older sister. The main difference in their pictures were this daughter didn't want her picture taken. She had a forced pleasant look on her face.

Daughter Lady Eleanor Coleman Wilson had the dark hair and dark eyes. She was standing next to her husband. She was tall and slender but not as pretty as Sally, Lisa or Mary. The way she was dressed and that matter of fact look on her face made me think that she was a businesswoman.

Then there was the ladies mother, Princess Audrey Lancaster Coleman. I had to say that Mr. Coleman lost when it came to whom his children looked like. The girls all looked like their mother. This lady's picture showed a person in charge. She had long ebony hair and the same blue sparkly eyes as Mrs. Robinson and Mary. She had managed to stay slim. She looked more like a queen than a princess did. I would say she came from money and fell into more money.

There were two sons-in-law. Edward Curtis Robinson married to Sally and Terrance Nance Wilson married to Lady. They both looked like they belonged in a rich sitting. Both men were about six feet tall, brown hair and both were slim. Mr. Wilson looked in better physical shape than Mr. Robinson did. This was quite a family that I am getting acquainted with.

As I sat there I began to think of questions that needed answers. The first question that came to mind was, "Is there another entrance in and out of the Robinson's home?" I would feel pretty stupid if the Robinson's had multiple entrances and exits. I will look into that soon.

The next question is to determine if Mr. and Mrs. Robinson have a daily schedule. I am sure Mr. Robinson has a regular work schedule and knowing it would be helpful. Mrs. Robinson told me that her husband worked for her father but to know the type of business he is in and his position would be helpful.

My thoughts were interrupted at eight twenty a.m. by a car approaching the entrance from the house. I reached for my binoculars and focused on the car. I could see it was a town car with one person in the backseat. It was Mr. Robinson. He drove off. I made my official first entry of the case; *Mr. Robinson left his home at eight twenty a.m. in the rear seat of a Black Town car.*

After Mr. Robinson drove away I found myself thinking about the task I had given Jamie. I had asked her to locate as much information as possible on the Coleman family. I didn't give her an opportunity to ask me for assistance or to answer any questions she may have had. I didn't know if Abe had ever had her involved in gathering this type of information. I'll have to be more caring in the future.

My thought was interrupted again as a Black Ford pulled up in front of the Robinson's entryway. A man was driving. He stepped out of his car and approached the Robinson's security guard. He handed the guard an envelope. They talked for a few minutes. Then he returned to his car and began to drive away.

At that moment I thought; this could be the car that is following Mrs. Robinson. Even though I had not seen Mrs. Robinson leave I decided to follow the Black Ford.

As I followed this car I wondered if the Robinson's guard kept a log of individuals that make deliveries? As my thoughts continued the Ford made a right turn. I followed. I was trying to maintain several car lengths between us when I saw the car's brake lights. The car pulled over and parked near a telephone booth. I eased past him.

I parked about four parking places in front of him. I stepped out of my car, crossed the street and began walking back toward the man. He was a good six feet tall, weighed probably one hundred eighty pounds, was dressed in a dark gray suit and he had a bald spot in the back of his head. I guessed that he was fifty-five to sixty years old.

Once I passed his location I returned to the side of the street he was on. I could see him holding the telephone with his shoulder and writing something in a small notepad. I looked at his license tag. I had left my writing pad on my car seat so I concentrated on the tag number.

When I returned to my car I wrote the license tag number down. It was J3615. That didn't seem right. I stepped out of my car and looked at my license tag. I determined there was a number in front of the J but I didn't see it. I only had a partial tag number.

I started my car and circled the block. I wanted to see if the Black Ford was still parked at the telephone booth. When I returned the car was gone. I looked at my watch. It was nine forty-five a.m. I decided to find a telephone and call Jamie.

When she answered the telephone I was shocked to hear, "Storm Investigations."

I had to laugh, "Jamie this is Mr. Storm." She began to laugh also. I asked her if there had been any calls.

"No."

I then asked her if she had obtained any information on the Coleman family.

"Yes. Mr. Coleman is the President and Chief Operating Officer of CMI Corporation.

I found myself saying, "I'm impressed but what does that mean?"

"CMI stands for Cole Mark Incorporated. CMI is made up of several different companies. The type of businesses are; Jewelry (both retail jewelry stores and the buying and selling of un-mounted gems), Interior Decorating stores, several wholesale stores that sells commercial furniture and appliances. The furniture and appliance business' sells to hotels, restaurants and other commercial businesses. CMI also owns several hotels and restaurants."

"Now here is a CMI business I am unable to gather any information on except for its name. It is CMI Investigations."

"CMI Investigations? What do they do?"

"I wasn't able to determine that."

"Is there anything else?"

"I was able to determine the name of the person that is in charge of each company. Mr. Robinson is the President, WorldWide Gems. That covers both the wholesale and retail jewelry businesses. Lady Eleanor Coleman Wilson is the President, Designs of the World. That is the interior decorating stores. Mrs. Wilson's husband, Terrance Nance Wilson is President, Executive Furniture and Accessories. A Samuel Theodore Burr is the President, Coleman Executive Hotels. A Mr. Anthony Mitchell Lancaster is the President, Lancaster's Restaurants."

"All of the CMI Executive's offices are located at 633 3rd Avenue, Manhattan."

"Jamie thank you this is great work." I looked over the list and said, "I guess the rich keep it in the family."

With that information I returned to the Robinson's home. I parked in my predetermined parking place and began thinking about the man that made the delivery to the Robinson's security guard. What was he delivering? Is he the man that is following Mrs. Robinson?

As I sat in my car my thoughts returned to CMI Investigations. What do they investigate? If CMI has private investigators why doesn't Mr. Coleman use them?

There were two other interesting facts. Why didn't Mr. Coleman provide pictures of Mr. Lancaster or Mr. Burr. Why? I don't think it was an oversight. I will look into their lives on my own.

I looked at my watch; it was eleven thirty a.m. Since I had left to follow the Black Ford I didn't know if Mrs. Robinson was still at home. How could I confirm that? That question made me remember my earlier question. Was there another entrance into the Robinson home? It was time I answered that question.

I started my car and drove slowly around the street in front of the Robinson home. At my first opportunity I turned right and began driving slowly. I arrived at the street corner and didn't see any entrance. I made another right behind the Robinson property. As I was driving along I saw a break in the curb.

I stopped my car and stepped out. I could see a cobblestone path. It was wide enough for a car. I began walking up the path. All of a sudden I came upon a guard shack. It was occupied by a man in the same uniform as the one at the first gate; he was reading a book. He had not seen me approach. I backed up slowly and returned to my car. I wasn't sure that this entrance lead to the Robinson's home but I felt that it did. As I made another right turn I confirmed that the cobblestone path was on the Robinson's property. I returned to my parking space in front of the home.

The more I thought about the other entrance the more I felt it was for deliveries but I couldn't ignore the possibility it was used by the family.

Since I wasn't sure whether Mrs. Robinson was at home or not I decided to end my surveillance for the day and return to the office.

On the drive to the office I began thinking about the Black Ford that I had gotten a partial license tag on. That reminded me of a detective that Abe had introduced to me. He had assisted me on my first case. He had joined Abe and me for drinks at Tennyson's. His name was Watson. What was his first name?

When I arrived at the office Jamie wasn't in. There was a sign on the door saying, "Out to lunch be back at one p.m." I walked into my office. Then it came to me. Detective Watson's first name was Tom.

I dialed the police precinct's number. I asked for Detective Tom Watson. In a few seconds I heard, "This is Tom Watson." I told him who was calling; we exchanged greetings. We talked for a few minutes about Abe's death then I asked him how difficult it would be to identify the owner of a Black Ford when all I have is a partial license tag number? He said it is possible but it will take sometime. Is this an official police request? I said, "No." Then Tom asked, "Who is your client?" I said, "If I tell you that I will lose my right thumb and big toe." He laughed then asked, "By helping you with this tag number am I going to be placed in a questionable position?"

I was silent for a moment; "I don't think so. If it comes to that I will turn the whole situation over to the police." He thanked me and indicated he would have the information for me soon. As I ended my telephone call I saw Jamie walking into my office.

She said, "I'm sorry for being late."

"You are the one that said you were late not me." I made Jamie aware of the telephone call to Tom Watson. I told her if I am out of the office when Tom returns my call to ask him to leave the information with her.

I discussed my morning with her. Once I finished that update I returned to the names and photographs missing from the group Mr. Coleman had provided. Why didn't he provide me pictures and identification of Mr. Lancaster or Mr. Burr? Why didn't he mention CMI Investigations?

I found the office telephone directory and looked up Anthony Mitchell Lancaster. As I looked at his address I noticed it was very close to the Robinson's house.

I also looked up Samuel Theodore Burr's address. He lived in Scarsdale but it was across town.

I then turned my thoughts to CMI Investigations. I opened the telephone directory and found that this Company's address is 633 3rd Avenue, suite 305 Manhattan. So it is located at the headquarters for CMI Corporation but it is on the third floor and all of the other CMI offices are on the sixth floor. Why is this company on a different floor?

I began to wonder how I could determine what type of business CMI Investigations handled. A thought came to my mind. Abe had introduced me to a Private Investigator that had been in the PI business for many years. Someone like that might have rubbed elbows with some of the CMI Investigators. I couldn't remember his name. The more I tried the more frustrated I became.

I walked out to Jamie's desk and asked her if she knew any of the private investigators Abe had interacted with. She indicated she had a list of individuals that Abe contacted or worked with frequently. I asked her for the list. As I began reading the names there it was, "Alvin Wilson." I asked Jamie to call Mr. Wilson and see if he was in his office. I would like to speak with him.

Jamie dialed his number and buzzed me.

Once I answered the telephone I reminded Alvin where we had met. We exchanged greetings and discussed Abe briefly. Then I said, "I have came across a company named CMI Investigations and I wonder if you had ever worked with them?" He was silent for a few seconds then he said, "I have heard of the company but I have never had any business dealings with them. This Company deals with corporate investigations. They are hired to investigate corruption within corporations. They also have been known to take cases involving the rich and famous types."

"Do you know the name of the person that is in charge?"

"A man by the name of Coleman."

"Do you know any of the investigators?"

"No. The reason I know this much about the Company is because of a case they handled a few years ago that had a lot of publicity." It had something to do with one of Mr. Coleman's daughters and the Italian government. This daughter had taken a large sum of money into Italy hidden in a suitcase.

"Do you remember the daughter's name."

"No but the New York Times ran several articles on it. My contact at the Times can provide you her name and probably copies of the articles."

Alvin provided his contact's name and telephone number. I thanked him for his help.

Once off the telephone I informed Jamie of the information Alvin had provided. I told her to call this man and make arrangements to meet with him and retrieve copies of the articles.

I began remembering Alvin. He is between fifty and fifty-five years old. He has been in the investigation business almost twenty years. He is about five-eight inches tall, weighs about two hundred pounds. He is totally bald. Abe had told me Alvin was a very good investigator. He also said that Alvin had many contacts throughout the City.

I was getting a headache thinking about the items Robert Coleman had not mentioned in our meeting. Why didn't he mention CMI Investigations? Why didn't he mention the prior event involving one of his daughters and money? Why were Mr. Lancaster and Mr. Burr names not included?

Jamie buzzed me. When I picked up she indicated that she could meet with the man at the Times tomorrow afternoon. I thanked her and reminded her I would be on surveillance tomorrow.

I began to think back on my conversations with Abe regarding cases and clients. He told me that our first and most important role was to our clients. As long as we did not break the law in solving our case in favor of our client we had accomplished what we had been hired to do. He always added if we had to stretch the law then we stretch it but remember don't break it.

Also if during our investigations we came across information that the police could use but it would place our client in harms way by providing it we would return to our original pledge. The client comes first.

I decided to end my workday and drove to Tennyson's to relax and unwind.

It was six p.m. when I arrived at Tennyson's. As usual the regulars were in their places. I took a seat at the bar.

As I began my first scotch and water I couldn't get Abe out of my mind. Thinking of Abe moved my thoughts to his ex-wife Kitty. Even though she is several years older than I am she is still a very pretty lady. I needed to call her and see if Abe's house has sold?

As I started my fourth drink I looked at my watch. It was seven p.m. and I was hungry. I drove to a restaurant close to Tennyson's to have some dinner. The restaurant wasn't very busy so I took a seat at the counter next to the daily newspaper. I scanned the paper while I waited on my meal.

As I turned to the society page I saw Mrs. Robinson starring at me. The article indicated she was the chairwoman of an organization raising money to expand a mission that provides beds for the homeless. The article returned my thoughts to Mr. Coleman and my unanswered questions. Maybe the articles at the Times will provide me a lead.

7

As I approached my door I could see a note taped to it. It was from the conscientious Oscar. It said, "Call *as soon as possible.*" I was not surprised but I was disappointed. I was hoping to meet with Mrs. Robinson again and read the earlier articles before meeting with Mr. Coleman.

I entered my living room then decided to check my mail. As I opened the box I found, of all things a note from Oscar saying, "Call me as soon as possible." One thing I will say about Oscar is that he is determined to get his message across. It was clear I needed to call him.

I must remember Mr. Coleman has given me more money than I thought I would ever see at one time. He sets my schedule.

I dialed Oscar's number and immediately heard him say, "Mr. Coleman wants to meet with you Friday evening at seven p.m."

"I will be there."

I thought about the information I would have to convey to Mr. Coleman. His daughter has contacted me and hired me to determine who is following her and why? I have her under surveillance. There is a man in a Black Ford that is involved. I am not one hundred percent sure what his role is. He may be the man that is following Mrs. Robinson. While at this meeting I need to obtain Paul Winford's telephone number. I want to be able to contact someone regarding the Coleman case other than Oscar, and Paul seems to be that person.

It is time to get some sleep and leave tomorrow's decisions to tomorrow.

The alarm began its unnatural sounds. Its vile noise rang in my ears. I am looking forward to the day I didn't have to hear it. Once the coffee was perking I called Jamie to ask her to begin her day retrieving the newspaper articles instead of waiting until this afternoon. That would provide me an opportunity to review the prior event involving one of the Coleman daughters before meeting with Mr. Coleman.

Once ready for the day I drove to the Newsstand and then on to the Robinson home.

As I parked I thought about the other entrance into and out of the Robinson home. I am not ready to think any of the family would use that entrance. They didn't seem to be people that would drive on a cobblestone path.

As I scanned the headlines I looked at my watch. It was eight ten a.m. I reviewed yesterday's notes to determine when Mr. Robinson had arrived at his front entrance. It was eight twenty a. m. I wondered how prompt he is. I found out in ten minutes. At eight twenty a.m. the same car and man came through the entrance. Mr. Robinson is a timely person.

At nine a.m. another car came to the entrance from the house. Through my binoculars I could see it was a woman. I looked quickly at the family pictures. It was Mrs. Coleman. My first thought was should I follow her? Then I thought why? I did wonder when she arrived at the Robinson's house. Last night or earlier this morning? I decided to log that Mrs. Coleman left the Robinson house at nine a.m. in a black town car and maintain my position.

At nine fifteen a.m. another car approached the entrance from the house. This car was also a black town car. I could see it was Mrs. Robinson. I started my car and fell in behind her. I left several car lengths between my car and hers. If the Black Ford began following her there needed to be ample room for it to fit between us.

Mrs. Robinson's car was headed in the direction of Manhattan. The morning traffic is making it difficult to maintain a safe distance between our cars without losing her. So far my black Ford is the only one following her.

Due to the traffic as we entered Manhattan I reduced the distance between our cars. Her car began slowing down and made a right turn into a parking garage. I made the turn rather fast and was nearly hit by a truck. The truck driver called me some unpleasant names. He needed to get control of his day. Even with my mind still on the truck driver and his need for therapy or a bloody nose I was able to keep Mrs. Robinson's car in view.

Her driver pulled into a parking space that was marked, "Private parking only." I slipped passed her and parked.

Mrs. Robinson stepped out of her car and entered the building that was connected to the parking garage. I followed her. She walked through the building out the front entrance and began walking down the street.

I dropped off my pace to determine if I was the only person following her.

She entered Macy's and walked through the store without even looking at any merchandise. She exited Macy's and entered a magazine shop. She didn't purchase anything there either; she just exited the shop. She continued walking down the street.

I began to get the message. She is trying to determine if anyone is following her. I wondered if she was good enough to spot me. She entered Rockefeller Center and exited through a door to the skating rink.

She then turned around and began walking in the direction of her car. She was determined to shake anyone that was following her. Then all of a sudden she hailed a cab. Crap! I will lose her now. But to my surprise I was able to hail a cab as her cab pulled away from the curb. I told the driver, "Don't loss the cab in front of you. I will make it worth your while." I love using that line. It is used in all of the gangster movies.

Once in the cab it appeared she was going in circles. I had my driver stop. I asked him to provide as much room as possible between the two cabs. Her cab turned right and I had my driver stop at the corner until several cars were between our two cabs. Within two blocks of her right turn her cab stopped and she stepped out.

Of all the places! She entered a Lancaster restaurant. I stopped in front of the restaurant.

I entered and told the matre'de I was looking for a friend that should be in the restaurant. He gave me that look; neither you nor your friends can afford this restaurant.

I walked slowly through the restaurant. I didn't see Mrs. Robinson anywhere. I stopped a waiter and asked him if he had seen Mrs. Edward Robinson. He said, "Yes. She was here but she left the restaurant though the rear entrance."

I asked myself, "Does this sound familiar?" Mrs. Robinson had told me about going into a restaurant and exiting out the rear door to determine if the man in the Black Ford was parked somewhere close.

I asked him to show me the exit. I walked out the door and looked both ways. There wasn't any sign of Mrs. Robinson in either direction.

As I entered the alley I could see the rear door of the shop next to the restaurant. I entered it and walked out it's front door onto 42nd Street. I looked up and down the street, no Mrs. Robinson.

Maybe following a wealthy lady was going to be more of a challenge than I thought. She smoked me today.

I hailed a cab and returned to my car. When I arrived at my car Mrs. Robinson's car and driver was still there. I have missed whatever she was doing in the City today but I will wait here until she returns to her car. As I updated my log I was interrupted when a Black Ford suddenly stopped in front of Mrs. Robinson's car. The car was blocking movement in the parking garage. The driver stepped out of his car and walked toward Mrs. Robinson's car. It appeared he was checking her license tag because once he read it he returned to his car and drove away. As it passed me I could see the car's license tag. It was 7J3615. This is the man and the Black Ford that made the delivery to the Robinson's security guard and then stopped at the telephone booth.

I started my car and began following the man in the Black Ford. He drove to a parking garage at 42nd Street and 3rd Avenue. I followed him into the parking garage. Once in the parking garage he exited his car. I followed him into the building attached to the parking garage. He entered the elevator. Since he was the only person waiting for the elevator I waited for his elevator to close. It stopped on the 6th floor.

I took the next elevator and exited on the 6th floor. Once I stepped off of the elevator there was a lady sitting at a desk in the lobby area. I saw a sign that read, "CMI Corporation." I walked up to the lady behind a desk and said, "Did a Mister Henry Tallman just step off of the elevator?" She looked down at a paper on her desk and said, "No."

I said, "I thought I saw him step on the elevator that closed just before I could enter it." She looked at me and said, "A Mr. Johnson just arrived. He is in a meeting with Mr. Coleman." I thanked her and apologized for troubling her.

I immediately felt like a blockhead, a numskull, and a jerk. What was Mr. Coleman doing? Did he have two investigators on the same case? So is Johnson the person following Mrs. Robinson? I would bet my fee on it. Since it was two-thirty p.m., I decided to return to the office. I wanted to see what Jamie had found on the old Coleman case.

On my drive to the office I thought, "Mr. Coleman seems to be making a fool of me. He has me chasing my tail following the man he hired to follow the person I was hired to follow. So I am one of multiple players in this rich man's game. I decided to determine how much of Mr. Coleman's money I had spent. I will call it business expenses then I will write him a check for the balance and tell him to find another fool to run in circles."

It was two fifty-five p.m. when I arrived at the office. There was a note on the door that said, "Jamie would return at three p. m." So I left the sign up and walked into the office. I started the coffee then entered my office. As I sat there my mind was blank except for a large question mark? Do I think I am a smart investigator? I shouldn't after being out foxed by Mrs. Robinson today.

My initial thoughts of Mr. Coleman were I liked him. I imagine he likes me also since he confirmed he can manipulate me. I bet he will be surprised when he discovers I have uncovered his mystery investigator. That will be a laugh on him.

Jamie came walking into my office with a stack of newspapers. Her first words were, "Phil if you lose or damaged any of these newspapers my life is over. I did not have time to wait on copies so when I was alone I just picked up the articles and left."

The first article was dated July 16, 1941. It said, "Miss Lisa Ann Coleman, 24 year old daughter of Business Mogul Robert Wayne Dunsworth Coleman, President and CEO CMI Incorporated detained in Italy."

The next article was dated July 20, 1941. It said, "Miss Coleman was missing a piece of luggage upon her departure from her ship in Italy. Ship's crewman finds bag without an identification tag. Bag given to the Ship's Captain. Captain opened the bag. Bag contained $20,000 American dollars. Miss Coleman identified the bag as hers. An agreement between the Italian Government and the FBI lead to the money being returned to the USA."

The next article was dated July 31, 1941. It read, "Italian government agrees to allow Miss Coleman to return to New York City where she will meet with the FBI."

Then the August 11, 1941 paper read, "Coleman family attorney, "Paul Winford" meets Miss Coleman on her arrival from Italy. Miss Coleman released on her own recognizance while awaiting discussions with the FBI and the New York City District Attorney."

Then the November 30, 1941 paper read, "All complaints against Miss Coleman dropped. No further information available from FBI or DA."

Jamie told me that there wasn't anything on the case after the November 30th article.

Well at least my case is different. Why didn't Mr. Coleman make me aware of this issue? It does seem relevant. If he had told me I wouldn't have had Jamie spend her time doing the research.

I looked at my watch. It was three fifty p.m. Since I didn't need to take the newspaper articles to my meeting I told Jamie to document the main issues and then she could return the articles to the Times.

I am ready to meet with Mr. Coleman but is he ready to meet with me? Will he be ready to discuss Mr. Johnson, Mr. Lancaster, Mr. Burr and the earlier event involving his daughter, Lisa? He better be because I am going to push for answers to each issue.

8

I arrived at the Coleman home at six forty-five p. m. I received the same instructions from the security guard as he waved me through the gate with the skinniest arm I have ever seen. I drove directly to the parking area. When I arrived, Bogey was waiting for me. I said, "Hi." Bogey gave me a stupid look and waved.

When we arrived at the door Mr. Butler greeted me. This time he took me directly to the Study. I walked to the hot seat directly in front of Mr. Coleman's desk and sat down. As I sat silently I began to feel uncomfortable. I looked at my watch. It was five after seven p.m. and Mr. Coleman had not appeared. I am disappointed.

I had no sooner completed that thought as Paul walked into the room. Maybe I am going to be dealing with the second team now. Paul greeted me and asked, "Would you like a drink?"

"Hello and yes a drink would be good."

"It's scotch and water?"

"Yes."

As Paul handed me my drink he said, "Mr. Coleman will be here but it will be closer to seven thirty p.m." Paul and I exchanged some small talk.

Paul asked, "How long have you been in the investigation business?" Why do people like Paul care how long I have been in the investigation business?

"Only a few months."

"What type of work did you do prior to investigation work?"

"I was in the Navy. I volunteered when Pearl Harbor was attacked."

"Did you see any action?"

"Yes. Let's see we saw action in the Marshall Islands, the Mariana Islands, Iwo Jima, Gum, Luzon, Manila Bay and some other places I can't remember. I was aboard the aircraft carrier USS Franklin. It was hit with two Japanese bombs earlier this year. It was a mess. Over seven hundred men on the ship were killed."

Paul acted like he wished he hadn't asked the question. "Phil, I have a great deal of respect for our veterans. I'm glad you made it through the war."

At seven thirty p. m. on the nose, in walked Mr. Coleman. He said, "Hello" and then apologized for making me wait. I thanked him and told him he was the boss; I worked his schedule.

He sat down behind his desk. He said, "Phil, how is your investigation going?"

"Your daughter contacted me and hired me. She indicated that someone is following her and the person is driving a Black Ford Coupe."

Mr. Coleman asked, "Does she have any idea who it is?"

"No."

I did one of those eye to eye looks and said, "She seemed to think it is someone that works for her father."

"She said that?"

"Yes." Mr. Coleman sat there looking at me without a word.

"Robert I believe she is right. The man does work for you."

"Why would you say that?"

"I'm not going to play games Robert; here's what I know.

"The man following your daughter is a man by the name of Johnson. Today, I followed him to your corporate offices. This Johnson was there to meet with you. At least that is what the receptionist sitting in the 6th floor lobby told me. I am too old to play games. I would like for you to explain why you have hired two investigators to accomplish the same task or Johnson will be the only investigator on this case."

"Mr. Storm you are better than I thought."

"Do you want to explain why you have Mr. Johnson and me both following your daughter?"

"Phil I am not accustom to explaining myself to my employees but in this case I will make an exception. When the issue first surfaced I was convinced that I needed to do something. I discussed it with Paul and we decided to hire an out of town investigator to look into the matter. Then I learned my daughter had contacted a local investigation firm. Once I was able to determine which firm she had contacted I also contacted that firm and the rest you know. I decided to continue with the out of town investigator until I had time to meet with your firm's investigator. Since I am satisfied with your investigative abilities I will discontinue using

Mr. Johnson soon. You have determined things I didn't think could be accomplished in the short time you have been on the case."

"So when are you going to end Johnson's employment?

"Soon. Phil, do not let Mr. Johnson trouble you."

"Here are some other questions I would like to have answered: why didn't you include photos of Mr. Lancaster and Mr. Burr with the other photo's you provided? Next, why didn't you inform me of CMI Investigations and last why didn't you tell me about the other incident involving your daughter, Lisa and a large sum of money in Italy?"

Mr. Coleman looked at Paul then at me. He had a puzzled look on his face. He began walking around the room. He looked frustrated, angry or totally caught off guard by my questions or my blunt approach.

He sat and said, "The issue several years ago has nothing to do with today. As for CMI Investigations, they do not and will not do any work involving my personal life. The earlier issue you mentioned was the last personal issue that they handled for me. They currently handle CMI business issues only."

"So you are telling me Mr. Johnson does not work for CMI Investigations?"

"Yes that is correct. As I previously stated he works for a company outside of this area. I told you privacy is a number one requirement when it comes to my family's business. Now with regard to Mr. Lancaster and Mr. Burr, I didn't see any need to include them.

"Mr. Coleman, I should be the one that decides who is included or excluded from this investigation."

Mr. Coleman interrupted me by asking? "Does my daughter know that you have discovered who is following her?"

"No she doesn't know. I am to meet with her on Monday."

"Where are you to meet her?"

"In my office. Your daughter is also trying to maintain privacy. Now if Johnson follows her to my office he will be asking you the same questions I am asking."

"Phil, I will see that Mr. Johnson does not follow her to your office."

"I will discontinue Mr. Johnson's services soon." The look on his face made me believe he did want me to stay on the case.

"Mr. Coleman, I will continue on your case but I don't want to have any problems with Mr. Johnson."

"Phil, can we get back to you calling me Robert?"

"Yes."

He asked me why I thought Mr. Lancaster or Mr. Burr was involved. I said, "I am not saying they are involved but they are in charge of CMI businesses. You had furnished pictures of all of the other individuals that are in charge of your companies."

"I'm impressed that you know that."

"The reason I bring up Mr. Lancaster and Mr. Burr is because it is as likely that someone within CMI is meeting with your daughter as someone from the outside. Since Johnson has been following your daughter has he provided you with who she is meeting?"

"No. I would not want to think it was someone within CMI."

I looked at Paul and said, "Can you provide me with Mrs. Robinson's daily schedule and travel plans?"

"Yes."

"May I have a telephone number I can use to contact you if it is needed? He said, "Yes and provided me his telephone number." I thanked him.

"Do you have any other questions or concerns at this time?"

"No." He shook my hand and said good bye. It was eight fifty p.m. as I left the house. Bogey wasn't waiting at the door to transport me to my car. I wondered what that meant.

Right now it really didn't matter. I was happy to walk to my car. Mr. Coleman's no disclaimer clause on Mr. Johnson's involvement still troubled me. Mr. Coleman never did offer me a picture of Mr. Lancaster or Mr. Burr. I will call Paul on Monday and ask him to provide information on Mr. Lancaster and Mr. Burr.

I drove straight home. As I approached my door I saw a note attached to it. This was becoming an all too often occurrence. This note was from Tom Watson. It said, "Phil, please call me." Since I had Johnson's name I decided to wait until Monday to call him. He can confirm that the driver was Mr. Johnson. I can't trust Mr. Coleman anymore. He could still be lying to me regarding who Johnson is.

My thoughts went to Mrs. Robinson. What would I tell her Monday? I will tell her the truth but not everything.

I came to the conclusion that she had to be aware that I have seen the same Black Ford twice. Once at the entrance to her home and then when I followed her into Manhattan.

I am too tired to continue thinking about work or anything else.

• • •

I love Saturday morning because I do not have to listen to the alarm clock. I will have breakfast and then call Kitty Alberson. I didn't have anything specific to discuss with her. I just want to see how she is doing.

After breakfast I returned home and called Kitty. As I dialed her number I thought what if she has company. What if a man is there? It wasn't long before I heard, "Hello". I said, "Hi Kitty this is Phil Storm."

"How are you Phil?" I could tell by her voice that she was happy to hear from me. Everything is good with me. How are you? "I'm doing great."

"Great" is much better than "Good" what makes you great?"

"The real estate lady I hired sold Abe's house. So now I am going to purchase a house of my own."

"That is what makes today great! Buying a house is something I have wanted to do ever since Abe and I split up."

I told her I was happy for her. Then I found myself asking her what she was doing today. She paused and said, "Nothing special I was thinking about going to a matinee movie."

"I was thinking about a movie today also. Do you think we could go together?"

"That would be nice. What movie are you considering?"

"I don't know I just needed something to help pass the day." Have you selected a movie?

"Yes but I'm not sure you will like it."

"What is the name of the movie?"

"A Tree Grows in Brooklyn."

I was hoping she would say, "Spellbound." But I told her that movie was fine. I asked her what feature she planned to attend?

"The one p.m. feature." I told her that was fine with me.

"I will pick you up at noon."

As I ended the call I asked myself what is the real reason I called Kitty. There is something about her I like. Maybe I felt safe with her since she was several years older than I am or maybe it is because she is an attractive lady or may be it is loneliness? All I know is I need to spend sometime with someone other than clients.

• • •

I arrived at Kitty's house at noon. She invited me in and asked me if I wanted anything to drink. I told her no. I found myself looking her place over. She said, "I'll get my coat and we can be off." She looked real nice. She was wearing a nice dress but it wasn't too much. I would say she wants to look good but didn't want to look like this is a special event. In my opinion, "That's what makes her a lady."

I would guess that Kitty was about five foot, four inches tall, weight about–I didn't want to guess. She had a good figure for her age.

The thing I like about her is the way she seems to be ready to handle every situation. As I look into her eyes my every thought is on her and what she has to say.

I was interrupted when she asked me to help her with her coat. I was glad she stopped my mind from thinking about her so deeply.

The movie was a girl's flick. Watching Kitty enjoy the movie was better than watching it. After the movie I asked her if she would like to have an early dinner. She said, "That would be nice." There is a nice restaurant within walking distance of the theatre so I asked her if she thought it was too cold to walk to it. She indicated the walk would be fine.

After we were seated in the restaurant Kitty asked, "How did you get your job working for Abe?"

"I was lucky. I was very surprised that he hired me once he realized I didn't have any investigation experience."

"That is the type of person Abe was. He would always take a chance on that type of person."

"What do you mean by that type of person?"

"Abe would always take a person that is honest no matter the outcome over someone that would try to lie their way through the interview."

I didn't know how to respond to her answer. I hoped my embarrassment wasn't showing. It was time to change the subject so I asked her to tell me a little about her and Abe. She smiled and said, "Abe and I met at a party given by one of my friends. Abe was to be my date but he didn't know it. Abe knew the boy friend of the girl having the party. We really hit it off that night. Three months later we were married. We were very happy for a long time. Then Abe's work became all he was interested in. He began spending more and more time on the job. Then he began spending time with some of his female clients. They weren't all business if you get my drift. Then it all ended." At that moment she sat quietly looking at her plate. My first thought was that Abe had stressed his creed to me in such harsh terms because he found out personally what happens if you get involved with a client or an employee.

I found myself wanting to hug her I could sense her hurt. I changed the subject. "How is your meal?"

"It is good. How is yours?" I think we both needed to change the subject. We both sat silently eating.

Kitty looked at her watch and said, "I don't want to end a very pleasant day but I told a girl friend that I would go with her to visit her mother who is in a nursing home. Her mother's mind is failing. Sometimes she is okay and other times she doesn't know anyone. It seems to help my girlfriend's visit if someone else is there."

"I think that is great." I paid our check and we began our return trip to my car.

As we walked I told her that her friend was lucky to have someone that would help her with a situation like that. Kitty smiled.

On the drive home I found myself asking her, "Do you think we could do this again sometime?"

"Yes I think that would be nice."

"I will call you before long." She stepped out of the car and waved good-bye.

As I began my drive home I found myself thinking about being alone. I really hadn't thought much about that until lately; that turned my thoughts to Jamie. I am alone and it appeared she is also. She never talks about any friends but I haven't offered her the opportunity to discuss any thing except work related items. I need to take time to talk with her about her life away from work. But I have never been very good at that.

Sunday morning looked to be a nice day. I decided to visit my mother after breakfast.

I arrived at her house at noon. She was eating lunch and she invited me to join her. I told her I had a big breakfast at ten a.m. and I wasn't hungry. As she ate we talked.

She began by telling me about her neighbors and what was going on in their lives. She told me about who was sick and who was in the hospital. She told me about her job. Mom looked good and acted like she felt good.

When she finished talking I found myself telling her about Abe's death, meeting his ex-wife, about Jamie and my job. She seemed pleased that I was sharing my life and friends with her.

After two hours I knew it was time for me to leave so she could go to bed. I told her good bye but I would visit again soon. As always she reached up and kissed me on the cheek and gave me a big hug. For the first time in a long time it felt good.

9

It was eight fifteen a.m. Monday, when I arrived at the office. Jamie was already there. I poured a cup of coffee and went into my office. Jamie walked to my office door and said, "Good morning." I was so ashamed that I had walked right past her without speaking.

I said, "Good morning and I apologize for not speaking earlier. I have a one-track mind and I am thinking about my meeting with Mrs. Robinson this morning."

"That's fine. What is the agenda for the day?"

"Mrs. Robinson was due in by ten a.m. and the outcome of that meeting will determine much of my day's activity. I said, Jamie, your job today is to smile and look pretty so if any potential clients come into the office they will see a smile greeting them." Jamie rolled her eyes and returned to her book.

Before returning to my desk I asked her about her weekend. "It was very nice." She told me that she had spent Saturday with her sister and her sister's children.

"How many children does your sister have?" "Three girls."

"Saturday evening we all attended a Christmas program that my oldest niece was in. After the program the girls came home with me and spent the night. Then Sunday before my sister arrived to pick up the girls we made cookies." Jamie seemed so happy talking about her nieces spending the night with her. There was a real joy in her face as she told me about the cookies and the mess they made preparing them for the oven. I was happy Jamie had family close and I was glad that I asked about her weekend.

Then I told her about going to the movie with Kitty on Saturday and the visit with my mother on Sunday. Jamie didn't know my mother lived in the City. She then told me her parents live in Queens.

At that moment Jamie's telephone rang. She returned to her desk to answer it. She buzzed the intercom and said, "Tom Watson is on the line."

I greeted Tom and he said, "I'm not sure the nature of your involvement with this car or driver but this car is registered to CMI Incorporated. I could not get the name of the driver. This Company is very private." I thanked him for the information and we ended the call.

At ten a.m. promptly Mrs. Robinson walked into the office. I heard her say good morning to Jamie. Jamie returned her greeting and asked her if she would like a cup of coffee. Mrs. Robinson declined. Jamie escorted her into my office. I stood, greeted her and asked her to have a seat.

I began the meeting by telling her about the Black Ford arriving at the entry to her home and that the driver left a package with her security guard. When the man drove away I followed him. After a while he stopped and made a telephone call. While he was on his call I was able to get a good look at him and I was able to get a parcel license tag from his car.

That tag information got me the name Mr. Johnson.

I have not determined any other information about Mr. Johnson. I am sure this is the man that is following you "Do you recognize the name Johnson?"

She gave me a blank look and said, "No, I don't recognize the name. Why is he following me?"

"That is still unknown. I did run into him again last Friday. I followed you into Manhattan. She looked like she had seen a ghost or worst.

She looked at me sternly and said in a sharp voice, "So you are following me just like the other man?"

"Mrs. Robinson, isn't that what you are paying me to do? I can only determine who is following you and why you are being followed if I am smarter than he is." She sat looking at me then at the ceiling. "I lost you at the restaurant so I hailed a taxi and returned to my car. I had parked close to your car. When I returned to my car your car and driver was still there. Before I left the parking garage this Black Ford pulled up in front of your car and sat there for a few seconds before driving off. Mrs. Robinson looked at me and said, "I'm sorry. You are right; you need to do whatever is necessary to determine why I am being followed."

"Mrs. Robinson I followed this man into the building where your husband works. Could this man be someone that is employed by your husband?"

She looked at me and I could see anger in her face once again. "No. Leave my husband out of this. You are way out of line. You must stay away from my family and keep them out of this." She showed a rough side that was very blunt.

I was completely surprised. "I'm sorry but to determine who is following you and why you are being followed means I have to cover all of the bases. You have to understand in my business I find husbands having wives followed and wives having husbands or girl friends followed. This is a routine question for me to ask."

She asked, "Do you mind if I smoke?" I said no as she lit her cigarette. She was working hard to get control of her emotions. Her face was flush, her forehead was wrinkled and her eyes were squinted. Then she said, "Again I am sorry. My husband and I are very much in love. Neither him nor any of his friends or employees would be following me."

"If you want me to continue on your case I will ascertain why this man is following you."

"Yes I want you to continue. I want to know why this man is following me and who hired him."

I told her that Johnson does not know I am following him. So you may continue to notice him behind you. Remember I will be behind him. She lit another cigarette and asked, "Do you have anything else to tell me?" I said no. She thanked me and said, "I'll see you next Monday at ten a.m."

As she left I knew my next order of business was to locate Mr. Johnson and determine what he knows. I didn't think Mr. Coleman would inform Johnson that I was on the case but what do I know about him? I didn't think he would have two investigators on one case either.

As I continued thinking about Johnson I guess he had not uncovered whom Mrs. Robinson is meeting or why. If he had Mr. Coleman would have paid me off. Still lots of questions.

I decided to have lunch and then return to the Robinson's house. I put on my coat and told Jamie I was returning to the Robinson's house to continue my surveillance.

When I arrived at the Robinson's house I circled the house and stopped at the cobblestone path. I stepped out of my car and walked to the security guard shack. When I arrived at the entrance there wasn't a guard insight. So I stepped under the gate and walked toward the house. I located the garage and entered through the side door. Once inside the garage I could see that there was room enough to park six cars. There was four parked. One was the yellow Chevy Mrs. Robinson had told me about, and then there was a black Town car, a black Ford Coupe and a black Ford Sedan.

So two cars were gone? Who besides Mr. and Mrs. Robinson drive their cars? I left the garage and walked to the side of the house. From there I could see the front of the house. There weren't any cars parked there. I returned to my car and drove to my parking spot.

Once parked I began to document the day's activities.

At three ten p.m. a car stopped at the entry gate. I raised my binoculars but all I could see was a woman's head. This person is known by the security guard because they were only stopped momentarily.

At three forty p.m. I saw a car coming from the house. It was the same car that drove in earlier. When it left the entrance I fell in behind it. We were headed in the direction of the Bronx. I decided to get close enough to read the license tag number. The car was a black Chevrolet sedan. The car made a sudden turn and pulled into the parking lot of a New York's Finest restaurant.

I pulled in behind the car and parked. As the driver exited the car I could see it was a young lady but all I could see was her back as she walked toward the restaurant. Then she stopped, turned, and returned to her car. I could see her face clearly then. It was the youngest daughter, Lisa Ann Coleman.

As she opened her car door she reached under the driver's seat and pulled out some thing small and placed it in her purse. I couldn't determine what it was. Then she closed the car door and walked into the building. I decided to wait and see what she was up to. While waiting I updated my notes with the description of her car and her license tag number. I noted that it was four ten p.m. I guessed it would take her an hour to eat.

I decided to enter the restaurant and have a drink then return to my car. I stopped after one. I needed to stay alert.

As I walked through the parking lot I found myself thinking about Kitty. I know so little about her. When we have been together I have been satisfied to listen to what she has to say versus asking questions.

The time was going by slowly. I decided to return to the bar for another drink.

I was back to my car at six forty-five p.m. Lisa's car was still in the parking lot. At eight p.m. I began to think that Lisa Ann had pulled a Mrs. Robinson trick by leaving the restaurant through a backdoor. But at this location their aren't any buildings close to the restaurant just more parking lot.

At ten fifteen p.m. Lisa Ann exited the restaurant alone and drove off. I followed her. What has this young lady been up to? It didn't take her over four hours to eat. What else could she have been doing? My initial meeting with, "Miss 1941 problem daughter was unusual in 1945."

Lisa Ann drove to the Robinson home. She lived at the Coleman house but at eleven fifteen p.m. she is dropping in on her sister. Was this unusual? I had a gut feeling that Lisa Ann didn't drive to a restaurant and spend over four hours eating? I didn't believe that for a second but I had no idea what else she could have been doing.

I wasn't sure whether to wait for Lisa to leave or not. She could be spending the night. I decided to drive around to the cobblestone path and walk up to the garage. If Lisa's car is not in the garage I will return to my parking place and wait a little longer. I was driving toward the cobblestone path when I saw a car enter the street from it. It was Lisa's car. So it is used. This will make my coverage of the Robinson house more difficult.

I was frustrated that Lisa had left by the cobblestone path. I repeat these Coleman women are tricky. I drove home.

The alarm began screaming at six a.m. Man was it a short night. I wanted to arrive at the Robinson's house early to insure that I didn't miss Mrs. Robinson leaving or Mr. Johnson returning. It was six fifty-five a.m. when I arrived. I was reading the morning paper when I noticed a Black Ford stop in front of the Robinson's house.

The driver stepped out of the car and approached the Robinson's guard. This time the guard gave him a package. As I focused my binoculars it was Johnson. I initially found myself getting angry, the thought of Mr. Coleman hiring two investigators to follow the same woman. I had to quit thinking about that and begin following Johnson. This was messing up my entire day.

Today will be the day I determine why Johnson is following Mrs. Robinson. I fell in behind him as he made his way toward Manhattan. He began slowing down and pulled off of the highway and stopped in front of a building named, "Ready to Buy Real Estate." What is going on now? He exited his car and entered the building. In less than five minutes he returned to his car and drove directly to 633 Third Avenue in Manhattan. Here we are again at the CMI offices. He parked. Today I take charge.

I reached into my glove compartment and removed my pistol. I placed it in my coat pocket. When Johnson returns to his car I will meet him.

It wasn't long before I saw Johnson returning to his car. I stepped out of my car and as he got close to me I rubbed my gun on his side. I told him to get in his car. He looked at me with a very surprised look. As he entered his car I said, "Don't move. I am getting in with you. We are going to drive and talk."

Once in his car I removed my gun from my pocket and laid it on my knee where he could see it. I frisked him. He didn't have a gun. I said, "Don't try anything dumb just drive."

"Where to?"

"Let's return to the real estate office that you visited before coming here."

When we arrived at the real estate office I said, "Park."

He complied. He asked, "Who are you and what do you want with me?"

"I am the one that will ask the questions and you are the one that will give the answers."

"What were you doing at this real estate office earlier?"

"I am from out of town and I was looking for a house."

"What were you doing at the CMI offices?"

"Well I was looking for a job. If I am going to move to the city I need a job."

I put the gun against his side and said, "Quit your lying. I know your name is Johnson and you are working for Mr. Robert Coleman." He gave me a look of disbelief and just sat looking out the window.

"Now shall we begin again? You have been following Mrs. Edward Robinson for days. Why?"

"You are right. I have been following her."

"Why?"

"You may not believe me but all I know is I was to follow her and determine who she meets."

"Well have you determined that?"

"I can't tell you that."

"Start the car."

"Why?"

"It appears that the only way I am going to obtain the answers to my questions is the hard way and there are more private places to have that discussion."

"Just a minute."

"Again, tell me who she has met with?"

"What happens to me if I tell you what you want to know?"

"You will drive away a free man. I am not a hit man."

"I'm not paid enough to get messed up."

"Johnson I am running out of patience. Tell me now!"

"Since I have been following her she has only met with one man and his name is Leo Filpatrick. This Filpatrick owns, "Ready to Buy Real Estate. I only discovered his name today. I reported it to Coleman, he thanked me and paid me off. I no longer work for him. I was on my way to my motel to pack my clothes and return home."

I looked at him and sensed he was telling me the truth especially after my Friday meeting with Coleman. I returned my gun to my coat pocket. "Drive me to my car." When we arrived at my car I stepped out of his car and stood watching him until he was out of sight.

Now Mr. Coleman; let's have no more surprises.

10

As Johnson drove out of sight I entered my car, reached for my pad and added Leo Kilpatrick to my notes. Since my day of watching Mrs. Robinson has been interrupted I'm going to return to the office and see what information I could uncover on Mr. Leo Filpatrick.

As I was driving I thought how odd it was that Coleman ended Johnson's investigation with the name of the person following his daughter. It could mean that Coleman knows Leo Filpatrick or maybe Johnson withheld information. I need to get acquainted with this Mr. Leo Kilpatrick.

When I entered the office Jamie was deeply involved in her book. I asked her how her day was going. She smiled and said, "It's going fine Mr. Storm as she returned to her book."

I retrieved my cup and was pouring a cup of coffee as she placed a marker in her book and indicated there had been two telephone messages. One from Kitty Alberson and the second call was from Miss Emerald.

I asked if either left a message. She said that Miss Emerald had received cancelled checks for forty and sixty dollars and neither check indicated the purpose of the expenses. Miss Emerald said that the reason for the expense should be written on each check so she could process it properly. I asked Jamie to call Miss Emerald and inform her that the forty dollars was her salary and the sixty dollars were my personal expenses connected to the Coleman case.

Kitty didn't leave a message other than to tell you to call her. I thanked Jamie and returned to my chair. As I sat drinking coffee I began to think about Leo Filpatrick. What does a man that owns a Real Estate Company have to do with my case?

I decided to call Alvin Wilson and see if he has heard of Leo Kilpatrick. In seconds I heard Alvin's voice. We exchanged greetings. Alvin was breathing hard. I asked, "You sound like you have been running."

"I have. I am overloaded with work. You are lucky to find me in my office."

I asked, "Alvin, have you ever heard of Ready to Buy Real Estate or Leo Kilpatrick?"

Alvin said without hesitation, "Why are you asking about him?"

"His name came up today while I was talking with a man regarding the case I am working."

"Stay away from that man. That name can be suicide!" I asked Alvin to explain. He said, "This man is one of the leaders in organized crime in this part of the country. Many people will tell you he is the number one boss. I have been told that it is certain death if you cross him." I was breathing heavy just listening to Alvin tell me about him.

"Is his real estate business legitimate?"

"The real estate business is legitimate, so are his upscale apartments, office buildings and restaurants. His storefronts are all legitimate. But his real money comes from gambling and other unmentionable enterprises that are just below the surface of those legitimate businesses. The thing for you to know is that this man is a crook, one of the biggest."

"Is there anyway I can get a list of his businesses?"

"Sure. I know a private investigator that has made his living working for The King."

"The King?"

"That is the title that he is known by." He is "Leo (The King) Filpatrick."

"How long would it take you to provide me the names of his businesses?"

"Not long. I'll get you the information but you must understand this man kills anyone that even looks like they are causing him trouble. He will kill them or he would have them killed. He is known to kill the messenger if he doesn't like the message." One other piece of information regarding Mr. Filpatrick is his status as a socialite. The socialites of the City love him. He is involved in many area charities.

"What is his involvement in your case?"

"I am not sure. All I know is one of my clients has been meeting with him. Filpatrick may have the answer needed to solve both of my cases. Alvin, I will appreciate any information you can provide me on Filpatrick and his business concerns."

"I'll call you with his businesses soon." We ended our conversation.

What have I stepped in? Mrs. Robinson is involved with the head scumbag of organized crime? Why? If I have to personally interact with this man I'm in something over my head. It would be nice to have Abe around to discuss this case with.

How are the Coleman's or Robinson's involved with this man? They have money, power and all of the social connections. Where does Filpatrick fit in?

It was lunchtime. I asked Jamie if she was going out to lunch. She said, "No."

"Let's go to lunch. Yes you and me." She smiled and said, "Okay." She placed her lunch note on the door, picked up her coat and off we went.

"Where would you like to eat?"

"It doesn't matter to me."

"Just give me a name."

"I usually go to a place called Tim's. It has very good soup and sandwiches."

"Do we drive to it?"

"No it's just two blocks from the office."

I had never heard of Tim's. When we arrived at the restaurant we found it crowded. A waitress approached Jamie and told her it would be a minute. You could tell the waitress knew her. We were stuck in a line. I have disliked lines since the Navy. They had lines for everything. I looked at Jamie and asked, "So do you eat here often?"

"Yes. If I go out to eat during the week I eat here. The waitress that spoke to me is a friend of mine." I looked at the waitress. She did seem to be about Jamie's age and she was almost as pretty. So Jamie does have friends and a life outside of work. I found that pleasant to know.

The waitress returned and escorted us to a booth. I enjoyed the meal. Tim's food was good but having lunch with Jamie was the icing on the cake. I enjoyed spending time away from the office with her.

On our return to the office I told Jamie that Alvin Wilson would be calling with information on Leo Filpatrick's businesses. I would like for you to look into each business and provide me the same information you provided me on the Coleman's. In fact this is connected to their case. I could sense her excitement.

I think Jamie enjoys doing research into the lives of our clients. At this point I believe that the personal information we gather in the Coleman and Robinson cases will be more important than the business information. If that were not true Mr. Coleman wouldn't have provided me pictures of his family. Now with Filpatrick I have an uncomfortable feeling that the business information will be more important than any personal information.

When we returned to the office I was troubled. Have I lost my focus? I need to continue surveillance of Mrs. Robinson but so much gets in the way. I followed Johnson instead of keeping my eyes on Mrs. Robinson and yes I gained valuable information but what was Mrs. Robinson doing while I was following him? I must remember Mrs. Robinson is my main focus.

While I was waiting for Alvin to return my call I began thinking about Lisa Ann Coleman. What part does she play in my case? Maybe nothing but I think all of the ladies in this family will be involved.

My intercom rang. It was Jamie wanting to know if I wanted to talk with Alvin or should she take down the information. I want to speak with him. We exchanged greetings. I thanked Alvin for his fast response. He said, "It was not hard to check on his legitimate businesses. Filpatrick owns or runs several restaurants named, "New York's Finest." He owns the real estate company named "Ready to Buy Real Estate." Some upscale apartments called "The City's Best" and an office building in Manhattan located at 633 3rd Avenue."

I almost wet my clothes. I said, "Alvin, what was that address again?"

"633 3rd Avenue in Manhattan, why?"

I pulled myself together and said, "I wanted to be sure I had the address correct." I thanked Alvin and ended the call.

I could not believe that. I wouldn't have to guess if the Coleman's knew Mr. Kilpatrick. They know him. The next coincidence was the restaurant known as New York's Finest Restaurant. That is the place that Lisa Ann spent several hours eating, or doing something.

I thought, "The information Alvin has provided is good but what I need is a contact into Filpatrick's underground businesses."

I buzzed Jamie and asked her to step into my office. When she entered I said, "Here are the names of Mr. Kilpatrick's businesses. See if Alvin's contact at the Times knows the name, Leo Kilpatrick. If he does see what information is available over the last few months.

I told Jamie that I was returning to my surveillance of Mrs. Robinson in the morning. She said, "Once I call the Times I am leaving for the day." I told her good night.

I decided to drive to Tennyson's. Once I arrived my thoughts turned to Alvin and the information he provided me on Filpatrick. He seems to have connections. He will be a valuable resource.

My thoughts moved from Alvin to Lisa Coleman. So Lisa is aware and maybe involved with Filpatrick or his people. Does that mean Mrs. Robinson is also aware of the unsavory part of Mr. Kilpatick's life? I would guess the entire Coleman clan knows him. But how much do they know about him? It didn't appear that Alvin knew any details about Filpatrick's illegal businesses.

I need a contact that knows detail information about Filpatrick's dark side. Who can I contact? I am stumped. I downed a fourth drink and decided to leave for the night. My bed was sounding good. I really hadn't slept much in the last couple of days. I will start with Mrs. Robinson in the morning while Jamie checks into Filpatrick's businesses.

The alarm was going off in one ear and the telephone in the other. I glanced at the clock and sure enough it was six a. m. As I lifted the telephone receiver I heard Jamie's voice. I automatically asked her what was wrong. She said, "Nothing is wrong I wanted to catch you before you left home. I talked to our contact at the Times last evening about Mr. Leo Filpatrick. He said he would meet with me at eight a.m. He said if I wanted to do a thorough search of Mr. Filpatrick I should plan on spending most of the day."

"Take whatever time is necessary. I want to know as much as I can about his public life."

I thought the information she retrieves will tell me about the public person but how can I get information regarding his dark side?

I stopped at the Newsstand for my morning paper. I was parked in front of the Robinson's house by seven a.m. I began reading the paper when I saw a car leaving the house. I looked at my watch; it was eight twenty a.m. Good boy, Mr. Robinson, you're right on time. I finished the paper and began letting my mind wonder.

It was ten twenty a m. when a second car came to the main entrance. It was one of the town cars. As it pulled out onto the road I could see Mrs. Robinson inside. Here we go.

I fell in behind her. Well this morning Mrs. Robinson's driver was not driving into Manhattan; we were driving in the direction of the Coleman's home. I dropped off the pace. Sure enough that is her destination.

I eased past the main gate and turned around. I found a parking place that provided a view of the Coleman's entrance. At five minutes after eleven a.m. Mrs. Robinson's car approached the front gate. I reached for my binoculars and identified Mrs. Robinson, Lisa Ann and a new lady, Mary Dawson Coleman.

I followed them into Manhattan. They pulled into the same parking garage that Mrs. Robinson had entered before and parked.

The ladies stepped out of the car and began walking into the building attached to the parking garage. They entered a clothing store. After about thirty minutes watching them I was beginning to think this was just a shopping trip.

As they exited one store Lisa Ann almost walked on me. It appeared they were returning to their car. I returned to my car and fell in behind them again.

Their car pulled up in front of the same Lanscater's restaurant that I had followed Mrs. Robinson to the day I lost her. They stepped out of the car and it drove away. I stopped in front of the restaurant to make sure they were going in. They entered the restaurant so I pulled up the block and parked.

I walked back to the restaurant and looked inside. I couldn't see them so I walked in and asked to use the restroom. The matre'de didn't like it but he let me through. On my way to the men's room I did see all three of the ladies sitting at a table. Upon my departure from the men's room I could see they each had a drink so I concluded they were here for lunch. I left the restaurant.

I walked across the street to a newsstand. I purchased a magazine and returned to my car to read it. I had a good view of the front door of the restaurant. After an hour and a half a black town car pulled up in front of the restaurant.

My three ladies exited the restaurant and entered their car. The town car left the city and pulled to a stop at the Coleman's house. Then in about ten minutes it was back on the road with only one woman in it. I had wasted this day shopping.

I decided to find a telephone and call Jamie. The telephone rang and rang with no answer. I guessed she was still at the Times office.

I returned to the office to review what Jamie was able to uncover or discover about Filpatrick. When I arrived Jamie's little note was on the door, "I'll be back by four p. m." I looked at my watch. It was three forty p.m. I made a fresh pot of coffee.

The office telephone began to ring. I answered it and heard Kitty's voice. We exchanged greetings. Then she said, "Is it all right to call you at your office?

I said, "Sure."

"Do you ever attend art exhibits?"

"No. Places like that never seem to be a place to go alone. Why?"

"I have tickets to a special exhibit in Manhattan on Saturday."

"In that case if you ask me nicely I'll be happy to attend the exhibit with you."

Kitty laughed, "Okay Phil, will you go with me?"

"Sure."

"The exhibit will be open from ten a.m. until seven p.m. I have been told that it will take about two hours to view the exhibit."

"Why don't we plan on arriving at the exhibit at four thirty p.m. and then have dinner after it?"

"That's fine but you don't have to take me to dinner."

"I would like to. I will pick you up at four fifteen p.m." She indicated that would be fine. We ended our call.

Kitty's call was great. Having something to look forward to felt good. It would be fun being with her again. Jamie came walking into my office. She had several papers in her hands. She said, "First let me tell you that Mr. Filpatrick is a very successful businessman. He is involved with several charities and city organizations."

She continued, "Before you begin to read through the articles I want to tell you that there is nothing to connect the Coleman's or Robinson families with Mr. Filpatrick."

"You didn't find any pictures of him with any of the Coleman family?"

"No."

"I felt frustrated. I just knew the two families would be entwined. I still want to read the articles. I was hoping this would link at least one of my families to him."

I began looking at the pictures of Mr. Filpatrick with other individuals while reading the attached articles. It didn't take me long before I found a face that was familiar. It was Paul Winford, Mr. Coleman's attorney beside Mr. Filpatrick. They both had big smiles on their faces and they were shaking hands. The article was about four months old. It told of a city charity that the two men were co-chairing.

So again without anyone saying anything it is clear that the Coleman's know Filpatrick. As I was reading the article my intercom buzzed. I answered it and Jamie said, "There is a Mr. Johnson on the telephone for you."

"I'll take it." What could this be? Why is Johnson calling me?

11

"Is this the Mr. Johnson I talked with yesterday?"

"Yes, the one in the same."

"What can I do for you?"

"It's not what you can do for me but what I can do for you."

"What's that?"

"You know when we met I told you the name I gave to Mr. Coleman was Leo Filpatrick?"

"Yes."

"Well once I returned home and checked in with my firm I began to ask questions about Mr. Filpatrick. I wanted to know why I was asked to follow Coleman's daughter and when I discovered whom she was meeting I was told to close the case and go home? That just didn't set right with me. Then when you put a gun to my side and told me you were following me I began thinking that Mr. Coleman was up to something more than just determining the name of who his daughter was meeting with."

I stopped Johnson and asked, "How did you locate my telephone number?"

Johnson laughed. "I'm good at what I do too. I saw you standing beside your car when I drove away. Once I was out of sight I stopped along side a building and when you drove by I followed you. I obtained your license tag number. With the license tag it was easy. I ran your license tag and that provided your name. Then I ran a search to see if you had a license for that gun you introduced me to and you do. On the permit it gave your occupation and the firm that employed you."

Johnson continued, "I have it on good authority that this Mr. Filpatrick is up to his neck in the rackets. I was told his restaurants are fronts for gambling. He has fully equipped casinos in the back of each restaurant and that is only the beginning. He is also involved in prostitution at the highest level. He uses his apartments to house his high paid professionals. Businessmen come to the City from all over the world and

Filpatrick takes care of their needs and their money. I was also told he is into B movies."

"You mean pornographic movies?"

"Yes. That's what I was told.

I asked Johnson, "Why are you telling me all of this?"

"Aren't you still on Coleman's payroll?"

"Yes."

"You are probably more involved with his issue than I was so that means you have more at stake than I did."

"When you placed your gun into my side I knew that."

"I am sorry about the gun."

"If you are interested in getting into Filpatrick's casinos contact a man by the name of Walter Ragsdale in the City. He hangs out at a place named "The Wharf in Harlem. Once you slide into Filpatrick's backdoor you will be in some very deep water; I hope you are a good swimmer. These people play hard ball. Killing is an everyday happening with that bunch."

"How does Ragsdale know about the casinos?"

"Ragsdale has been in prison for armed robbery and attempted murder. When he was released there wasn't much honest work for him. His uncle is a dealer at one of the casinos and his boss found Walter a job as an errand boy."

"Walter will do anything for money. As long as you can pay his price he will assist you. I am telling you this because Coleman upset me when he received the name of the person his daughter was meeting but terminated me before I could ascertain why? All I want from you is the outcome of your case. That is if you make it to the end."

"Johnson, I thank you for this information. This is exactly the information I have been looking for. I will make it through this case and I will provide you the outcome."

"What is your telephone number?"

He provided his number. I asked him where he is located. "In Boston." I thanked him and ended the call.

I sat in my chair and began to swirl. If Johnson is telling me the truth I have a way into Filpatrick's backroom businesses. So Lisa Ann was not eating for several hours; she was gambling. That makes more sense than a four-hour meal.

I hit my intercom button and asked Jamie to come into my office.

I thanked her for the newspaper articles and told her they helped out a great deal. She seemed very happy that she could help. I told her who I had been talking with and what information he had provided.

I then gave Jamie my notes, pictures and newspaper articles on the Coleman Case. I told her we needed an out of the way place to keep this file since it contained the Coleman family pictures and names.

"Phil, let me show you something." I walked with her to a picture on the wall behind the coffeepot. She removed the picture and there was a rectangular slot. It was about nine inches wide and twelve inches deep. She said, "Abe had it made for just this type of information." She could see the amazement in my face. "I hadn't thought about it until you said put the file in a safe place."

"That will work just fine."

I looked at my watch and it was five minutes after five p.m. I said, "Jamie, it's quitting time." If you need me in the daytime for the next few days call my home number; I may be there.

Once Jamie left I knew my next step was to drive to the Wharf Bar. I didn't like the location of the Wharf Bar but if this man Ragsdale will assist me in gaining access into Filpatrick's backrooms it will be worth it.

As I entered the bar I could tell by the looks that the locals hadn't decided whether I should be there or not. I took a seat at the bar and ordered a drink. When the bartender brought my drink he asked, "Are you from around here?"

"Yes I live and work in the Bronx."

"What brings you here?"

"I am looking for a man by the name of Walter Ragsdale."

"Are you a cop?"

"No. I think Ragsdale can assist me in a business matter."

"Do you know Ragsdale?"

"Sure I know him."

"Does he come into the bar often?"

"Yes almost everyday."

"Is Walter here now?"

He looked over by the pool table and then back by the pinball machine and said, "No not right now."

I was on my third drink and beginning to feel hungry. I waved at the bartender to bring my tab. When he arrived I said, "If Ragsdale comes in while I am gone let him know I will return after dinner. Will you do that for me?"

"Sure I'll tell him. Who do I tell him wants to see him?"

"Ragsdale and I haven't met yet; just tell him a friend of his named Johnson from Boston asked me to contact him." The bartender said, okay. I paid my tab and left an extra good tip.

As I left the bar I noticed the City crews were hanging Christmas decorations. I need to remember to purchase a Christmas present for my mother.

With Christmas on my mind I thought this year I will buy Jamie, Miss Emerald and Kitty gifts also. It has been several years since I have had friends worth buying gifts. I realize how that sounds but the truth is the truth. It is going to be a good Christmas this year.

I finished my meal and returned to the Wharf Bar. I approached the bartender and asked if Ragsdale had shown up. He pointed to a man at the pinball machine and said, "That is Walter."

I thanked him and said, "Send him a fresh drink on me." Then I decided to wait and walk the drink to Ragsdale myself.

Walter was about thirty-five years old. You could tell by the way he was dressed and his unruly hair he didn't care how he looked. His physical condition was solid. When I shook his hand his gripe was as hard as a rock. He had on a short sleeve shirt showing his biceps. He must have spent most of his time in prison lifting weighs.

As he finished his game I said, "Hello my name is Phil Storm I would like to talk with you for a few minutes. Do you have some time?"

He looked me over as I handed him his drink and said, "Sure let's talk." We took a seat in a booth.

"I understand you can assist me in finding some action? I enjoy a friendly card game now and then."

He looked at me for several seconds before he said, "Are you a cop?"

"No."

He asked, "Who told you I could assist you?"

"A man by the name of Johnson from Boston."

"Are you in the same business as Johnson?" Now I was in a tight spot.

"No, but Johnson and I became acquainted the last time he was in the City."

Walter reached over and felt the material my coat was made of then he said, "It will be expensive."

"I'm not rich but give me a price?"

"It will cost you two hundred dollars."

"What does that buy me?"

"It will buy you a way into the casinos."

"Where are the casinos located?"

"Are you familiar with the New York's Finest restaurants?"

"Yes."

"Each restaurant has a private casino. The two hundred dollars buys you a membership to the casinos. So I will be allowed in any of the casinos?"

"All but one." I asked him how I will know the one I cannot enter. He wrote down an address and handed it to me.

"How will the casinos know I'm a member?"

"You don't need to worry about that. I will provide a membership card."

"When will I receive my membership card?"

"As soon as you provide me the two hundred dollars."

"I can have you the money tomorrow. Can you meet me here tomorrow about five p.m.?"

"Make it at six p.m.

"Six p.m. it is."

"I will be doing some checking on you. I hope I don't come across anything funny or the deal is off." Ragsdale stood and returned to the pinball machine.

I sat there for a few minutes thinking about this meeting and my clients. This meeting seemed to have more to do with Lisa Ann than Mrs. Robinson. I've never seen Mrs. Robinson in a casino.

Lisa may not have anything to do with why Mrs. Robinson is being followed but I would bet money she is linked to my case in some way. Lisa visits Filpatrick's casinos and Mrs. Robinson is meeting with him. My sixth sense tells me this entire family is involved in some way.

Johnson had been able to determine that Mrs. Robinson is meeting with Filpatrick and he had informed Mr. Coleman. Why didn't Robert provide me that information and ask me to speak with Filpatrick regarding his meetings with his daughter?

I wonder if the meetings between them will continue. The only way to determine that is to continue following her. I do think having access to the casinos has relevance in both cases. It will be interesting to see if any other members of the Coleman family visit Filpatrick's casinos.

It was seven a.m. sharp when I arrived at my parking place at the Robinson's house. I began reading the morning paper. As usual there was no activity from the Robinson's until eight twenty a.m. when Mr. Robinson left for work.

I thought to myself, If only I enjoyed crossword puzzles. Once I finish reading the newspaper there isn't anything to do but daydream. This morning is passing slowly.

Then at eleven ten a.m. a town car approached the entrance to the Robinson's home. I reached for my binoculars to see who was in it. It looked like Mrs. Coleman but I wasn't a hundred percent sure. These Coleman women look enough alike at a distance that they can fool you. The car entering the driveway broke the monotony of the long morning.

It was twelve fifteen p.m. when the same town car exited the entryway. The woman in it is Mrs. Coleman. I thought should I follow her? These Coleman women are shrewd. I decided to wait and see if Mrs. Robinson had any travel plans today.

It didn't take long to realize I had made a good decision. At twelve twenty p.m. a town car came to the entrance. It was Mrs. Robinson. I told myself that I would not lose her today.

As I fell in behind her car I decided to leave several car links between us in case I am not the only one following her. It appears she is going into Manhattan.

Once in the City her town car drove into the same parking garage as in earlier trips. I stopped short of her car and parked. No one exited her car. I could tell her car was still running. I started my car in case she decided to leave.

After sitting with our cars running for about five minutes another car pulled up beside her car. She exited her car. Someone in the other car opened the rear door and she stepped in. Once the door was closed the car drove away.

I pulled in behind it. Who was this? The car began driving through the City and stopped in front of Filpatrick's real estate office where I had seen Johnson. The man and Mrs. Robinson exited the car and walked into the building. In a few minutes they returned to the car and it drove off.

As I followed I thought about Johnson's visit to the real estate office. It had been very brief also. So was she just making a delivery? That reminded me of the two times I had seen Johnson at the Robinson's entrance. One time he was delivering a package and the other time he was picking one up. What was in the packages? I began to believe that Johnson wasn't as much help as he could have been. I need to contact him and have him explain what he was delivering to the Robinson's guard and to the real estate office. That would take less time than trying to determine it for myself?

My thoughts were interrupted when the car in front of me returned to the parking garage. Mrs. Robinson exited the mystery car, returned to her car and then drove away. Her driver drove her straight home. It was one thirty p.m., Mrs. Robinson is home and I am going to lunch.

While driving to lunch I remembered my need to make a trip to the bank and withdrawal the two hundred dollars for Ragsdale. Once I complete that I will return to the office and call Johnson. I was hopeful Johnson would know what was in the packages he had delivered.

Jamie was seated at her desk when I entered the office. She had her million-dollar smile ready for me. We exchanged greetings. She said, "There hasn't been any calls."

I entered my office and dialed Johnson's telephone number. I heard, "Williams and Johnson Investigations, this is Bond." I asked him if Johnson was available. He indicated that Johnson was on another line, could he take a message? I gave Bond my telephone number and asked him to have Johnson call me. I indicated it was very important that I talk with him. He indicated he would pass the message along. I ended the call.

In a few minutes my telephone rang. It was Johnson. We exchanged greetings. "Johnson there are a couple of questions I would like to ask you?"

"Okay shoot."

I said, "When you were on the Coleman case you made a delivery and a pick up to the Robinson's security guard. What was in the packages?

"I would guess it was money by the way the package felt. The delivery was made at Mrs. Coleman request.

When I saw you in Filpatrick's real estate office what were you doing?"

"I was delivering a similar package for Mrs. Coleman."

"Do you have any idea why these deliveries were made?"

"No. That family is very closed mouth."

"Is there anything else you can tell me about your involvement with the Coleman case?"

"No you know everything that I do." I thanked him and ended the call.

So, Johnson was the delivery boy for the Coleman and Robinson payoffs. This took me back to the beginning of the case. My first meeting with Robert was to discuss large sums of money being withdrawn from Mrs. Robinson's accounts. I thought to myself, Mrs. Robinson and Mrs. Coleman are two classy ladies; why are they giving money to Filpatrick?

If it wasn't money what could it have been? Drugs? No matter what was in the packages it is still very unusual that women of importance and notoriety would be making the deliveries themselves. I can't understand why they would put themselves in that type of position.

I can see it in the newspapers, Sally Lancaster Coleman Robinson and her mother Princess Audrey Lancaster Coleman arrested? Maybe counterfeit money trafficking, payoffs to the mob or drug trafficking? What was causing these ladies too personally interact with a known thug.

What is driving this case? I will be meeting with Mrs. Robinson in four days and I would bet money that her father would be calling before that.

I had to meet Walter Ragsdale in a few hours. I hope his assistance pays dividends because this case has hit a brick wall. If money is changing hands what is the reason? Is it blackmail, gambling debts, or payment for drugs? What else could it be? What am I overlooking?

Jamie walked into my office and said good night. I told her good night. Then I said, "Jamie, remember I am continuing my surveillance of Mrs. Robinson tomorrow."

At five twenty p.m. I entered the Wharf Bar and ordered a drink. As I began walking to an empty booth I was hoping that Ragsdale would be on time; I am hungry.

At five fifty p.m. Ragsdale came through the door. I stood and asked him what he was drinking as I waved at the waitress.

As Ragsdale was waiting for his drink he asked, "Do you have the money?"

"Yes" as he handed me a card. It was a small card with New York's Finest written across the top. Just below the name it had the number 653B. I asked Ragsdale, what the 653B meant. "That is your ticket into the casinos."

He reminded me of the one casino I could not enter. That didn't bother me because it wasn't the one that I had seen Lisa in. I handed him the two hundred dollars.

"What do I need to know in order to gain access to the casinos?" He indicated that when I enter the restaurant I am to show the matre'de my card. He will have a waiter escort me to the entry of the casino. Then once I am in the casino I will go to a main window to purchase chips. Cash is not used for gambling ever. Remember that.

I asked him, "Why?" He said, "If the casino is raided it would be said that all the activity was just friends having fun. No one is losing or winning money." I thought that was revolutionary.

He continued, "While you are in the casino all your drinks are free. You can use cash to tip the waitress or the cigarette girl. There is one last thing you must know and always remember while you are in the casino. All of the ladies that enter the casino have the same name, Mrs. Smith, and all of the men are known as Mr. Smith."

"What is that all about?"

"If you don't know any names you can't tell anyone who was in the casino can you? Don't go around asking questions. Do you understand?"

"I understand. Thanks Ragsdale." I left the bar. I know Filpatrick holds my answers but who will be his mouthpiece?

12

With my casino card in hand I stepped into my car and decided to try out my new card. It was eight thirty p.m. when I parked at the New York's Finest Restaurant where I had seen Lisa Ann Coleman.

I entered the restaurant and held my card in front of the matre'de. A waiter escorted me to the entrance of the casino. It was just like being seated in the restaurant but faster.

Once inside the casino I stopped at the main window for some chips. I decided to play a few hands of blackjack. Before I began gambling I ordered a drink.

There were two blackjack tables without any business. So once I had my drink I sat down and tried to look like I was interested in gambling. The casino was only about half full. I imagined many of the individuals that patronized this place were late night gamblers. I decided to be a high roller and play dollar blackjack. Since I only had twenty-three dollars I needed to play slow or I would not be playing long. After playing five hands I was up two dollars.

I gathered my chips and walked to the roulette wheel. I placed a dollar chip on red and one on number twenty-one. In a very few seconds I had lost all of my winnings. I decided to play again. I placed two-dollars on number seventeen. I won. So now I was playing on the house. Before I placed another bet I decided to find the waitress and get another drink.

As I approached the waitress I saw a familiar face entering the casino. It was young Lisa Coleman or I should say a young Mrs. Smith that looked like Lisa Coleman. She wasn't alone. She was with a Mr. Smith. I focused on him. I wanted to remember his face.

With my drink in hand I returned to the blackjack table. After losing three dollars I decided to leave the casino and wait in my car for Mr. and Mrs. Smith to depart. I planned to follow them and see where that would lead me.

Since I had arrived at the restaurant early I was parked in a perfect place to watch anyone leaving.

At eleven fifteen p.m., I spotted Mr. and Mrs. Smith leaving the casino. As I watched them walking across the parking lot I fumbled for my pencil and writing pad. I wanted to write down the license tag of the car they were in. In minutes I realized they were in separate cars. Lisa was in front of Mr. Smith. I was able to write down his license tag number as he was leaving the parking lot. I had Lisa's tag number.

As we pulled onto the highway I could tell this wasn't going to be easy. It was dark but there weren't many cars on the highway. I didn't want Mr. Smith to make me, so I stayed as far behind him as I could without loosing him. It appeared we were driving into the City.

Once in the City Mr. Smith pulled into a parking garage. I turned my lights off and followed him in. I was able to find a parking space just as I entered the garage. I stepped out of my car and walked across the parking garage. I saw Mr. Smith's headlights go off. He stepped out of his car and Lisa met him.

Lisa and Mr. Smith entered an elevator in the garage area. I approached the elevator and watched it stop on the twenty-fifth floor. I didn't notice the name of the building when I pulled into the parking garage. I wish I could have joined them on their elevator ride but at midnight in a building I wasn't familiar with I could have stepped off of the elevator with no where to go but join them. I would have looked pretty silly trying to explain that.

I took the elevator to the first floor where I was met by a security guard. He asked me where I was going. I told him that I had seen a friend getting on the elevator in the parking garage but the door closed before I could join him. He went to the twenty-fifth floor.

The security guard looked at me and said, "This is an apartment building and you will have to call your friend and get permission from him before you can leave the lobby."

I looked at the guard and said, "Maybe I should just leave it alone." The guard returned to his desk. I returned to the elevator and exited in the parking garage.

I wanted to determine the name of this building. In my part of town you don't find security guards posted in the lobby of apartment buildings. So where am I? When I arrived in the front of the building I could see its name, "The City's Best." Well here I am again, at one of Filpatrick's properties. This is the name of the apartments that Johnson had told me was for high priced party girls.

What was a girl like Lisa doing in a place like this? I am very confused. Why am I watching Lisa when my clients are Mr. Coleman and Mrs. Robinson? The investigator in me tells me that all of the Coleman women are involved in at least one of my two cases. I am sure this Coleman daughter and this location are both pieces of the puzzle needed to solve my cases.

Mr. Coleman is the father of all of them and I believe they are all involved in some way. As I stood here looking up at the front of "The City's Best" apartment building I made myself a promise to discontinue following Lisa unless I could connect her actions directly to my cases.

My immediate issue is to determine if it is worth waiting to see if Mr. Smith and Lisa leave tonight or tomorrow morning? It is a few minutes after midnight.

The private investigator in me wanted to stay so I could follow Mr. Smith and determine his identity. Then it hit me. This man lives here. Why would he bring his lady friend to a place like this if he didn't live here? I want to arrive at the Robinson's house by seven in the morning so it is time for me to go home.

On the drive home I wondered if Tom Watson would help me determine the name tied to this license tag number. I didn't like involving him when my requests were not official but if he doesn't want to assist me he can tell me.

Since it was one a. m. when I fell in bed the alarm clock was exceptionally frustrating when it began its ring at six a.m. I needed a shower and some coffee. With the coffee in me I was ready to start my day. I drove to the Newsstand for a morning newspaper.

I arrived at my routine parking place at seven-ten a.m. If I hadn't stopped for a newspaper I would have made it by seven a.m. Today is Friday so I will see Kitty tomorrow and I will see Mrs. Robinson on Monday. The case is moving very slowly. As of today I don't have any new information to pass along to Mrs. Robinson.

I began thinking about her case. Is Mrs. Robinson being blackmailed?

When we meet Monday I will ask her if she is being blackmailed. How will she react to that?

At eight twenty a.m. a car came from the Robinson's house. It was Mr. Robinson. He is an on time machine. At eight thirty a.m. another car came to the Robinson's entrance. It was Mrs. Robinson and she was driving the Ford Coupe. She wasn't using a town car today. Interesting.

As I fell in behind her. It only took a few minutes to realize she wasn't going into Manhattan. It became clear she was going to her parent's house.

At eleven thirty a.m. her car exited the Coleman's house. There was another woman in the car. I fell in behind them. I couldn't tell for sure but I thought it to be Mrs. Coleman. They were heading in the same direction as the casino I had visited last night. We began picking up traffic which made it easier to stay close without being made.

At eleven fifty-five a.m. their car exited the highway and entered the parking lot of the New York's Finest Restaurant. I was right about their destination.

I stopped short of the parking lot and watched the ladies exit their car. I confirmed it is Mrs. Coleman with Mrs. Robinson. After they entered the restaurant I parked.

I sat in my car deciding what to do. If I enter the restaurant and they were seated close to the front I could be seen. If they weren't in the restaurant I couldn't enter the casino without being seen.

I decided to enter the restaurant and have a waiter escort me to the casino. As we walked toward the casino I could see my two women seated at a table with a man. I pointed at their table and asked the waiter if he knew the three people at that table. He said, "Yes I know them. The lady on the left is Mrs. Robert Coleman, the woman on the right is her daughter, Mrs. Edward Robinson and the man is Mr. Leo Filpatrick." I thanked him for the information.

I entered the casino and looked around.

Since I knew where the ladies were I decided to return to my car and wait for them to leave.

As I walked back though the restaurant I could see my friends each with a drink. Once outside the restaurant I moved my car to a parking lot across the street. I didn't want to be noticed when the ladies exited the restaurant.

So now I have seen the King. Wow! This is a meeting of the top Coleman women and the King of the Gutter. Filpatrick is involved in my case and so is Mrs. Coleman. Now I need to connect the dots. This meeting had to be about something illegal.

At twelve fifteen p.m. the two ladies exited the restaurant and returned to their car and drove to the Coleman home. I tagged along. In fifteen minutes Mrs. Robinson returned to the front of the Coleman house alone. She pulled onto the road and drove home.

I decided to leave the Robinson surveillance and drive to the office. In route to the office I stopped for a sandwich. It was one forty-five p.m. when I arrived at the office. Jamie was at her desk reading. We exchanged greetings. I walked into my office and updated my case notes from last night and this morning. Once I had finished the notes I gave them to Jamie.

I returned to my office and called Paul Winford. I wanted to see if there had been any other unusual withdrawals from Mrs. Robinson's account. I didn't know what Paul would say, but I would love to have the same information on Mrs. Coleman. I decided to ask him for Mrs. Coleman's account information also. You can't even get a no if you don't ask the question.

I dialed Paul's number. Someone answered his telephone. I asked, "Is Paul available?"

The lady asked me, "Who is calling?"

"Phil Storm." In a few seconds Paul was on the telephone. We exchanged greetings.

I asked Paul, "Will you check to see if there has been any unusual withdrawals from Mrs. Robinson's account lately?" "What period of time?" "Since I've been on the case." "Fine."

"Paul, before we end our conversation I would like to ask you something else."

"All right."

"Paul, if I asked for the same information regarding Mrs. Coleman's account would you have to get permission from Mr. Coleman before you could provide it?" He didn't say a word.

"Paul, if you could provide me this information I will explain it to Mr. Coleman when we meet."

Paul was silent for several seconds before saying, "Phil why do you need that information?"

"I think there is money leaving Mrs. Coleman's account and going directly to Mrs. Robinson. If that is true it is relevant to my case. Paul, I don't want to upset Mr. Coleman but I do want to solve this case.

"So you will need the same time period?"

"Yes. I need unusual checks written to Mrs. Robinson or unusual cash withdrawals."

"Can you tell me anything about what part this information may play in the case?"

"Paul I was hired to follow Mrs. Robinson and determine whom she meets and why she is meeting them. The case came about because of unusual withdrawals of money from Mrs. Robinson's account. I realize that initially the unusual withdrawals were connected to trips abroad. Currently it appears that the same thing is taking place in the City.

"What if Mrs. Robinson has no unusual withdrawals but her mother does? Paul, I will be honest with you. I think Mrs. Robinson is being blackmailed. I haven't determined the reason but I feel she is receiving financial support from her mother.

"You know you will need to explain this to Mr. Coleman soon?"

"Yes. This is Friday and I meet with Mrs. Robinson on Monday. I would like to receive this information before I meet with her. So Paul, will you help me?"

"This isn't something I would normally do. I am not sure I should be looking at Mrs. Coleman's account. I never have but I will make this one exception. You have presented a logical and practical need for the additional information. You will be the one that explains the request to Mr. Coleman."

"I will make sure he is aware that I requested the information and I will explain why I requested it."

"I will try to have this information to you before Monday."

"Paul, my meeting with Mrs. Robinson is at ten a.m. Monday." I ended the call.

I felt the Monday meeting with Mrs. Robinson would answer some questions even if Paul couldn't provided me Mrs. Coleman's financial information prior to my meeting. I was going to pressure Mrs. Robinson on the blackmail issue.

I put business aside and walked to Jamie's desk and said, "What plans do you have this weekend?"

"Not much. I am going to my sister's house Saturday. Her husband works on Saturday and we are going to take her children to see Santa. That is always fun. Then we will return to my sister's house and decorate her Christmas tree. The kids have so much fun doing that."

"It is nice having family close this time of the year."

"Yes. I don't know what I would do with myself if it wasn't for my sister and her family living close." I'm not sure what I would do if I didn't like to drink. *Where would I go what would I do?*

"What are you doing?" I really didn't want to tell her about my plans with Kitty and I knew why. Jamie is someone I would love to spend time with. As much time as possible but until I determine if Abe's rule regarding no involvement with a client or employee is my rule I will continue seeing Kitty.

So I said, "Remember when Kitty called earlier in the week?"

"Yes."

"She wanted to know if I would like to go to an Art Exhibit with her Saturday? So that is where my Saturday will begin. Then after the museum we are going to have dinner."

"That will be nice. She seems like a nice lady."

"She is a nice lady."

"Jamie do you decorate a Christmas tree at your place?"

"No there isn't any reason since there isn't anyone there but me. What about you?

"No I don't see the need either. I will be at my mother's on Christmas day."

I said, "Jamie if you want to leave for the day it is fine. I am going to stay in case Paul Winford returns my call."

"Okay Phil, I'll see you Monday."

I walked to the coffeepot and poured the remaining coffee into my cup. As I returned to my office I began thinking about Kitty. I wondered why a lady like her didn't have a steady boyfriend or a husband. She seemed to have all the qualities a man would look for in a wife. Here I am saying that after only being with her a few hours. I did see those qualities in her. She is several years older than me but I shouldn't let that be a deterrent if we want to spend time together. Why do I always bring that fact up when I talk to myself about her? If we enjoy being together age shouldn't matter.

I looked at my watch. It was six p.m. and I hadn't heard from Paul. I was going to contact Tom Watson and see if he would help me with Mr. Smith's real name. Since it is late Friday I will call him on Monday.

I began to wonder if I should return to my favorite restaurant's backroom to see if Lisa and Mr. Smith would be there again. Lisa's activities may not be apart of my case but then it may figure in somewhere.

Besides I don't have anything else to do tonight. I decided after dinner I would drive to the casino.

It was seven thirty p.m. on a nice but cold night as I drove to the casino. While driving I began thinking about Christmas.

What type of gifts should I buy Jamie, Miss Emerald, Kitty and my mother? I thought I will ask my mother for gift ideas for the ladies. I knew if I do ask her for ideas I will have to explain in detail my relationship with each one of the ladies. I could ask Kitty for some ideas for my mother. A woman's touch would be good.

As I approached the restaurant I could tell by the number of cars in the parking lot it would be packed. The casino was wall to wall people. I don't think I had ever seen so many Mr. and Mrs. Smith's in my life.

I decided to have a drink and watch the people. As I was mingling in the crowd I spotted my Mr. and Mrs. Smith. Lisa was dressed to the nines. She was a very pretty young lady. She was carrying a drink in one hand and chips in the other. Mr. Smith was following her with a firm grip on her waist. He definitely wanted all to know she was with him.

As I watched the two of them I thought maybe Lisa is the one being blackmailed? Her older sister and mother were making the payoffs. If so what did they have on her? Gambling, or her relationship with a man that probably makes his living pushing something illegal for "The King".

I needed to get deeper into "The Kings" dirty world. As I watched them I knew if I stay until they leave I will end up at the City's Best apartments again. So I finished my drink and drove home.

It was eight fifty a.m. when I awoke on Saturday morning. It felt good waking up without the noise of the alarm clock. I decided to have breakfast at the Coffee Shop. Then I would drive to my mother's apartment.

This Christmas issue seemed to be more important than in past years. Of course my last few Christmas's had been overseas. But even if I had been in the States I wouldn't have had any special people in my life. I said to myself, "My mother is special but I knew what I meant by the comment."

I arrived at my mother's apartment at twelve twenty p.m. She was eating. She asked me to join her. I told her I had finished breakfast less than two hours ago. I said, "Mom I need your help. I have three ladies who I want to buy Christmas presents. One is a young lady that works for me, one is the former wife of my boss that died and one is an older lady that handles the accounting records for my business."

My mother said without hesitation handkerchiefs, headscarves or bath salts. I said, "Thanks for the great ideas."

"If any of the ladies are real special maybe a necklace?"

Was I impressed! "Thanks mom. Those are great ideas."

As expected she asked, "Is one of them special?" "No mom they are just good friends." I may have lied a little but to my surprise mom left it at that.

After the Christmas conversation mother updated me on all of the neighbors. I looked at my watch and it was five minutes after two p.m. I told mom that I had an appointment at four p.m. and I needed to stop at home prior to the appointment. She seemed to be happy about the visit and that I had involved her in my private life. It was a very enjoyable visit.

On my drive home I decided to buy Kitty a necklace but I was still in limbo as to the other ladies.

It was four p.m. when I parked in front of Kitty's house. As she came to the door I could see I had dressed properly for the day. I had worn a suit without a tie. She was dressed in a nice dress but it wasn't an evening gown. She looked great. There was a twinkle in her eyes, giving her a look of happiness.

Once we arrived at the museum I found myself walking from item to item watching Kitty as she looked at each piece. Once in awhile she would turn to me and ask what I thought of a certain piece. Most of the time we agreed. After we had completed viewing the exhibit I asked, "Are you ready for dinner?"

"Sure."

"There is a restaurant within walking distance of the museum, do you think it is too cold to walk to the restaurant?"

"No. The walk will be fine." Once we had arrived at the restaurant and placed our order I asked Kitty to assist me in deciding what to buy my mother for Christmas.

"Does your mother attend church?"

I sat there a minute with an empty head? You know I'm not sure? Why?"

"A Bible from her son would be a nice gift."

I looked at her and said, "Do you go to church?"

"Most of the time. Remember my friend whose mother is in a home?"

"Yes."

"She calls me every week to see if I will go to Church with her. She is married but her husband doesn't attend Church so I usually go with her. So the first personal thing I have learned about Kitty is she attends church. That's a start at getting to know her better.

Once we had completed our meal we window-shopped our way back to my car. As we drove I told her that this had been a very enjoyable Saturday and I was glad she invited me to join her. She agreed. "So would it be acceptable to have dinner together in the future?"

"Yes. I would like that."

When we arrived at Kitty's house I walked around and opened her door. As she stepped out of the car she said, "Thanks Phil, don't be a stranger." Then she walked to the door. I waved at her as she opened her door. I returned to my car and drove home. I came to the decision that Kitty only wanted to be my friend and nothing more. I decided that was enough. It was nice to have her as a friend.

13

Monday morning I arrived at the office at seven thirty a.m. I was drinking coffee when Jamie walked in. She said, "Boy you are an early bird today."

"Good morning young lady."

"What's on the agenda for today?"

"I have a ten a.m. with Mrs. Robinson. I am hoping to receive a telephone call from Paul Winford before ten a.m. If he doesn't call before ten a.m. but calls while Mrs. Robinson is here put the call through."

I was getting nervous about my meeting with Mrs. Robinson. I didn't have any idea what type of response she would have when I accused her of being blackmailed.

Just a few minutes after nine a.m. my telephone rang. Jamie answered it and then hit my intercom button. She said, "It is Mr. Winford."

I answered the telephone. We exchanged greetings and then he said, "Phil there were not any unusual withdrawals from Mrs. Robinson's account but there were several unusual withdraws of cash from Mrs. Coleman main account over the time period you requested."

I asked Paul to provide me the amounts of the withdrawals. He indicated that each withdrawal was for five thousand dollars. I asked Paul to hold the line. I wanted to look at my notes and compare his dates with the dates when Johnson had delivered packages to Mrs. Robinson's security guard, Filpatrick and the date when Mrs. Robinson and Mrs. Coleman met with Filpatrick.

I asked Paul to give me the dates of the withdrawals. As I looked at the first withdrawal date I saw that it was two days before I saw Johnson make his delivery to the Robinson house. The second withdrawal was also two days before his pick up at the Robinson's entry. The third withdrawal was the same day that Mrs. Robinson and Mrs. Coleman met with Filpatrick.

Paul said, "Phil, are you still on the line?"

"Yes. I was just checking the dates of the withdrawals against my case notes."

"Is this information helpful?"

"Yes. The dates of the withdrawals do correspond with activity I am seeing. Paul, I will be more specific when we meet with Mr. Coleman." Paul asked me when I was planning to meet with him.

"Why don't you call Mr. Coleman and schedule a meeting anytime after today." Paul indicated he would contact Oscar and have him schedule the meeting. I asked Paul to provide Oscar my office telephone number. Paul agreed and we ended our conversation. I was ready for my meeting with Mrs. Robinson.

Mrs. Robinson is like her father when it comes to promptness. Straight up ten a.m. she walked into the office. Jamie greeted her and asked her if she would like coffee. Mrs. Robinson said, "No, but thank you."

She walked into my office, looked at me and said, "What do you have for me?" She is so matter of fact. No greeting just straight to business.

I looked her straight in the eyes and said, "Mrs. Robinson I think you are being blackmailed and I think this Mr. Johnson has been used to deliver some of the payoffs."

She sat up straight in her chair and said, "How did you come up with that notion? And who is this Mr. Johnson?"

"While I was watching the entrance to your home this Mr. Johnson made one delivery to your security guard and on one other occasion he made a pick up from your security guard. Can you explain that?"

"There are many deliveries that come to that guard each week. I did not receive anything from a Mr. Johnson. Why am I being blackmailed?"

"I don't know I was hoping you would tell me?"

"There isn't anyone blackmailing me. Who is this Johnson person?"

"I was hoping when you told me why you were being blackmailed you would tell me who he is or at least who his employer is."

All of a sudden Mrs. Robinson stood and faced me and said, "Mr. Storm you are fired! You have not provided me with anything but a lot of incorrect and empty nonsense."

She returned to her seat, removed her checkbook and began writing. She ripped out a check and handed it to me. It was for the remaining five hundred dollars she had told me she would pay me when I completed her case.

"Madam if you no longer need my services you do not owe me any additional money." I handed the check back to her. "Can't we sit down and talk about this some more?" She laid the check on my desk and ran out the door without a word. Man was I surprised. She had a look of anger in her eyes as she yelled at me.

As I looked at Jamie I could see confusion and concern in her face. I stood there for the longest time staring at Jamie. I could not believe what had just happened. I finely said, "Well Jamie I didn't handle that very well".

"I believe you hit a nerve." That brought me back to my senses.

"I hit a nerve."

I thought, "Why did Mrs. Robinson get so upset?" If she isn't being blackmailed she could have said, " Phil that is not true. You are on the wrong track. You need to get more information regarding the man who is following me. The answer to why he is following me will come out once you determine who hired him. Once you determine that you will know I am not being blackmailed."

I wish I had handled the meeting different. I am sorry I allowed her to leave but I was so stunned I couldn't say anything.

Maybe I should have told her that her father hired Johnson. But since I didn't know why Mr. Coleman had hired him just telling her who hired him would have probably ended up with the same response.

I remember her saying in our first meeting that it had to be her father that hired the person following her. So if I had confirmed that without the why part being answered I am sure she would have walked out anyway.

Unless Mr. Coleman takes the same action as Mrs. Robinson did when he becomes aware I had Paul provide me information on his wife's finances I will continue trying to solve his case.

I was sitting at my desk still thinking about the way Mrs. Robinson left when I heard my intercom buzz. I answered my telephone and Jamie said "A man named Oscar is on the telephone for you." I thanked her. I greeted Oscar. He said, "Mr. Coleman will meet with you at seven p.m. Tuesday evening at his home." I told Oscar I would be there and ended our conversation.

Once I ended the call my thoughts returned to Mrs. Robinson. She was so upset. If she isn't being blackmailed why did she get so upset?

Where does Mr. Leo (King) Filpatrick fit in? Why is she and her mother involved with him? Still more questions than answers.

I needed to obtain more information about Filpatrick and his illegal businesses. My only connection to Filpatrick's dark side is Walter Ragsdale. Since he provided me with access to the casinos maybe he could connect me to the B movies and the City's Best prostitute businesses. Maybe the pieces of the puzzle I need to solve my cases lies hidden in this rotten part of the City?

I called the Wharf Bar. When the bartender answered I asked him if Ragsdale was there. He said, "No." I thanked him and ended the call. I decided to drive by the place later. I wasn't ready to provide any personal information to Ragsdale.

Now it was time to call Tom Watson and see if he would assist me one more time. I buzzed Jamie and asked her to call Tom. In a few minutes Jamie buzzed me to let me know Detective Watson was not available but she had left a massage for him to call me as soon as possible.

I looked at my watch and asked Jamie, "Do you have lunch plans?"

"No. I was going to take care of an errand instead of eating."

"Why don't you go to lunch with me and then you can take care of your errand."

"The free lunch talked me into it."

"Are we going to the same place?"

"If you are buying we can go where ever you like."

"Your lunch place is fine."

It was nice having lunch with Jamie. Once we finished lunch she was off to take care of her errand and I was on my way to the Newsstand to purchase the morning newspaper prior to returning to the office.

It was two thirty p.m. when Tom returned my call. We exchanged greetings. "Tom, I'm sorry that each time we talk I am asking for something."

He said, "That's fine. What's up?"

"I have another license tag number that I need to connect with a name. The man driving this car seems to be involved with a person that is associated with my current case."

"Give me the number." I gave him the license number. "I will get back with you." I thanked him. I can not continue using a police detective for unofficial information.

It was three fifty p.m. when I left the office to drive to The Wharf

Bar. When I entered the bar Ragsdale was playing a pinball machine. I approached him and asked, "Can I buy you a drink?" He looked at me and then at his watch. He said, "Haven't got time for a drink right now."

"I need to talk with you for a few minutes."

"I can't right now. I am expecting someone any minute and when they arrive I will be leaving with them."

"When can I meet with you?"

"Later today."

"How about six p.m.?"

"Fine."

"Could we meet at Tennyson's?"

"Sure. I'll see you there at six p.m." I thanked him.

I was glad he would meet me at Tennyson's. I didn't like coming to Harlem. This Bar couldn't be in a worse area but if I had to continue coming here to meet Ragsdale I will since he is my only led into Filpatrick's dark world.

With my meeting set I returned to the office where I found Jamie reading her book. She looked up as I entered the door and said, "Take a look at what I bought?" She held up some very small clothes. I knew the items were Christmas presents for her sister's children. "I have so much fun shopping for my nieces."

I could feel the Christmas spirit looking at the children's clothes. I needed to attend to my shopping before long. I thanked her for showing me the clothes.

I poured a cup of coffee and headed for my office to read the paper. The news seemed to be the same as the last time I read it. As I sat reading Jamie buzzed me. I picked up the telephone.

She said, "It is Tom Watson."

When he came on the line I said, "Hi that was fast."

"When I gave your license number to the lady that does the tag look ups, she remembered that she had looked this license tag number up yesterday. Phil, I don't know whom you are representing but you have come in contact with a bad boy. This is Eugene Ransom. He is one of King Filpatrick's top men. Phil, do you know whom King Filpatrick is?"

I said, "I have heard he is a man who has two heads. One head seems to be honest while the another one isn't so honest."

"I just wanted to make sure you knew about his bad side. We have our eyes on him so be very careful while around him. Phil, if possible leave him alone."

"Tom I don't think I will be in direct contact with either Mr. Ransom or Mr. Filpatrick. Ransom is someone that is involved with a person in my case. I will be careful and thanks." We ended the call.

Again the Robinson/Coleman case leads back to Filpatrick. This man, Ransom is directly involved with one of my client's family members. Does that mean he is involved in my case? It appears to me that if Mr. Coleman would talk with Filpatrick he could solve his case without me. But because he is writing the checks I will continue investigating Filpatrick for him.

It was six p.m. when I walked in the door at Tennyson's. I walked to the bar and Jerry pointed to a booth where Walter was seated. I ordered a drink and told Jerry to send another one over for Walter. I sat down in the booth with Walter. He said, "What's goin' on now?"

"I need your help again."

"What on?"

"On two items. First, if I was alone and needed a quick date where could I find one? Second, if I was going to invite some of the guys over and we needed some big boy entertainment where could I find it? Any idea, Walter?"

The waitress set our drinks down and walked away. Walter said, "I might be able to put you in contact with a person that could help you but it is expensive. I removed a fifty-dollar bill from my pocket and put it under his hand. He looked at it and said, "If this guy has a brother you have a deal."

I sat there looking at him.

"If I give you this guy's brother how many more people will I have to pay?"

"If you need a date you'll have to pay for the date on delivery. If you need big boy entertainment you'll have to pay for it on delivery. But there aren't anymore middlemen to pay. What do you say?"

I slipped the second fifty-dollar bill to his side of the booth. "I'll give you a telephone number and a name. When you're ready call the telephone number and tell the person that answers the telephone that Walter R. recommended you. That will get you in the door."

"It sounds easy. What's the name?"

"When you call ask for Just Helpful."

What?" Walter repeated, "Ask for Just Helpful.

"Is this like knowing everyone in the casinos as Mr. and Miss. Smith?"

"Is there goin' a be a problem over a name?" I said, "No problem Walter I'll do it your way."

"Do not write the telephone number down. Memorize the number. I hope you have a good memory?"

"When I pay a "C" Note for a telephone number I will remember it." I called the waitress over and paid our tab and we parted company. I needed to have dinner.

Once I finished dinner I drove home. As I mixed a drink I began to question how this new information could assist me with my case.

As I sat staring out of my only window into the darkness I decided to call the telephone number and ask for a meeting with Just Helpful. I will take the pictures of the Coleman women and ask Just Helpful if he had ever seen any of them. If he does recognize anyone I imagine money will assist me from there.

I know if Mr. Coleman ever discovers that I have shown his family photographs to a man by the name of Just Helpful my fingers and toes would never be the same but it is worth the risk. Since I am at a stand still any lead is better than just sitting. I know something in Filpatrick's illegal businesses is going to provide me the break I need to solve my cases.

I looked at the clock. It was nine thirty p.m. I didn't think a man by the name of Just Helpful kept regular office hours.

I have a meeting with Mr. Coleman tomorrow night. Any additional information I can provide will be helpful. There it is "Helpful" so maybe Just Helpful will provide answers?

I dialed the telephone number. A man answered. I said, "Walter R. told me to call and ask for Just Helpful. Is he in?" The voice said, "just a minute." Another voice came on the line and said, "What can I do for you?"

I asked him, "Is this Just Helpful?"

"Yes this is he."

"I would like to set a time to meet with you and check out your merchandise?"

"What?"

"I would like to check your merchandise?"

"If you are into pictures you can come around anytime."

"Good."

Does this include big boy entertainment?"

"Yes, there is a listing that includes the stars picture."

"That's good enough for me. When can we meet?"

"When do you want to meet?" I said tonight.

"Fine."

He gave me an address and said, "When you arrive enter and take a seat in the lobby; someone will meet you there."

"Fine. I'll be there in about twenty-five minutes."

When I arrived at the building I was surprised. It was a nice looking building. Once I entered the room I turned around and looked at the door I had just opened. On the top of the door there was a device that would alert someone that there was a guest.

I sat in the waiting room for a good ten minutes. Then a man entered and asked me what I wanted. I told him, "I have a meeting with Just Helpful."

This man is probably six foot four inches tall and muscles everywhere. I noticed that he was missing the bottom half of his left ear. The only thing he had more of than muscles were tattoos. His arms were mostly blue with what appeared to be tattoos on top of tattoos. He was totally bald and he had tattoos on his forehead and around the lower portion of the back of his head. He told me to follow him.

Mr. Halfear escorted me into an office where there was another man. This man was as small as Mr. Halfear was large. The little man was sitting behind a desk that was too large for him. He was partially bald. He wore glasses with very thick lens. He was smoking a cigar.

I asked him, "Are you Just Helpful?" He looked at me and said, "That's what they call me." I had the envelope with the Coleman pictures in my hand.

"What's in the envelope?"

"Some pictures. I would like to see if one of your clients looks similar to any of the pictures. It's a thing with me. I go for girls with certain looks."

He asked me if I was a cop. I knew he had to ask that question. He is aware of entrapment. I told him no. If you need to confirm that with

Walter R. call him. He said, "Let me see the pictures?" He seemed to be a smart little man.

I handed him the pictures of the ladies. Then he asked, "What else do you have in there?"

"I have pictures of men but you won't need to deal with them." He gave me a long look. I smiled and said, "I'm straight. I'll show you the men's pictures if you need to see them?"

He began looking at the ladies pictures. I reached over and put Lisa's picture in front of him and said, "Have you a lady that looks like her?"

"No."

"Are you sure?"

"I know my stock."

Then he picked up another one of the pictures and said, "I can show you this one." The picture he was holding was of Mary Dawson Coleman. I said, "You have a movie with a girl that looks like her in it?"

"No. I have her merchandise."

"Can I see it?"

"Stay here."

I was confused. The out and about daughter is Lisa Ann. She was the one in Italy before the war with the money issue, she is out and about with a scumbag gambling and staying in the apartment building where the high dollar girls live and this man is telling me he has a movie with Mary in it? What is going on?

He came strolling back into the room with a large book and some small canisters. He sat at his desk and asked me to come around and look over his shoulder. I walked around his desk and he opened the book. Sure enough there was a picture that looked just like Mary Coleman.

I asked, "Is this girl in some of your movies?"

He pointed down at the canisters and said, "These are three of her films."

"She is in your movies?"

"She's the star. Her movies are good sellers."

"How many movies has she made?"

"I don't know but this tells me I should have six but all I could find was three. I can contact one of our other outlets in the morning and see if they have her other movies."

I asked him the price of the movies.

"Twenty-five dollars each." I reached into my pocket and pulled out seventy-five dollars and asked for the three canisters. He handed them to me.

The Coleman ladies pictures were lying on his desk. As I reached over to pick them up I asked, "Are you sure you haven't seen this girl?" I pointed at Lisa's picture again.

"She's not one of mine." I asked him to load the movie and prove to me that the girl in my picture is really in the movie?

"Sure come with me."

He led me into a little room with three chairs and a small table with a projector on it. In the front of the room was a screen. He took one of the movies out of the canister and loaded it on the projector. He turned off the lights and started the movie. As the movie began I sat surprised. If it wasn't her it was a look a like. After watching it about three minutes I told him he could stop the film. He placed the movie into the canister and returned it to me. I thanked him and I left the building.

As I was driving home I tried to understand what I had uncovered! My thoughts returned to the reason I was hired by Mr. Coleman. I was hired to follow his daughter, Sally and determine whom she was meeting and why.

Then I determined that Mr. Coleman had hired an investigator prior to hiring me to do the very same thing. Then when I began watching Sally I discovered Mr. Coleman's daughter Lisa was involved with one of King Filpatrick's scumbags. Now I have determined that Mr. Coleman's daughter Mary is a star in pornographic movies.

By the time I arrived at my place my mind was swimming in questions.

How many family members are involved? I do believe that Mr. Coleman is a smart man but I don't think he had any idea what I was going to uncover. I have been working under the assumption the unusual money withdrawals would lead me to some tainted or corrupt item in Mrs. Robinson's life. Is that a wrong conclusion?

Since I have been on the case Mrs. Robinson has not left the country nor has there been any large amounts of money moved from her accounts. Currently the money is coming from Mrs. Coleman. Why rout the money through Mrs. Robinson if it is going to end up with Filpatrick? Especially since the last payment went directly from Mrs. Coleman's account to a meeting with Filpatrick.

I decided it is Mary that is being blackmailed. Her sister and mother are acting as middlemen between her and Filpatrick. I now have proof that Filpatrick has the kind of information on Mary that would make it easy to blackmail the Coleman family.

Filpatrick can hold the Coleman's hostage forever. I am sure they would rather pay than have the world know about Mary's movie career. I couldn't determine any other reason why they would continue to pay Filpatrick.

I said, "Remember Phil, your case isn't about Filpatrick. It is to determine who is following Mrs. Robinson and why? I have identified whom and now I believe I have identified the why.

Mary is being blackmailed. I need one more meeting with Mrs. Robinson. At that meeting I will provide her the who and the why.

What drives the Coleman ladies to personally associate with trash like Filpatrick? It is late and I am mentally drained. I need to rest so I can fight the good fight tomorrow.

14

I rolled over and looked at the clock. It was eight fifty a.m. Since I had decided not to follow Mrs. Robinson today I intentionally didn't set my alarm. As I rolled out of bed I called Jamie. When she answered the telephone we exchanged greetings.

I said, "How is your day?"

"It is fine. Mrs. Robinson called and wants to meet with you. She said she would call again at noon to schedule a meeting." I was quite surprised but very happy. I told Jamie to schedule a meeting with her anytime this afternoon. I ended our call.

I arrived at the office at ten thirty a.m. Jamie greeted me with another good morning as she filled my coffee cup and handed it to me. I said, "Hi kid and thanks for the coffee. Why are you serving me coffee?"

"I looked at your coffee cup earlier this morning and decided to wash it before something began growing in it. So since it was right here I just filled it." I smiled and walked quietly to my office. I thought that was nice of her. I admitted to myself that I usually rinsed my cup with left over cold coffee and considered it clean.

At noon Jamie buzzed me and told me Mrs. Robinson wants to meet at two thirty p.m. today. I thought good timing. I will meet with her this afternoon and with Mr. Coleman this evening.

Jamie walked into my office and asked, "Can I take a little extra time when I got to lunch today?"

"Sure take what time you need. Would you bring me a sandwich when you return?" She agreed. I gave her some money and she left the office.

At one fifty p.m. Jamie walked into my office with my sandwich. Then she returned to her desk. In a few minutes she returned to my office. She had a large sack in her hands. She began pulling toys out of the sack. I knew her sister's children were going to have a great Christmas. Jamie had a look of a small child as she showed me each toy. She is enjoying shopping for her nieces.

The telephone began to ring as Jamie was replacing the toys in the sack. She answered it and laid the receiver on her desk and returned to my office for her sack. I could see that the call was for her because she began taking each toy out of the sack again as she talked on the telephone.

At two thirty p.m. Jamie brought Mrs. Robinson into my office. I greeted her and asked her to have a seat. She started the meeting by saying, "I needed to meet with you and apologize for my behavior at our last meeting. Do you think I am still being followed?"

"No, I didn't think so."

"I am not being blackmailed. There are some problems within my family but I believe they will be resolved soon so I will not need your services any longer. I hope you will accept my apology."

"I certainly accept your apology but I don't think I had solved anything. I want to return the last check you gave me."

"Mr. Storm you have earned the money so please keep it."

She seemed so relaxed and she sounded so matter of fact that her problem would be resolved soon that I decided to keep the check and let her go in peace. I will tell her father what I have uncovered.

"Thank you Mrs. Robinson; I hope you and your family have a very Merry Christmas."

"I hope your Christmas is merry also," as she walked out the door.

Why did she say the family problems would be resolved soon? I knew if I had asked the question she wouldn't have answered it. Well, good-bye Mrs. Robinson. I gave Jamie Mrs. Robinson's five hundred-dollar check and asked her to see it made its way to Miss. Emerald.

Since I kept Mrs. Robinson's check I decided to give Jamie a Christmas bonus. I would give her twenty-five dollars the Friday just before Christmas. As I thought about giving her the bonus I wanted to jump up and say, "Merry Christmas to all and to all a good night." The telephone ringing returned me to reality. Since the intercom didn't buzz I knew it was for Jamie.

I don't have anything to do until my meeting with Mr. Coleman. I wasn't looking forward to telling him about his daughter but he was paying me to solve his case. He knows Filpatrick was the one meeting with Mrs. Robinson but I am sure he doesn't know why.

I arrived at the Coleman entrance at six thirty-five p.m. I was early but I had to wait somewhere until seven p.m. The security guard waved me through the gate.

When I arrived at the parking area there wasn't anyone waiting to escort me to the house. Then as I was stepping out of the car I could see Bogey approaching in his cart. When he arrived I said, "Good evening." He looked at me and smiled.

Without a word he drove me to the front door. I began to think that Bogey and I would never become close friends. That was funny. I didn't have any desire to know any other thugs. Walter Ragsdale and Just Helpful are plenty.

The door opened and there was Mr. Butler. I was sure he would always be nameless. Without a word he guided me to my normal meeting place. It seemed unusual that none of the Coleman employees had anything to say.

It was six forty-five p.m. when Paul Winford entered the room. I stood and we greeted each other. Paul asked, "A drink Phil?"

"Yes that would be nice." He poured two drinks and handed me one.

"Phil, Mr. Coleman is very upset with me. When I made him aware I had reviewed his wife's financial information his face became bright red and he began banging his fists on his desk. I have never heard him swear or scream."

I thought, "Maybe I will be totally finished with the Coleman family today. I thanked Paul for preparing me for Mr. Coleman's reaction. "The information was pertinent to the case."

Mr. Coleman walked into the room. He didn't say a word. He walked over and mixed himself a drink and then sat down behind his desk. He killed his drink without a word. I wondered when the action would start. I can handle the yelling much better than the silence. Then Mr. Coleman stood and said, "Phil, I am as disappointed with you as I am with Paul. You had Paul over step his boundaries when you asked him to look into my wife's financial information. As I told Paul this type of information will never be available to either of you again. You are not to review my wife's affairs unless you have my permission. Am I understood?"

"Yes I understand."

"Now update me."

"I will recap the case. You already know that Mr. Johnson determined that your daughter was meeting with Mr. Leo Filpatrick. I can inform you that she has met with him once since Johnson has been taken off of the case. I can also tell you Mrs. Robinson is passing Mr. Filpatrick money when they meet. I have not determined the reason for the payments but I am close."

"Let me tell you about my most recent meetings with your daughter. I have met with her twice since I last met with you. In the first meeting I told her that I believed she was being blackmailed. She became very angry. She said that was not true and she fired me. She did not want me bothering her further. She walked out of my office. Then the next day she called me and wanted to meet. I met with her. She said she wanted to apologize for her actions. She indicated she was not being blackmailed. She said this whole situation is a family problem that will be resolved soon and she did not need my services any longer."

Mr. Coleman looked at me as he poured himself another drink. "What do you think she meant when she said a family problem?"

"I am not sure but I think Filpatrick is involved. I also think when she refers to a family problem she is referring to her extended family not her immediate family. I would say she doesn't want anyone to know that Filpatrick is involved."

Mr. Coleman looked down at the floor and for the first time I thought he doesn't know what is going on. He looked up and said, "A family problem. So Phil what is the problem?" I couldn't bring myself to tell him about Mary.

"Sir I am close to determining that but I will need Paul's help."

Mr. Coleman immediately said, "Neither one of you will talk to my wife or review any information about her again."

"I don't need any information regarding your wife. I need Paul to assist me in scheduling another meeting with Mrs. Robinson. When she first came to my office she told me never to call her at her home. She would meet me in my office. I need to talk with her again.

Mr. Coleman asked why. I said, "She is the person with the answer to the statement "It is a family problem." If you will give me a little latitude I believe I can get that question answered with one more visit with her."

Paul asked, "How can I help Phil?"

"I need to know Mrs. Robinson's schedule over the next few days. Maybe I could show up at an event long enough to ask her to meet with me?"

"I can provide you her scheduled charity events. That might offer a brief moment for you to ask for your meeting."

"That would be perfect."

Mr. Coleman then said, "What information do you have to share with her?"

"Sir, can I hold off telling you that until after I meet with her again? I want to be sure of the information first."

"I don't like all of this secrecy when it has to do with my family but I will give you a little more time."

"Phil I will call you tomorrow with her schedule." I thanked Paul.

Mr. Coleman said, "Phil I want to meet with you as soon as you have met with my daughter."

"I will advise Paul as soon as I have had that meeting." At that moment Mr. Coleman left the room and Paul escorted me out of the house. I found it odd that Mr. Coleman never referred to his daughter by her name. It was only as his daughter.

As usual I am alone in my car driving home reviewing my meeting. I thought the meeting went well. I didn't tell Mr. Coleman any real details and he accepted that. When I meet with Mrs. Robinson I will tell her all I know. I will hand over the movies if she will agree to confirm that Mr. Filpatrick is blackmailing Mary and that the cash payments are coming from her and her mother.

I detoured on my way home to eat; my early afternoon sandwich was gone. I pulled into a small restaurant along the highway. While I sat eating I began thinking of Miss Emerald. I will also give Miss Emerald a Christmas bonus. I finished my meal and drove home.

I noticed the morning was very cold as I entered my car. The door was frozen closed. Once in my car my mind returned to the Christmas bonuses for Jamie and Miss Emerald. To my disbelief it was going to be after eight a.m. before I arrive at the office. I am slipping.

As I entered the office I could here the telephone ringing. Jamie hurried to answer it. I thought whom now? Jamie buzzed me and told me it was Tom Watson. I answered the telephone and said, "What can I do for you?"

"It's what I have for you. When I arrived at the precinct this morning I was made aware of a murder that took place last night. The body of Eugene Ransom was found in a car in a parking garage in Manhattan."

I found myself asking Tom, "Was he alone?"

"I think so. Why?"

"I'm not sure why I asked that. My mind is somewhat befuddled today."

"Since you had some interest in him I thought I would let you know."

"Thanks Tom I appreciate this information." He ended the call.

I hope Lisa isn't involved. My next thought was more positive. One more scumbag bit the dust. I will follow this in the newspaper to see if Miss Lisa's name is mentioned. This girl can really pick friends.

The telephone rang again. Jamie buzzed me to inform me that Mr. Winford was on the telephone. I thanked her and answered the telephone. We exchanged greetings.

"There are two very good opportunities for you to talk with Mrs. Robinson." The first opportunity is Thursday at about eleven thirty a.m. She will be a guest at a luncheon. All of the guests are to be there at eleven thirty a.m. but the event does not begin until noon. Paul provided the address.

The next opportunity is at a charity drive ceremony Friday at ten a.m. Mrs. Robinson is not on the program but she is to be there because she is on the charity board of directors. Again she should be available just before the ceremony begins. I thanked Paul for his help.

Before ending the call Paul said, "Remember Phil, you will need to contact me or Oscar once you have met with Mrs. Robinson. I could sense in Robert's voice last night that your comment regarding "This is a family problem" has him very concerned." He ended the call.

Since my chance meeting with Mrs. Robinson couldn't happen until tomorrow I decided to go Christmas shopping.

I approached Jamie and informed her that I would be out of the office for a few hours. I will return before five p.m.

My first stop was the bank. I needed cash. As I left the bank I began to think about what to buy my mother. I decided to give her twenty-five dollars cash. I will place the money in a Christmas card and lay the card on top of some nice handkerchiefs. That way she would have a present from me and she could buy herself something nice later.

I drove to a local store that would have all of the items I was going to purchase. I started in the jewelry department. I approached a young lady behind the jewelry counter. I asked her, "If someone was buying you one of these necklaces which one would it be?"

She placed a necklace in her hand and said, "This is the one I like." It was very dainty. I agreed.

She asked me if I wanted the necklace wrapped. I said, "Yes, but I have more shopping."

"Continue your shopping. When you have selected your other items bring them to me. I will take them to our gift wrapping area."

It was only a few minutes later I returned to the young lady with all my selections. I explained each separate gift to the young lady. She then instructed me to come to the gift wrapping area in about fifteen minutes to pick up my gifts. I walked around the store looking at men's shirts then I walked to the gift wrapping area. The gifts looked great.

I didn't want to leave the gifts in my car so I drove home. While at home I called Jamie. She indicated that everything was quiet. I told her I was going to have a late lunch and then return to the office.

When I returned Jamie indicated that Tom Watson had called. I returned his call. We exchanged greetings then he provided me an update on the Ransom case. He indicated that a woman's compact had been found under the passenger seat of Ransom's car. It had a small card in it. It is some type of card used by one of King Filpatrick's joints. It has the name, New York's Finest across the top."

I asked Tom if there was a number on the card. He said he didn't remember. "Why?"

"I'm just nosey."

"Just a minute. When he returned to the telephone he said the number was 35A. Phil, do you know what that means?"

I had to think fast.

"You remember when I asked you for Ransom's license tag information?"

"Sure I remember."

"Tom, the person that was involved in my case had a similar card."

"If you determine the significance of the card will you let me know?"

"Yes." He thanked me and we end our call.

I wondered if Ragsdale could provide me the name that would match the card number. Well if I ask him it will have to be tomorrow because I only have a few dollars cash and Ragsdale doesn't seem to do anything for free.

I looked at my watch. It was three thirty p.m. As I was getting a cup of coffee I noticed Jamie was deeply involved in her book. I asked, "What are you reading?"

"The Collected Poems by W. H. Auden."

"So you like poetry?"

"I like some. My sister loaned me this book; she said it was released a few months ago."

I thought about Tennyson's. It seems like someone is trying to tell me something. I patronize a bar where poetry is read, my secretary is reading poetry and Kitty is taking me to art exhibits. Are they trying to improve their social standing or mine?

Whatever their logic is it is nice to have both ladies in my life. I didn't respond to Jamie. I poured a cup of coffee and returned to my office.

With nothing else to do I reread the newspaper until Jamie left at five p.m.

I decided to stop at my favorite local restaurant and have dinner.

With my meal finished I drove to Tennyson's.

When I arrived at Tennyson's I took a seat at the bar and ordered a drink. When Jerry brought me my drink he said, "That buddy of yours, Ragsdale, is here." I turned as Jerry pointed him out. I told Jerry to have the waitress bring Ragsdale another drink.

I walked over and said, "Do you mind if I sit down?"

"No it's a free country."

"Yes I remember that."

He asked me, "Did you have any trouble with Mr. Helpful?"

"No, he was helpful. Walter did you get that! He was very HELPFUL ah! ah!" The look on Walter's face and his lack of a comment made me believe he didn't get it.

"There is one question I have for you. Does the number on the card you gave me identify me by name somewhere? In other words can I be held accountable if I lost the card and someone else uses it?"

"Did you lose your card already?"

"No I haven't lost it but what happens if I do?"

"Are you playing detective? If you have a question about your card just ask. Don't beat around the bush."

"I saw one of the cards lying in the seat of a woman's car. She was hot so I wondered if there was a back door to getting her name."

"What was the number?"

"It was 35A."

Ragsdale looked at me and said, "That is a very special person."

"So you know who it is?"

"No but I can tell by the number that this person has access to any of the casinos. What's the name worth to you?"

"I am tapped out so it can't be worth anything to me tonight."

He looked over at me and said, "Buy me another drink I'll be right back."

I waved at the waitress for a new round of drinks. Ragsdale went to the telephone in the far corner of the bar. I sure hoped I hadn't stepped on my tongue. Ragsdale returned to our booth and sat down.

"Where did you say you saw this card?" I said, "In a car parked on one of the casino parking lots. As she stepped out of her car a man met her and they entered the casino together. I assumed she got into the casino on his card. When I entered the casino I spotted her but as you know there is no names in there." He smiled I knew that was good.

"Storm, you don't run in the same circles as this one." I knew my thoughts were correct. The card the police had found was Lisa's.

"Okay Walter let's drop it. I finished my drink and told Ragsdale good night and I drove home.

Alarm clocks are evil. Every morning would be so much better without them. After cursing the alarm clock and the fact that I was not born rich I drove to the Newsstand. With my newspaper I drove to the office to see the brightest light of my day, Jamie and her smile.

I arrived at the office at seven fifty-five a.m. As I was walking in I heard a voice behind me. Good morning there Mr. Storm. I turned and there it was Jamie's radiant smile. "Good morning"

"What is the occasion?" I asked her what she meant. "Why the necktie today?"

"I am going to have a brief meeting with Mrs. Robinson at one of her charity events and I wanted to look the part."

"You're looking good. Go read your newspaper I'll start the coffee."

I walked into my office and began reading the paper. I was curious to see if there was anything new on the Eugene Ransom murder. I found an article on the lower part of the front page. As I read the article it was clear that Lisa was not connected to Ransom yet. His death was considered a homicide and the article indicated that the police thought it was tied to organized crime. It did not mention Filpatrick's name or any organized crime bosses. It was just a vanilla article about another homicide, nothing more.

Jamie bounced into my office with my coffee cup in her hand. I told her, "A man could get use to this type of treatment."

She smiled and said, "As long as it's paid for." My Navy mind thought that comment over for a few seconds but this is Jamie not a woman in some port. I cleared my mind and returned to the paper.

It was eleven a.m. when I left the office to meet Mrs. Robinson. I arrived at the meeting place at eleven twenty a.m. In a few minutes I saw her approaching. She was dressed to the nines.

She saw me and hesitated for a moment. Then she walked up and took my hand and said, "What brings you here this morning?" She had a big smile on her face.

When she took my hand my pulse beat quickened. I looked at her. She knew what she had done. I said, "I need to see something beautiful to help me make it through the day." As soon as I said that, I knew it was inappropriate. She smiled back but was silent.

"Mrs. Robinson, I would like for you to meet with me one last time. I have some information I would prefer to share with you versus your father. It will not take long."

"Well Mr. Storm it can't be here."

"Oh I know that but if you would call my office I will make myself available whenever you can meet."

"I'll call your office later today."

I thanked her and said, "I hope you have a wonderful day."

Once I arrived at my car I unbuttoned the top button on my shirt and loosened my necktie. I am sure it was a woman that invented the necktie. It had to be.

I was pleased that she agreed to meet. I hoped she hadn't just blown me off. I returned to the office ready to convey all of the information I had uncovered on Mary to her. I didn't have to wait long. My intercom buzzed. Jamie said, "It is Mrs. Robinson."

"Thanks for returning my call so promptly."

"Would you be available if I came to your office now?"

"Yes."

"I will leave for your office now." I thanked her and ended the call.

When Mrs. Robinson arrived I could see she was more relaxed than on either of her last two visits. I asked her to have a seat. "What I have uncovered is a family matter and I felt it should be discussed in person. I hope this information will not upset you but this information needs to be discussed."

Her relaxed appearance began to tense a little. "Soon after I began your case I discovered that a Mr. Johnson was following you. I also determined it was your father that had hired him. On one occasion this Johnson passed an envelope containing money to the security guard at your front gate. Then on another occasion he picked up an envelope containing money."

"Thanks to Johnson I know you have met with a man by the name of Leo Filpatrick. Your mother accompanied you to that meeting." I could see she was beginning to tense up. I stopped and asked? "Would you like a glass of water?"

"That would be nice." I buzzed Jamie and asked her to bring Mrs. Robinson some water. I waited until Mrs. Robinson had her water before I continued.

The water didn't seem to help relax her. I continued, "It is my opinion that Mr. Leo Filpatrick is blackmailing your sister Mary." Mrs. Robinson began to cry. I sat there as she removed a handkerchief from her purse and dried her eyes.

"Does my father know about this?"

"No. He does know you have met with Mr. Leo Filpatrick but he does not know about your sister, Mary's involvement."

"You have to keep it that way."

"Let me continue with my information then we can discuss what information is passed along to your father. I know why Mr. Filpatrick is blackmailing your sister and I know that your mother is financing his blackmail payments."

"No, Mr. Storm, you have it wrong?"

"What do I have wrong?"

"Mr. Filpatrick is a family friend and he is helping us with this matter. Yes, he is helping us with Mary."

"How can that be? He is a criminal."

"There are times when we are all criminals." I was speechless.

"So you know about Mary?"

"Mary is a frail young lady that made some bad choices. I admit her life is in shambles. Currently she is attempting to put her life back together. The entire family is helping her. Or almost the whole family."

"I imagine that those canisters are of Mary?"

I looked down at my desk and then at her. I felt cheap.

"Yes they are of Mary."

"So you know. What you don't know is that Mr. Filpatrick is collecting these canisters so Mary can have a normal life. Yes, we are paying him for his service. You have discovered our family's *dirty little secret* but there is one person that can never know about it. That is my father. Yes, the powerful Robert Wayne Dunsworth Coleman does not know nor will he ever know this secret about his family. You cannot tell him. This information will kill him. His trust in his wife has kept him from this information and with your help he will never know."

I could not believe what I was hearing. Leo (The Top Scumbag) Filpatrick is their friend and co conspirator? How can this be? I looked at Mrs. Robinson. She had a look of certainty on her face. She knew after telling me this story through tears, I couldn't tell anyone. She was my client and things we say in private must be kept private.

I had to ask? Who is blackmailing Mary?

"Mr. Storm, all you need to know is that those people are much nastier than Mr. Filpatrick. He and his connections are our only hope in putting this issue to bed quietly."

"Madam, what were the monies you took aboard a few months ago? What was the twenty thousand dollars taken from your sister Lisa in Italy to be used for? I deserve some answers if you expect me to assist you in keeping this information from your father. I am willing to help you, Mrs. Robinson but I need to understand." I thought to myself, what a mess I am in. Have I forgotten that Mr. Coleman is also paying me for information regarding Mrs. Robinson's meetings? He is paying a lot of money.

Mrs. Robinson looked at me and said, "So you will help me?"

"Yes but you must remember your father is also my client. I owe him answers. I have told him whom you are meeting. So what do I tell him when he asks why?"

"Let me answer your earlier questions as complete as I can. All of the money transactions have been to satisfy the collection of the canisters. When I was working without the power of Mr. Filpatrick I was failing to do anything more than keep up with the on-going demands."

"My mother packed the $20,000 dollars without Lisa knowing the money was in her bag. The money was a payment. Lisa was to call mother when she arrived in Italy. The bag was locked and Lisa was not to unlock it, just deliver it. When the Ship's Captain was given a bag without an identification tag he opened it. Lisa had reported that one of her bags missing. She identified the bag as hers. The rest is history. The authorities contacted my father. My father contacted my mother because she had assisted in packing Lisa's luggage. My mother told him that the money was there for Lisa to purchase clothes while she was aboard. My father's trust in his wife meant she did not have to answer any other questions. He used his political power to have the bag returned without further questions. My father isn't dumb but like most fathers he doesn't want to believe anything sinister or evil about his children."

I changed the subject by asking? "Do you know whom your sister Lisa has been seeing?"

"I am not familiar with Lisa's friends. What are you implying?"

"I have seen Lisa with a man by the name of Eugene Ransom. I have seen them on several occasions. Does that name mean any thing to you?"

"No, should it?"

"He was found dead in a car a few days ago. Mr. Ransom lived at the City's Best apartments. This building is populated with ladies of the night. It is one of Filpatrick's businesses.

Mrs. Robinson just rolled her eyes. "The police found a card in his car that can involve Lisa. I know that for a fact."

"Well if that information surfaces I know that father's attorneys will handle it. It is not an important issue."

"Madam, it may become important if the police determines it is Lisa's card."

"That item is for father's attorneys. It may be in the papers for a few days but it will be forgotten as old news is."

"How can I meet with your father regarding this case and not make him aware of Mary's issue? Madam, do you have any suggestions?"

Mrs. Robinson looked at me with a half smile and said, "Tell daddy I became unlucky while dining at the New York's Finest and that I promise not to let it happen again."

"You want me to tell him that you lost all that money gambling?"

"Yes."

"Will he believe me?"

"Sure he will. Aren't you the one that said Mr. Filpatrick had less than honorable businesses? Father is aware of his side businesses."

"Madam my head is spinning."

"Trust me he will believe it as long as you are convincing. Just stand up and tell him his daughter lost money gambling and the withdrawals and meetings were to repay the gambling losses. Just remember he really doesn't want to believe his children will do anything wrong. A little backroom gambling will be considered childish and mischievous but not criminal. Just remember that."

"Madam, if you will answer my two remaining questions I will tell your father this lie."

"What are the questions?"

"The first one is, how did your father discover you had contacted Abe's firm?"

"Let me answer that question with a question. He discovered it the same way I knew he had hired Johnson when you and I first talked. Mr. Storm, my mother told me. And you ask how did she know?

My mother has always made it her business to have contacts within her husband's businesses. That way she can assist herself and her children when needed."

"Paul Winford told my mother that he had contacted an outside investigation firm to look into some money issues involving me and she told me."

I stood and like a little kid I said, "I need to take a couple of minutes, please excuse me." I walked out of my office and headed for the men's room.

Paul has been playing for both teams and he sure knows how to keep a straight face. Johnson and I have been played. The Coleman women have played us like children. Of course that is why Mrs. Robinson used the term "Childish" when describing the way her father would see her haphazard approach to gambling. That is how the Coleman women handle the Larger than life businessman that thinks he runs the show. Mr. Coleman thinks Paul works for him when in fact Paul works for Mrs. Coleman.

When I returned to my office I said, "Mrs. Robinson I am sorry but it isn't everyday I discover I have been employed to solve a case that is already solved."

"No Mr. Storm the case will not be solved until you meet with my father and provide him the facts. That is why I insisted that you take the second payment. I knew this day would come. Mr. Storm, you have earned every penny of your fee."

"Mrs. Robinson, I think you have answered my second question. That question is, "How did your mother know to use Johnson to deliver the money?" I imagine Mr. Winford was involved again?"

"Yes, that is right."

"So I presume Paul convinced Johnson not to inform your father about the deliveries?"

"Mr. Storm that is something you will have to ask Paul."

"I'm not going to let Paul know that I am aware of his involvement with both sides of this case."

I stood and walked over to Mrs. Robinson. I looked down at her and said, "Thanks for seeing me and helping me understand this case. Mrs. Robinson, if I hadn't asked for this meeting how would you have kept me from telling your father the truth?"

"I hadn't determined that because I wasn't sure how much you knew."

"So I made it easy for you?"

"Mr. Storm you are a very good investigator. I really didn't think you would uncover Mary's secret and I wasn't going to tell you that part. So by being such a good investigator you did make it easy for me and I appreciate that."

I felt like I needed to pay her for solving the case. But when I stand before Mr. Coleman and make him believe a lie I will have earned every penny of both fees.

Mrs. Robinson was waiting to see how much information I would uncover on my own. Then she would fill in the necessary blanks to prepare me for the lie I would have to tell her father.

At this moment I had a thought. If I ever marry I'm not having children. I would wonder about every interaction with them. Are they out foxing me today? This would be especially true if my children were all daughters. This case has convinced me of that.

It was almost four thirty p.m. when Mrs. Robinson left. Based on my original plan I should be calling Paul Winford to advise him that I had met with Mrs. Robinson but instead I am going to leave for the day.

My mind was spinning by the time I arrived at Tennyson's. I needed a drink. I thought if I wait a few days to schedule my next meeting with Mr. Coleman that would give Mrs. Robinson ample time to contact her mother. Then her mother can contact Paul and he can contact me with the time and date of my next meeting with Mr. Coleman. That two faced Paul. I won't let that happen but my call to him will wait until tomorrow.

After a few drinks and dinner I was ready to end my day. Once at home I undressed and went to bed. As I lay there I thought about my day. It had been a very interesting day. As a private investigator I learned a very important lesson. There are days that the client takes charge of the case without telling the investigator.

15

I arrived at the office at seven thirty a.m. I made coffee and began reading the newspaper. As I sat reading the paper the telephone rang. It was Paul Winford. "Phil, I am glad you are in. There is another Coleman issue that you may be able to assist with."

"What's that?"

"Have you read the newspaper lately?"

"Sure I read it daily."

"Then you know about the death of Eugene Ransom?"

"Yes."

"The police wants to speak to Miss Lisa Coleman regarding him. They consider her a person of interest. I am meeting her within the hour to discuss her knowledge of Mr. Ransom. Would you have any thoughts why the police would think Lisa knows Mr. Ransom?"

This man is good. Do I have any thoughts why the police believe Lisa knows Ransom? I am sure Paul knows about their relationship.

I thought, I would just play dumb. "I will tell you what I know about Lisa and Mr. Ransom. Lisa and Ransom were involved. I have seen them together."

"Where have you seen them?"

"I have seen them on two occasions at one of Filpatrick's casinos. I also followed them from there one night to the City's Best apartments where Ransom lived."

"Phil, your involvement with the Coleman family is much broader than I would have guessed."

I thought if he only knew. "Paul the entire family has been a part of my investigation."

"Phil, have you seen them in any public establishments?"

"No."

"So do you have any idea how the police connected her to Mr. Ransom?"

"There was a lady's compact found under one of the seats in Ramson's car. In the compact was a card. This card has the name "New York's

Finest" across the top and it has a number on it. The card is issued to gain access into Filpatrick's casinos. This particular card is assigned to Lisa. That information is only known by Filpatrick's organization. So unless there is a leak in Filpatrick's organization no one would know the name assigned to the card. Of course there are a lot of well-known individuals that visit the casinos. But those people would not provide the police information because if they did it would indicate they were involved in visiting an illegal establishment. I think the police are just fishing."

"Phil, I am more impressed with you each time we talk. So if the police discuss this card Lisa can simply indicate that she has no idea what the card is for."

"Yes. Paul I am more impressed with you each time we speak also."

"Is there anything else I should know Phil?"

"No."

"Thanks Phil."

"Before we end our conversation I want you to know I have met with Mrs. Robinson and I am ready to meet with Mr. Coleman."

"I will have Oscar schedule the meeting." We ended our call.

I returned to my newspaper. The large numbers of Christmas ads made me think about my mother. I would visit her on Sunday and confirm her plans for Christmas Day. Since I have missed the last two Christmas's thanks to Uncle Sam I shouldn't take anything for granted.

At noon I approached Jamie and said, "I am approving Friday afternoon off for you and me. You can get an early start on your weekend."

"Do you want to go to lunch before we end the day?"

"Yes, that would be nice." Jamie cleaned the coffeepot and placed my cup on the little sink behind her desk. Then we were off to lunch.

Jamie is such a happy person. She always has a smile on her face. It is nice being around her. When we arrived at the restaurant we were seated immediately. I could see her waitress friend working the other side of the restaurant. We ordered our meal.

"What are your plans for the weekend?"

"I am going to visit my mother Sunday. That is all I have planned. What about you?"

"I am thinking about going into Manhattan. The City is so pretty this time of the year. All of the stores are full of people just hurrying here and there. I don't like going alone so I will see if my sister can join me."

Our meals were delivered. As we began eating I thought to myself. I wonder if Jamie would like to see the City with me. I don't like visiting the City unless there is a specific reason and spending the day with Jamie would be enough of a reason.

"Would you consider letting me drive you into the City tomorrow. We could see the City dressed in it's Christmas best." She gave me an unusual look. I thought I have placed her in an uncomfortable position. She may not want to go with me but because I'm her boss she may not want to tell me no. "Jamie it was inappropriate of me to ask you that. "I apologize."

We finished eating and began to leave the restaurant when she said, "Why not. If you still want to see the City together let's do it."

"Are you sure? I want you to know it is just going to be two friends out to see the City dressed in her Christmas splendor."

"Okay let's do it."

"What time would you like to leave?"

"I'll be ready anytime after nine a.m.

"I'll pick you up at ten a.m."

"Are you sure you want to drive into the City? We can use public transportation."

"I'll drive."

"I'll see you at ten a.m." I returned to my car as she walked to her bus stop.

I decided since it was early afternoon I would drive to my mother's place now. Then I would have my Christmas day plans firmed up.

It was one p.m. when I arrived at my mother's place. As usual she was home. She had been washing a few clothes in the bathroom. She had them hanging over the shower curtain rod.

She wanted to know why I wasn't at work. Just like a mother, a worrywart. I told her I set my own hours not to worry. I asked, "What is the plan for Christmas Day?"

"I'm preparing Christmas dinner for a few of my friends. You are coming?"

"Sure. What time?"

"Dinner would be at two p.m."

"What can I bring?"

"Have you started cooking?"

"No but I know where there are some good deli's."

"I just want you here nothing more."

"I'll see you Christmas day."

Once in my car I began thinking where can I go instead of Tennyson's? As usual I couldn't come up with anywhere else. So I drove to Tennyson's.

It was nine p.m. when I waddled out of Tennyson's. The drive home was a blur. When I approached my door there was a note taped to it: "Be at his house at nine a.m. Saturday." Oscar had signed the note. I was glad. I wanted this case over.

Then it hit me. I must call Jamie. She is excepting me tomorrow at ten a.m. I didn't want to miss my day with her but I didn't want to postpone this meeting with Mr. Coleman either.

I dialed Jamie's number. Once she answered I informed her that Mr. Coleman wants to meet with me at nine a.m. tomorrow. So we will have to set a later departure time or schedule it another day."

"Phil, let's make it another day. Earlier in the evening I was talking with my sister and she indicated her husband is going to be home tomorrow. So I will call her and have her go with me. We'll go another day. I'll see you Monday morning. Thanks for calling. Good night." I was asleep as soon as my head hit the pillow.

I woke up and looked at the clock. It was seven thirty a.m. I had failed to set my alarm. It didn't matter I had plenty of time to make my nine a.m. meeting. I started the coffee and stepped into the shower.

On my way to the Coleman's I stopped for a morning paper. I wanted to see if there was anything new on the Ransom case. With paper in hand I entered the Coffee Shop for breakfast.

I wouldn't have to say anything to Paul or Mr. Coleman about Lisa. There she was on the front page. Under her picture it said, "Lisa Ann Coleman daughter of Robert Coleman CMI Corp. Head." This time they didn't list all four of his names.

The article stated, "Well known Socialite Miss Lisa Coleman and Deceased Crime Figure Mr. Eugene Ronsom have been linked. A source has indicated the two have been seen socially on several occasions. The most recent date was earlier in the evening of his death."

Paul nor Mr. Coleman could keep her out of the newspaper this time. Sometimes money can't keep mouths closed.

I arrived at the Coleman's entrance by eight fifty-five a.m. The security guard waved me through. I hurried to park my car. Bogey was waiting. I said, "Good morning" as I joined him on his cart. Bogey said, "Morning" and nothing more.

I stepped out of the cart at the front door and rang the bell. Same old story. Mr. Butler met me. I was shocked when he said, "Good morning sir." I said, "Good morning." He escorted me into my normal meeting place. I sat down in the hot seat. Mr. Coleman and Paul entered the room together.

We exchanged greetings. Mr. Coleman started the conversation by thanking me for the information I provided Paul regarding the other matter. Why didn't he say the information regarding Lisa and Ransom? It was almost like if he didn't say Lisa then it was just a matter not family or personal. Maybe Mrs. Robinson was right he just didn't want to know any thing unpleasant about his family. I said, "I am glad it helped."

"What information do you have on our other matter? Again, not the case regarding Sally or Mrs. Robinson just our other matter."

"Mr. Coleman, in a nutshell the money withdrawn from your daughter's account were monies, as your daughter put it, to satisfy some unlucky times dinning at the New York's Finest and similar places in France and Italy. Your daughter informed me that it was stupid and she hoped her husband would not have to know about it. She indicated it would not happen again. The meetings with Filpatrick were to make payments for her unlucky visits to his establishments. This case boils down to a person spending more money than she should have on a bad habit."

When I quit talking Mr. Coleman sat looking at me for several seconds then his look turned into a stare. The silence was stretching into minutes. His look wasn't on the Christmas season; it was more a look that said, "Where did I go wrong raising my children." Finally, He said, "Phil, do you truly believe my daughter's story?"

"Yes Sir I do. As you know Johnson led us to Filpatrick. I was able to find money movements from family accounts just before meetings between Mrs. Robinson and Mr. Filpatrick. I was able to determine that Mr. Filpatrick does have casinos behind his restaurants. If you would like I will continue to follow your daughter. I will have Paul provide me a monthly update to determine if there continues to be unusual withdrawals from Mrs. Robinson's accounts. You are paying me very well so I will continue my surveillance and updates as long as you feel they are needed."

At that moment Paul said, "Robert I believe Sally's story. Remember in early 1944 there was a similar event? Robert you may remember it was during the time when she and Edward were having words."

"That is enough Paul. This isn't the place for past family issues. Phil, it will not be necessary for you to continue."

He reached into his desk drawer and removed a check resister. He began writing a check. In a few seconds he handed me a check for three thousand dollars and he said, "Thank you Phil. If I need any outside assistance in the future I know whom to ask." Without another word he left the room.

I looked at Paul as he said, "I hope you have a wonderful Holiday Season Phil." Before I could say anything in return Paul was also gone. I was standing in this large room alone. When the Coleman's are finished they are finished. I walked to the front door and reclaimed my hat and coat and walked to my car. I didn't see Mr. Butler or Bogey. I felt like I was the only cast member left alive when the play ended.

As long as the Coleman women can keep Mr. Filpatrick quiet, Mr. Coleman will continue to be in charge of the family business' and oblivious to his family's *dirty little secrets.*

It is December 15 and all is well with the Coleman family. As I drove home I felt like nothing was solved. Filpatrick was working with the Coleman's to clear Mary's issue but it wasn't over yet.

That meant Mrs. Coleman would have to continue delivering money to Filpatrick. Filpatrick's men would continue rounding up the nasty little canisters. As that continues, Paul Winford will continue to see that Mr. Coleman, and Mrs. Coleman both feel good about their family.

I decided to drive to the Coffee Shop for dinner. Once I had finished dinner it was on to Tennyson's.

The next time I looked at my watch it was nine p.m. I knew it was time to go home. If I didn't leave now I wouldn't be able to find my car, let alone drive it home. I had really over done it. How stupid I am.

16

T he thing I despise as much as the alarm going off in the morning
is the telephone ringing in the night. As I located the telephone
I looked at the clock. It is eleven-thirty, no wonder my eyes won't focus I
have only been in bed a couple of hours. I said, "Hello, Phil here."

A very familiar voice said, "Hi Phil, this is Paul Winford. Phil I am
sorry to wake you but I need your assistance."

"What is it Paul?"

"Lisa Coleman is missing. She had the family driver take her into the
City to meet a lady friend to shop and have dinner. She had instructed
her driver to wait in town. At nine-thirty Lisa called her driver and indicated she was taking a cab from Lancaster's Restaurant to his location at
633 3rd Avenue. She never arrived. The driver called me at ten-fifteen
p.m. to ask what he should do? I told him to return to the Coleman's
home. Phil this must be looked into immediately!"

I said, "Paul, I will drive to Lancaster's. The doorman should be able
to provide me the name of the Cab Company that picked Lisa up. The
dispatcher can provide the driver's name that made the pick up and then
he can provide us Lisa's drop off location."

"Phil, I will call the restaurant and get that information in motion."

"Thanks that will speed things up."

Then Paul informed me that he would be going to the Coleman's
home once we ended this telephone call. He asked me to contact him
there once I had determined where Lisa had been taken.

As I was dressing I thought, Ransom dead and now Lisa missing?
Are the two happenings connected? I only thought that my employment
with the Coleman family was completed. Once dressed I drove to the
Lancaster restaurant and identified myself to the doorman. He informed
me that the Yellow Cab Company picked Lisa up. He provided me the
telephone number of the dispatcher.

I called the dispatcher. He had already talked with the driver and
provided me the address where Lisa was taken. I looked at the address. It
wasn't 633 3rd Avenue. I asked the dispatcher if the driver was available.

"No, but I can contact him." I asked the dispatcher to have the driver meet me at Lancaster's.

In fifteen minutes the cabby arrived. I asked him if there was anyone with her when she entered his cab. He indicated that she was alone. I asked him where he took her. "He indicated initially he drove her to 633 3rd Avenue but when she was stepping out of the cab two men pushed her back into the cab and then they joined her. They gave me this address. I dropped all three of them off there. It was the address of the City's Best Apartments. I didn't have to wonder any longer if Ransom's death had any thing to do with Lisa's disappearance.

I left the restaurant and drove to the City's Best Apartments. Why did they bring her here? I parked in the garage and walked into the lobby. I knew there would be a security guard there.

I approached the security guard and asked him if a young lady entered the lobby this evening and asked to enter Eugene Ransom's apartment? He said, "I'm not sure. There are many people coming into the building."

I said, "Sir, if you would like I will call the police and have them ask you this question?"

"I think the person you are speaking of was in the lobby at nine forty-five p.m."

"Was she alone?"

"No. There were two men with her."

"Where did they go?"

"I can't tell you; our tenants expect privacy."

"The young lady was not a tenant. Again I will say, you can tell me if she went to Eugene Ransom's apartment or you can tell the police."

"Yes that is where she went."

"Is she still there?"

"No, she and one of the men returned to the lobby at ten thirty p.m."

I asked the guard how she looked. He indicated that she looked scared. I don't think she wanted to be with the men.

"When they departed did they leave by cab?"

"Yes."

"What cab company?"

"It was the Yellow Cab Company."

I asked the guard if I could go upstairs and look around. He indicated he couldn't allow that. I said, "Then I am calling the police."

He stood looking at me for several seconds. "You're a troublemaker."

"You have that right. Do you want things to get worse?"

He then handed me the key to Ransom's suite. "Sir, don't take all night up there."

When I entered the suite I found it a mess. Someone had ransacked it. I began looking through the mess. I walked into the bedroom. I found a picture of Lisa on the floor. Not far from the picture was a heel that had been broken from a woman's high heel slipper. Crap! The lights went out.

I woke up on the floor of the bedroom. There was blood running in my left eye. I had also been kicked in the ribs. Lisa's picture and the broken high heel were lying beside me. I stood, picked up Lisa's picture and the broken high heel then returned to the lobby.

When I arrived at the guard's desk he could see the blood on my face. "So you provided me company."

"I'm not going to die for anyone."

"You saw who did this to me?"

"Yes I saw them. It was the same two men that were here earlier with the girl."

"Describe them."

"They were both white and spoke with an accent. One was about five foot-eight, a hundred and twenty pounds. He had brown hair and I would guess he was about thirty-five years old. The other man was about six feet tall, a hundred and seventy or eighty pounds. He was balding and I would guess him at about forty-five to fifty years old."

"Were they in a car?"

"Yes, they were in a black four door Cadillac. It looked new." I asked him how the men got past him. He said, "The little man entertained me with a big gun and the big one went upstairs."

"Did they indicate why they wanted access to the suite?"

"No. They walked up to me and the little guy said, give me the key to Ransom's suite. I told him I could not do that. He pulled out a gun and put it against my head. I gave him the key. He didn't say another word."

I told the guard to call the police and inform them that two men broke into Ransom's suite while holding you at gunpoint. "The place is a mess."

I needed to contact Paul. I located a telephone and updated him.

"Should I call the police?"

"Not yet. I know a person that maybe able to tell me who we are dealing with."

"Keep me updated. Mr. and Mrs. Coleman are very upset." I will.

I returned to my car and drove to the Wharf Bar. I was hoping to find Ragsdale. Maybe he'll know who has her.

It was one forty-five a.m. when I arrived at the Wharf Bar. I approached the bartender and asked if he had seen Ragsdale. He said, "Walter is in the backroom playing cards." I asked him to tell Ragsdale I wanted to talk with him immediately. The bartender left the bar. In a few minutes he returned and said, "Have a drink, Walter will be with you soon."

I found an empty booth, downed a drink and ordered another one. I was tired and my body hurt. Walter approached me and asked, "What's so important?"

"You knew Eugene Ransom?"

"Yes, I knew him."

"Eugene Ransom had been dating Lisa Coleman. Do you know who she is?"

"The dame whose card you found."

"Tonight she was kidnapped. The men that kidnapped her drove her to the City's Best Apartments and one of the men took her to Ransom's suite. After awhile Lisa and the man returned to the lobby and they left. I went into the suite about two hours later and the place was a mess. While I was looking around someone came up behind me and put me on the floor. I pointed to my head and eye. "I am being paid to find Miss Coleman."

"Walter can you assist me in determining who has taken her?" Walter sat silently for several seconds. Without a word he stood and walked to the telephone at the other end of the bar.

In a few minutes he returned and said, "Level with me. What business are you in?"

"I am a PI and I am working for the Coleman family.

"It may become messy from here on in and it will be expensive."

"Walter, what information do you have for me?"

"The Russians have her?"

"Why?"

"They know she was Ransom's lady friend. They believe she has information that is very important to them."

"Walter, how can I determine what the information is?"

"I may be able to set up a meeting with you and them."

"If you can do that it is more money in your pocket." Walter returned to the telephone.

When he returned to the booth he said, "They will allow you to talk to the woman."

"That is a good start. Give me your price Walter."

"It will cost you one thousand dollars." I nearly past out but indicated I would get him the money Monday."

Walter told me to provide him a telephone number that the Russians could use to contact me. I gave him my home number. "I will drive home and wait for their call."

"I'll give you time to get home then I will provide them your telephone number."

As I was leaving the bar I wondered how Ragsdale contacted the scumbags so easily. At this point I couldn't worry about that but I did wonder. Currently the important thing is to return Lisa to her family.

Once home I poured a shot of scotch and called Paul. He was pleased that I had contacted the men holding Lisa. He wanted to hear from me as soon as a meeting was scheduled.

"Phil, I want you to understand that money is not an issue. Lisa's safety and return to her parents is the number one issue."

"Paul, I had to pay a thousand dollars to setup the meeting." He said, "You will be paid for all expenses and more once Lisa is home."

"Phil, Mr. Coleman wants me to inform you that you are to do whatever is necessary to return his daughter."

I am finding it hard to stay awake. I made coffee while waiting for my call.

As I watched the coffee perk I tried to think of what type of information Ransom would have given or discussed with Lisa. Why do men like Ransom provide their ladies with information they can't tell anyone else?

What if she doesn't have the information her kidnappers are after? I don't think her kidnappers will believe that without applying pressure. I cannot allow that to happen.

Then my tired mind switched from Lisa to Ragsdale. Ragsdale left a card game, walked to a telephone and contacted the people holding Lisa. How was he able to accomplish that with one telephone call? Who is this Ragsdale? With one telephone call he made a thousand dollars. It was too easy.

Ragsdale is more than an errand boy for Filpatrick's organization! It also means that Filpatrick's organization is in the middle of this?

I sat silently drinking coffee. At six a.m. my telephone rang. I answered it, "Phil Storm." The voice on the other end of the line said, "Be in front of the Wharf Bar at seven a.m. Make sure you are alone."

"I'll be there." The telephone went dead.

I called Paul with the update. He asked me if I had any idea what they are after."

"No. But I should know after the meeting. I will update you then." Paul thanked me.

I drank another cup of coffee. The warm coffee seemed to be helping me stay awake.

I arrived in front of the Wharf Bar at six fifty-five a.m. I opened my glove compartment to make sure my gun was there. I didn't plan on using it but I would use it if it would prevent me from taking another beating. As I closed my glove compartment a car pulled up next to me.

A man about six feet tall exited the car and walked around to my door. He said, "Get out." I stepped out of my car. He patted me down. Then he said, "Give me your car keys."

"Why?"

"Do you want to talk to the girl?"

"Yes."

"Then give me your car keys." I handed him the keys. He returned to his car.

In a moment Lisa began walking toward my car. I opened the passenger door. She entered. I said, "Lisa Coleman?"

"Yes, I am Lisa Coleman."

"My name is Phil Storm. I am a private investigator working for your father through Paul Winford."

Lisa looked haggard. "Have they hurt you?"

"They have pushed me around and caused me to ruin a shoe." I told her that I had found the heel in Ransom's suite.

"Lisa I was in Ransom's suite and I saw the mess these men made. I can only help you if you help me. What is it that they think you know?"

"Eugene had a book with client information in it. These men want that Client Book."

"Do you have the book?"

"No and worse I don't know where it is. One night when Eugene and I were having drinks he told me how important he was to Mr. Filpatrick as long as he had this Client Book. When I was taken to Eugene's suite the man with me asked me to provide him this book. I told him I didn't know where the book was. He didn't believe me. Do you believe me?"

"Yes I believe you but we need to talk about where the book could be. I am convinced it isn't in Ransom's suite."

"Lisa is there any place other than his suite where the book could be?

"It might be in his car or at his club."

"What club?"

"The 42nd Street Men's Club."

"Lisa, I will locate this book. You have to trust me."

"Sir, do I have choice?"

"I'm afraid you don't."

I returned Lisa to the Russian's car and told the driver he would have to give me some time to locate the book. He said, "You have until noon."

"Do I meet you here at noon?"

"I will call you at noon and provide a meeting place. If you try anything funny she dies."

"I understand."

Once the scumbags drove off I decided to check out the leads Lisa had provided. My mind shifted to my stomach. I am very hungry. I decided to have breakfast and then I would call Paul and let him know I had talked with Lisa.

When I finished eating I went to the men's room and washed my face. Staying awake was getting more difficult. I called Paul and informed him I had met with Lisa. I asked him if he knew anyone that is a member of the 42nd Street Men's Club?

"Yes I am a member."

"You maybe a lifesaver."

"What do you mean?" I told him the men that are holding Lisa are looking for a book of client information that Eugene Ransom maintained."

"When I spoke with Lisa I asked her if she knew the location of the book. She said no, but since it wasn't in his suite her only other thoughts were that it was in his car or at this club."

"Does the club have storage areas for personal items?"

"Yes, each member has a locker." Can you assist me in locating Ransom's locker?

"Yes. I will leave for the club when we complete this conversation." I thanked Paul.

It was ten a.m. when I arrived at the 42nd Street Men's Club. I was standing in front of the Club when a car approached and stopped. Paul stepped out as someone drove away in the car. I asked Paul if that was his car. "Yes."

"Where is that man taking it?" Paul indicated there was member parking is in the rear of the Club.

"Paul, I have to be home by noon to talk with Lisa's kidnappers."

We entered the Club and Paul approached a man seated behind a desk. Paul said, "Randy can I speak with you privately for a moment?"

"Sure Paul, let's go to the Cigar Lounge." The two men walked off. I thought, "The Cigar Lounge?"

After five minutes the two men returned to the lobby. Randy handed Paul a key.

"Come with me." We walked into a room that had lockers on one wall. Paul placed the key in a locker and it opened.

"Phil, this is Eugene's locker."

Paul began looking through it. He removed a small writing tablet and handed it to me. I began turning the pages. I stopped on a page where the word Princess was written followed by the words Pride & King and then the numbers 5553091nycp3s.

I stood looking at the letters and numbers. I asked Paul, "Does this make any sense to you?"

"Well Princess is Mrs. Coleman's first name. The 555 3091 is probably a telephone number but it isn't one that I recognize. The other code doesn't mean anything to me."

I rapidly flipped through the remaining pages. There wasn't anything else of interest. I said quietly to myself, Why would Mrs. Coleman's first name be written in this scumbag's tablet? This lady hangs out with a bad crowd. The Coleman women continue to surprise me. Maybe social grace and criminals do run in the same circle.

Paul and I returned to the lobby. I asked Paul if there was a telephone I could use. "Yes follow me." We walked into a room with several large desks.

Each desk had a telephone. I sat down and dialed the number we had found in Ransom's tablet. A woman answered the telephone and said, "The Pride's residence."

"Is Mr. Pride available?"

"Yes may I tell him who is calling?"

I didn't have time to lie. "Tell him Phil Storm needs to speak with him."

"Laddie, someone by the name of Phil Storm for you."

I heard a man's voice say, "Pride speaking."

"Mr. Pride my name is Phil Storm did you know Eugene Ransom?"

"Yes I knew him. Why?"

"I found a tablet of Ransom's and in it was a number/letter code written on one of the pages next to your name. I wonder if you can assist me in determining what it means. The code number is nycp3s. The name Princess was written next to it. Any idea what it means?"

After a few seconds of silence Mr. Pride said, "Who are you?"

"I'm a PI working a case. My client's daughter is being held by some men that believe she knows the location of a book that was last known to be in Ransom's possession. Your telephone number and these other code numbers may help in locating that book. I do not want to cause you any trouble. I just want to return my client's daughter to him uninjured."

"Give me your code again?" I repeated the code. Pride said, "It is probably where a boat is tied up."

"What do you mean?"

"nycp probably stands for New York City Pier. Then the 3s is probably the slip number where the boat is moored. That's my guess."

"Thanks very much sir."

"If this comes back to bite me I will find you."

"I understand."

I turned to Paul who had been sitting silent while I was talking to Pride. I asked him, "Do the Coleman's have a boat?"

"Yes they have a yacht named Princess."

"We need to find this boat. I have a feeling Ransom stashed the book where no one would look, the Coleman yacht."

17

It was eleven twenty-five a.m. when we arrived at my place. My body ached. I couldn't think about drinking anymore coffee. I knew a shot of scotch would put me to sleep. The two of us sat silently looking at my living room wall awaiting our noon telephone call.

As we waited I said, "Paul, is there anyway you can confirm the location of the Coleman's boat?"

"Yes," as he walked to my telephone. I heard him ask someone for the telephone number of Captain Casey.

Then he dialed another number and said, "Captain Casey?" Is the Princess in her slip? Then he said thanks and ended the call. He turned toward me and said, "She is in her slip."

At noon my telephone rang. I heard, "Is this Storm?"

I said, "Yes."

"Do you have my merchandise?"

"No I will need a little more time. I am doing everything I can to locate the Book."

"If you are messing with me you and the girl will die."

"I'm not messing with you but it is taking longer than I thought."

"I will call you at five p.m. and no more extensions."

"Let me speak with Lisa?" I heard a quivering voice say, "This is Lisa."

"Lisa this is Phil. Hang on a little longer. You will be home before the day is over."

"Thanks Phil." The telephone went dead.

Paul said, "Before we leave I need to update the Coleman's."

"Tell them we have talked with Lisa and she is fine."

"If we don't return Lisa soon I am sure Mr. Coleman will bring others into the investigation." Then Paul placed his call to Mr. Coleman.

I wondered who the others would be. At that moment Paul sounded just like Mr. Coleman. No names, he will bring others into the investigation. I can't determine if they don't mention names for secrecy or to keep emotions out of the issue.

As we were driving to the pier I asked Paul, "How long have you worked for the Coleman's?"

He said "ten years."

"So you know the family quite well?"

"Yes."

"How well do you know Lisa?" Paul looked out the car window and was silent. I said, "What's wrong?"

"I know her personally. We had a brief relationship a few years ago."

"What did Mr. Coleman think about that?"

"As far as I knew Mr. Coleman was not aware of it. Mrs. Coleman recommended that we end the relationship but by that time I was yesterday's news to Lisa. So it was easy to end. When Lisa ends something it is over."

I could tell it was only over as far as Lisa was concerned. I asked, "So is she strong enough to put up with the men that have her?"

"Yes. Once she is back home she will act as if it was just another outing. Phil, Lisa can be as cold as the North Pole." I knew it was time to change the subject. I couldn't help thinking about the Coleman women. Maybe I should be feeling sorry for Lisa's captors instead of her.

We arrived at the pier. Paul indicated that we would need to stop at Captain Casey's home. He is the Captain of the Coleman's yacht and he has the key to the secure slip area where the yacht is moored.

Captain Casey was found in a small house a few yards from the pier. He was probably thirty-five years old, tall, slim and very good looking. I imagined the Coleman women liked going to sea with him.

After a brief discussion with Paul the Captain walked us to the slip area and unlocked the wire gate. He asked Paul if he needed to join us. Paul looked at me and said, "I don't think so." With that comment the Captain handed Paul the key to the slip area and told him to lock the gate behind us. Paul locked the gate and we walked to slip 3.

Paul was correct when he said the Coleman's owned a yacht. It was a yacht not a boat. I guessed it was at least sixty feet long. She was a beautiful thing. Until now if a vessel was less than nine hundred feet it was a boat to me. The aircraft carrier I served on was just over nine hundred feet from stem to stern.

We boarded the Princess. I was glad we had several hours to look her over. There were two lower decks. One had a kitchen and sitting area.

The other was the sleeping area. I asked Paul to begin in the kitchen area while I begin in the sleeping area. I told Paul to search this boat as if he was a prospective buyer.

I looked over every inch of the sleeping area without finding anything. I walked upstairs too determine if Paul had found anything. Paul was walking around with a discouraging look on his face. He said, "I haven't found a thing."

"Paul we can't give up. Let's change search areas."

I had been searching the upper deck for about twenty minutes when Paul came up the stairs and asked me to follow him below. We returned to the sleeping area.

We approached one of the beds and Paul told me to push my hand down the side of the mattress. I ran my hand along the side of the mattress until I felt something rectangular in shape. I reached into my pocket and removed my knife. I made a slit in the mattress and reached in. There was a small book. I opened it and looked through it. I then handed it to Paul. "I bet this is what the Russians are after." Paul opened the Book and began studying each page. As he looked up at me he had a very satisfied look on his face.

He said, "Do you really think the men holding Lisa will release her once we provide them this Book? Remember you and Lisa can identify them. Then Paul looked at his watch and said, "It's three p.m. We have two hours to formulate a plan."

"What are you thinking of?"

Paul said, "I think we need to contact Mr. Filpatrick and let him assist in gaining Lisa's release. He has a great deal to lose if this Book finds it way into the hands of the Russians."

"Are you crazy? In my opinion if Filpatrick is involved he will take the Book and then kill us all."

"Phil I must tell you about Mr. Filpatrick. He may be involved in illegal businesses but he is a friend of the Coleman family." Of course I knew that but I wasn't going to tell Paul.

I said, "What are you saying?"

"You must believe me when I tell you Mr. Filpatrick will see that nothing happens to Lisa or us."

We returned to the Captain's house. Paul asked to use Captain Casey's telephone. The Captain showed him to an extension in the bedroom. It was three fifteen p.m. While Paul was on the telephone

I thought, criminals come in all sizes and social classes. My rich and respectful family sleeps with their enemy. Paul returned from the bedroom and said, "Phil, give me the Book and return home.

"What? Give you the Book and return home? Where are you going?"

"From this point on the less you know the better."

I said, "Paul you want me to return home and wait for the five p.m. call without the Book? That is like pointing an empty pistol at someone. At least with this Book I have a bargaining tool. Paul, I need to understand what you are going to do?"

"You will have a book to provide the Russians prior to five p.m. You will give them that book and they will be satisfied.

Ransom's book is too important for it to be in play. Once you and Lisa are out of harms way Mr. Filpatrick's people will take over."

"Paul I have one question? What if they don't turn Lisa over to me? I'm the one on the front line. Where will you be?"

"Phil, we don't have time for this, please return home. I promise you will be fine and once Lisa is returned to her parents you will be paid handsomely."

Like I had good sense I drove home without the book. I didn't like this situation at all. When would this other book arrive? Was I going to be a hero or a sacrifice? It was four twenty-five p.m. when I arrived at home.

I had been there thirty minutes when there was a knock at my door. I opened the door and there stood Paul. He stepped in and handed me a book. I opened it and flipped through the pages. It did look very similar to one we had found. Paul said, "Do you feel better now?"

"Yes, but you are playing with our lives."

"How would you handle it?"

"I would provide the Russians the correct Book and hope they would live up to their end of the deal."

Paul said, "So shall we do it your way or mine?" I thought what a mess. If I do it my way and they didn't release Lisa as soon as they received the correct Book we both are dead. If I do it Paul's way and they don't release Lisa we still have the Book to bargain with. I said, "Paul, let's do it your way."

Again at exactly five p.m. my telephone rang.

"Do you have the merchandise?"

"Yes."

"Meet me at the same place at five forty-five p.m."

"I'll be there. Can I speak to Lisa?" Lisa came on the telephone. I said, "Lisa this is almost over. You will be home in a couple of hours.

"Thanks." The telephone went dead.

I turned to Paul and said, "We are to meet in the parking lot of the Wharf Bar at five forty-five p.m." Paul dialed a number and repeated the location and time. "After you make your delivery take Lisa home. I will call you early Monday morning and make arrangements for you to receive your fee."

Paul left and I drove to the Wharf Bar. I will be glad when this mess is over. I don't like doing business in Harlem. I arrived in front of the bar at five thirty p.m. As I sat in the parking lot waiting I could feel my body shaking.

At five forty-five p.m. the Russians entered the parking lot. They motioned for me to follow them. They drove to the rear of the parking lot behind several cars. I positioned my car so both cars were facing each other. I could see Lisa.

The largest of the two men stepped out of their car and motioned at me. I stepped out of my car and walked a few steps toward him. Then I stopped. I said, "Let Lisa out of the car." He had the man that remained in the car to open Lisa's door. She stepped out and joined the man facing me.

"I want you and Lisa to meet me halfway." We began walking toward each other until we were standing face to face.

I handed this large ugly man the Book. He opened it and began reading. He looked at me and shook his head in a positive manner. Then it happened. He removed his gun from his pocket and said, "Begin walking to our car." I said, "Blockhead, what are you doing?"

"I am going to make sure this is the correct Book."

I was in a mess up to my neck and so was Lisa. She had depended on me and I had depended on Paul. I told myself if I live through this mess someone will pay.

We were pushed into the backseat of their car. The large man climbed in with us. The driver started the car and we began our journey. I began to panic. I had to make a move.

I looked at Lisa's door. It was unlocked. I decided the next time the car stopped I would reach across Lisa, open her door and jump. I had to think of old number one first then I could assist Lisa.

All of a sudden the car in front of us stopped. We plowed into the rear of it. As I reached for the door handle there was a gun blast. The noise was deafening.

As I looked up I could see our driver slumped over the steering wheel. I looked at Lisa. She had blood all over her. The large man in the backseat rolled out of the car. I looked up, someone grabbed me and placed me in a car. Lisa was already in the car. The car drove away.

I was still dazed when someone picked me up and helped me out of the car. Then I looked up and I saw Paul. He looked like he was talking to me. All I could hear was the loud ringing noise from the gunfire.

Paul seemed to be yelling. "Phil, are you okay? Here is your car do you think you can drive yourself home?" I just sat there. I wasn't sure if I was hearing Paul or what I wanted to hear. I found myself asking, "Is Lisa alright?"

Paul yelled, "She is fine. She is on her way home. Phil it is all over and everyone is fine. I told you it would be fine."

As I sat in my car I asked, "Who are these people Paul?"

"Phil they are the good guys and that is all you need to know. Just go home and get some sleep. I'll call you Monday morning."

I started my car. Here, I am in Harlem again. My head aches and my ears are ringing.

My thoughts went to Lisa. Would she be all right? This experience made Mary's problem look very small. Lisa had blood all over the front of her clothing and on her face.

By the time I arrived home I was wide-awake. I couldn't get the Russians or Lisa out of my mind. The Russians didn't get what they were after. Would they continue to try? Would they attempt to locate Lisa again? Would they come after me? As far as I knew the two men that could identify Lisa and I were both dead. Had they past our names to others? If Lisa is as tough as Paul had indicated I imagine she will make it through this situation.

My thoughts switched to Paul. This man is very connected to Filpatrick's people. In less than two hours he had a group of hit men in place. I wonder how many situations like this Paul has been involved in. He is Mrs. Coleman's silent partner, and it appears he holds a similar position with Scumbag Filpatrick.

I must get some sleep. "I may not hear it but I need to set my alarm."

I remember setting the alarm because it was going off in my ear. As I reached to turn it off I thought, "I can hear." I looked at the clock. It was six o'clock, Monday morning.

I rolled out of bed fully dressed. I made coffee, then undressed and started the shower. My ribs were tender, my eye were black and almost closed.

I am very hungry. I dressed quietly and began my morning routine by stopping at the Newsstand then on to the Coffee Shop for breakfast. As I waited for my breakfast I found it hard to believe what had happened within twenty-four hours.

I wouldn't believe it if I had not been involved. I wonder if Paul would call me and ask me to indicate a fee amount or if he will just send me a check for a predetermined amount? My guess would be the latter.

As I began reading my newspaper two articles on the front page caught my attention. The first article read, "Two men found dead in Harlem." That article indicated that the police were considering this a homicide because it appeared gang related.

The men were found near a bar in Harlem that has mob affiliations.

The second article read, "Three men found dead in a car in the lower Bronx." These killings also appear mob related.

I guessed the two men killed outside the Wharf Bar were the Russians but I had no idea about the other group. I finished breakfast and made my way to the office.

I arrived at the office at seven thirty-five a.m. I walked directly into my office and continued reviewing the paper.

My telephone began ringing. I answer it and heard Oscar Williams voice say, "Mr. Storm I have some very upsetting news to convey to you."

I asked, "What's that Oscar?"

"Mr. Paul Winford is dead."

"Paul is dead? How? Where? When?"

Oscar said, "Paul and two other men were killed last evening. Someone shot them in a car."

"Is that the article in the newspaper about the three men shot?"

"Yes sir."

"Oscar, do you have any details?"

"No. Mr. Coleman wanted me to convey this information to you."

Crap! Paul's dead.

This private investigator profession is a dirty business.

I said, "Oscar I was with Mr. Winford until about six p.m. last evening. What time was he killed?"

"Mr. Storm, I do not know."

"Oscar, I need you to ask Mr. Coleman to call me. I was working for him through Paul this weekend and I need to discuss my fee. Also I would like to hear from you if you become aware of any detailed information regarding Paul's death.

"Mr. Storm, I will convey your information to Mr. Coleman. I am sure he will return your call."

I was in shock. It appears that Paul was still with the two men that knocked off the Russians. Someone must have been following them. Who could it be?

It almost had to be other members of the Russian mob? Are they aware that the book they received is a phony? Do they know who has the correct Book? Who does have the correct Book? What am I involved in?

18

J amie came dancing into the office with her radiant smile. She is such a pretty lady. I walked out to meet her. She stopped me and said, "What happened to your eye. It looks terrible."

"I'll tell you later. How is Jamie?"

"I'm fine. The Christmas season is so much fun."

I asked, "Did you make it into the City Saturday?"

"Yes, we had a great time. We walked all over Manhattan. Someday we are going to be rich enough to shop in all of the stores in Manhattan. The City is so pretty at Christmas."

"Well I am glad you had a good day."

Jamie asked, "How was your weekend?"

"Jamie come have a seat." Once in my office I told her that the Saturday morning meeting with Mr. Coleman was the most uneventful part of the weekend.

Then I told her about the Saturday night telephone call regarding Lisa Coleman's disappearance and the details that it took to return her home.

Then I told her about Paul Winford's death. I didn't include the shooting event that Lisa and I were involved in.

Jamie said, "Phil you had a horrible weekend."

"Well it was different. The worst part was that Paul was killed."

"Mr. Winford seemed like a nice man when I talked with him on the telephone."

"Yes, He was a nice man." I thought, "His problem was he walked a tight rope without a net. You can only serve two bosses so long before one of them let you down." That made me remember the need to go to the bank and withdraw Ragsdale's money.

I finished my coffee and told Jamie I needed to make a trip to the bank. Before I leave I want you to call Miss Emerald and inform her that she is invited to join you and I for lunch Friday. This will be our Christmas luncheon. Have her meet us at the office by eleven thirty a.m." I picked up my coat and left the office.

While driving to the bank I thought, "I do not want to return to the Wharf bar." It could be a dangerous meeting. I withdrew the money for Walter and the Christmas money for Jamie and Miss Emerald. I located a telephone and called the Wharf Bar. The bartender answered the telephone. I asked him if Walter Ragsdale was there. He said, "No." "Can I leave a message for him?"

He said, "Yes." Have Ragsdale call Phil. I provided my office telephone number and ended the call. I was hopeful Ragsdale would meet me at Tennyson's.

I returned to the office at ten forty-five a.m. I decided to contact Alvin Wilson. The last time I had spoken with Alvin he indicated that his business was booming. Since I have closed the Coleman cases maybe he has something I can assist him with until a new client comes along?

I placed the call. A lady answered his telephone, "Wilson Investigations, Mary speaking." I said, "Mary my name is Phil Storm I would like to speak to Alvin."

"Mr. Wilson isn't in the office. He indicated it would be after three p.m. before he would return to the office."

"Have him call me then." I provided her my telephone number and ended the call.

Now I was waiting on Mr. Coleman, Ragsdale and Alvin to return my calls. Here it is eleven a.m. and I had nothing to do. As I began reviewing the newspaper the telephone rang. Jamie buzzed me and indicated it was Detective Watson. I said, "Good Morning Tom how are you today?"

"I am swamped after yesterdays killings."

"So those killings were in your precinct?"

"No. I have been assigned to an Organized Crime Taskforce. When there is a crime that appears to be mob related my team is assigned the investigation."

"What can I do for you today?"

"I just wanted to tell you that the murder of the two unidentified men close to the Wharf bar maybe connected to the Ransom murder."

"What ties them together?"

"When their bodies were taken to the morgue we had their pictures taken. Once the pictures were developed one of the men on the taskforce took them to Ransom's apartment building. The security guard identified the two men as being at his apartment Saturday evening. Ransom's apartment had been ransacked. Since you were interested in the Ransom case I thought you would want to know."

"Thanks, Tom."

"Phil, do you know anything about the two men that were killed?"

"No? Why?"

"The security guard indicated that another man came into the lobby Saturday night and requested access to Ransom's apartment. The guard said he would bet money the man was a private cop. He provided a very good description of the man and Phil, I would bet money it was you."

I thought what do I say now? "Tom I was at Ransom's apartment this weekend. I have a female client that had been seeing Ransom prior to his death. She told me that Ransom had a picture of her and she wanted me to retrieve it. The guard provided me access to his suite to retrieve the picture and that is what I did.

"You are going to tell me whose picture it was aren't you?"

"Tom, this lady must have complete privacy."

"Phil, if you are impairing my investigation you and I will have a problem."

"I will tell you her name but please keep it confidential."

"I will keep it confidential if possible. Now Phil, who is the lady?"

"Her name is Lisa Coleman."

"We have already interviewed her regarding Ransom and there doesn't seem to be any reason to talk with her again."

"Phil, I have one more question? The security guard indicated that this private cop returned to the lobby with a nasty gash on his head and eye. Phil, if I could see you right now would I find a gash on your head and maybe a black eye?" I thought, "I need to discontinue using policemen for information." I felt this was the time to start lying.

"No Tom. My head and eyes are fine. I told you why I was in the building."

"Phil, stay clear of this case. I feel there is going to be an opportunity for innocent people to get hurt by being in the wrong place at the right time. When the real criminals get upset they don't care who dies."

"Thanks for the heads up."

"Phil, if your name continues to appear as I work this investigation I will have to bring you in and have an official interview with you. I am not threatening you just stating the facts."

"I understand. Stay healthy Tom." We ended our conversion. I need to stay out of Tom's sight until my face heals.

Jamie stepped into my office and said, "Are you going to lunch?"

I looked at my watch it was eleven thirty-five a.m. "No, but if I give you some money would you buy me a sandwich?"

"Sure." Jamie left the office.

After Jamie left, I began thinking about Paul. All I could focus on was how confident he had been last Sunday. He made sure Lisa was on her way home and he assisted me to my car. He was taking care of everyone but there wasn't anyone taking care of him. How quick life can end.

My telephone began to ring. I picked up the receiver and heard the voice of Walter Ragsdale. He said, "Do you have my cash?"

I said, "Yes. Can I meet you at Tennyson's after five this afternoon?"

"My day is very busy. I need you to bring the cash to the Wharf Bar this evening."

"So there isn't any chance of meeting at Tennyson's?"

"No I did you a favor, now you need to do this for me."

"Fine Walter I'll be there this evening." I ended the call.

I didn't want to go near the Wharf Bar after Sunday. I didn't feel safe in Harlem but without Ragsdale's assistance Lisa wouldn't be at home and I may need his assistance in the future.

My telephone rang again. It was Oscar. He said, "Mr. Storm, I have prepared a check for you in the amount of five thousand dollars. I have been instructed to deliver it to you. Will you provide me with a time and place?"

"I will be at my office until five this evening. You can deliver it here."

"Sir, I am to tell you that Mr. Coleman thanks you for your assistance this past weekend. He also wanted me to ask you if five thousand dollars was sufficient?"

"The amount is more than sufficient. Please tell Mr. Coleman thanks for me." Oscar thanked me and ended the call.

I am a wealthy man. I have over eight thousand dollars. I wish I had never earned the last five thousand dollars. It has blood on it.

Jamie entered my office and placed my sandwich in my hand. She told me she had talked with Miss Emerald and she would meet us for lunch Friday.

I asked, "What is Miss Emerald's first name?"

Jamie smiled at me and said, "Olivia."

"That name fits her."

As I ate my sandwich I thought if Alvin didn't have a case I could assist him with something will turn up.

The rest of my day was spent talking with Jamie about Christmas's of the past. I told Jamie about my last two Christmas's spent overseas and how lonesome they were. At five p.m. Jamie did her little house cleaning chores then said good night. I was a little frustrated that Alvin hadn't called.

I arrived at the Wharf bar at five thirty p.m. I did not see Ragsdale so I asked the bartender if Ragsdale was here. He said that Walter was in the backroom. I asked him to tell Walter that I was here. The bartender walked off.

I knew he was headed for the backroom where Walter drinks and gambles. I am sick of backrooms. In a few minutes Ragsdale approached me. He said, "Got it Storm?"

"Yes, I have the money but let's sit down somewhere."

"Come with me." We walked through the door Ragsdale had entered from and walked to the far end of the bar in the backroom. I handed him the money. He counted it. He looked at me with a smile and said, "Man, you have made my Christmas. If I can help you in the future just let me know."

"I'll do that." Then I turned and walked out of the bar. I wanted out of Ragsdale's part of town.

As I started to open my car door I felt a hand on my shoulder. As I turned there was a man with a gun in my face. I then noticed a man on my right side and one on my left. All three of them had guns drawn. I said to the man directly in front of me, "What do you want?"

With a heavy accent, "You are coming with us."

I turned my back to him and began to open my car door while saying, "I don't think so." As I reached for my door handle I saw stars.

I woke up in the back floorboard of a car with a man on each side of me. My head was throbbing. I rubbed it then looked at my hand. It was covered in blood. I made another bad choice. I tried to pull myself off of the floor and onto the seat but when I moved I felt sick. So I remained in the floor.

As I lay slumped in the floor it became hard to breathe. I was wedged between two very large men. I said, "Do you guys have enough room? I feel like a sardine can you each move over?"

I heard one of the men say, "Let's just throw him out in the street. He will have plenty of room then." The wise guy hit my head. I made another bad decision.

The car stopped. The two men stepped out of the car. I heard one of them say, "Get out or I'll throw you out." I didn't want that so I slowly pulled myself to my knees and began to stand. I managed to stagger out of the car.

I followed my new friends into a building. Inside the building was a bar, pool tables, pinball machines and several tables. There were eight to ten men in the place. My friends walked through that room and into another room.

The largest man pointed to a chair and told me to sit. This man was six feet six inches, probably weighed two hundred fifty to three hundred pounds. He was huge. He had a scar down the left side of his face. When you looked at him all you saw was mean.

As I sat there a man came into the room through a side door. He was a little man, probably five feet five inches tall and weighed about one hundred thirty pounds. He was well dressed. He had blonde hair.

After several seconds of studying my face the little man said, "Well Mister it looks like they have brought me damaged goods?" He looked at the man that had hit me and said, "Sammy what happened?"

Sammy said, "Andre this guy is a smart mouth and he doesn't follow instructions. He gave us some crap and walked away from me when I asked him to get in our car. I didn't see any other way to get him here."

Andre smiled. He had a pleased look on his face when he heard the man's response. He said, "Well Mister I don't have to tell you what will happen if you don't mind your manners." I looked at him without a sound.

He continued, "I need your help. What is your involvement with Mr. Eugene Ransom?"

"I didn't have any involvement with Ransom."

"I don't believe you sir. Let me try again. You were in Mr. Ransom's suite a few nights ago and on a separate occasion you were seen with his lady friend. Are you still going to tell me you were not involved with him?"

I sat there for a few seconds and thought. Was it going to be worth another beating to keep my mouth shut? I decided to answer his questions as complete as I could.

Then it hit me. This man is Russian. Ragsdale again. That is why he would not meet me at Tennyson's. He had it set up. I would pay him for helping me find Lisa and now he is getting paid for turning me over to the Russian mob. I must discontinue using Ragsdale.

I said, "I'll tell you what my involvement with Mr. Ransom and his Lady friend is."

Andre smiled and said, "That's a smart answer. Maybe you aren't as dumb as Sammy thinks you are."

I said, "I had been working for his lady friend's father on another matter. When she did not arrive at a predetermined meeting place Saturday night I was asked to look into that matter."

Andre interrupted me and asked, "What is your line of work?" I said, "I am a private investigator."

"What were you investigating for the lady's father?"

"He has another daughter that is having trouble staying away from the slots and crap tables. She had lost more than she could pay. All her father knew when he hired me was that some men were bothering her. He wanted me to determine why. I had finished that case when Mr. Ransom's lady friend disappeared. So I was asked to locate and return that daughter.

"I located a man that put me in touch with the people that had the lady. That individual scheduled a meeting. We met. They wanted a Book that Ransom had. They didn't find it in his suite so they thought the lady might know where it was. Sir, to make a long story short, the Book was located and delivered to the men holding the lady. Then they pulled a fast one.

"Instead of giving me the lady for the Book they shoved both of us into their car and began to drive away. Then all hell broke loose. There was shooting. Someone grabbed the lady. I made it to my car and I drove home. The next thing I knew was in the Monday morning newspaper. That's where my information ends."

My little friend said, "Thanks for your story but I still think you are holding back?"

"I have told you everything."

"Sir, I think you know you delivered the wrong book?"

"Sir, I delivered the Book I was provided by a man named Paul Winford. That is all I know about the Book."

"Mister, providing the wrong book is what ended Mr. Winford's life. Do you want to join him?"

"No I don't want to join him but I don't have the Book. If Mr. Winford provided me the wrong book he is the only one that knows the location of the correct Book."

"Mister, you are a private investigator. You found the lady and the people holding the lady. So now all you have to do is find the right Book."

I sat in front of Andre thinking about my situation. If Paul gave the Client Book to Filpatrick I have no way to retrieve it.

I wanted out of this place so I said, "Sir all I can tell you is I will attempt to find the Book. Can you tell me how I will know I find the correct book?"

Andre said, "I'll say it again. You are the PI and your life depends on you finding the correct book."

Andre looked at Sammy and said, "Return him to his car." Then he said, "Mister to make sure you accomplish what you are supposed to I want your home and work addresses as well as your telephone numbers. Please don't lie to me." I provided him the information.

"Sammy, when you deliver him to his car follow him home. Mister what time do you arrive at work?"

I said, "I'm there by eight each morning, why?"

"Sammy may need to stop by for a cup of coffee some morning."

"Keep Sammy out of my life."

"Mister I can't do that until we have the Book. You can consider Sammy a friend that may stop by anytime. I will give you until December twenty-third to locate the Book. Please don't disappoint me. If you disappoint me I will have a meeting with Ransom's pretty little lady friend. By the way what is her name?"

"Just leave her out of this. You deal with me."

"I will leave it that way for now but if you fail to provide the Book I will have Sammy visit the Lady." At this point I knew it didn't make any difference what I said; he wanted the Book. Andre left the room. Sammy and his friends walked me to their car.

19

As I was driving home the unknown was troubling me. I began wondering whom and when I would be hit across the head again. That pain was almost as bad as my current headache. I need a drink. I was at a loss. If Paul kept the Book where would he have stashed it?

I bet Ragsdale is also looking for the Book. I am sure that is how Andre's men found me. Paul did play both sides so he could have told Filpatrick the Russians have the Book and kept it himself. If so where is it?

I arrived at Tennyson's at nine p.m. I decided to find a corner table and drink alone. As I sat with drink in hand I thought, "Paul was a smart man. I need Paul's home address as well as access to his Manhattan office and his office at the Coleman home.

Who will assist me in gaining access to his offices? I know his house is a part of the police investigation so I will have to be careful going there.

Maybe Mrs. Robinson would be my ticket into Paul's offices.

I looked at my watch. It was ten thirty p.m. I could feel the alcohol relaxing my tired beat up body. I needed to stand and drive myself home. As I stood I nearly fell down. Why do I do this to myself? The drinks are good and the feeling helps me make it through the nights but I over do it on a regular basis.

I regained my balance and pointed myself toward the door. As I approached the door whom to my wondering eyes did appear? It wasn't a funny little man and eight tiny rain deer it was big Sammy. Man I didn't need this. I had forgotten that he was going to follow me home. Just my luck; a big gangster for Christmas. I looked at him and staggered to my car. If he could follow me I would have to let him tuck me in.

I parked my car and looked around. Yes Sammy was there. I motioned for him to follow me. I opened my door and through open my arms and said, "This is home Sammy." Without a word he pushed me away and left. I was able to remove my coat and shoes before I hit the bed.

● ● ●

That diabolical alarm clock began its unnatural sounds and my head was pounding. I undressed and sat in the shower. While in the shower I decided to by-pass coffee at home and drive to the Newsstand and then on to the Coffee Shop.

As I entered the Coffee Shop I began trying to determine how I could contact Mrs. Robinson. I decided to call Oscar and see if he was in a position to give me her social schedule. If he couldn't help me I would just park outside her house and follow her. It is the eighteenth of December and I have until the twenty-third. Ho! Ho! Ho!

This Christmas is going to be one to remember. That made me think of Kitty. I needed to make arrangements to deliver her Christmas present.

I will need to be careful I do not want Sammy to locate her.

I arrived at the office at seven fifty-five a.m. To my surprise Jamie was there and the coffee was ready. We exchanged greetings. She asked, "What happened to you?"

"Would you believe I fell down a flight of stairs?"

"No Phil. Tell me what happened?"

"Right now it is better that you don't know. I am not one to keep secrets from my partner but it is in your best interest right now." I then asked her to call Oscar for me.

As she turned to walk back to her desk she said,

"Phil, be careful."

"Jamie I am trying to."

She buzzed to inform me that Oscar was on the line. I said, "Good Morning Oscar."

The little man said, "Thank you sir and good morning to you."

"Oscar, I need your assistance. I need to contact Mrs. Robinson. Mr. Winford assisted me in this matter before his death. He would check her social calendar and provide me dates and times of her scheduled events. Then I would meet with her briefly to schedule a meeting. She does not want me to contact her at her home. Can you help me?"

"I think I can obtain that information."

"Will you assist me?"

"You are not going to upset Mrs. Robinson are you?"

"No Oscar I am not going to upset her. I am going to provide her information that I think she will be happy to receive. So I am a liar."

"I will gather the information and call you later today." I thanked Oscar and ended the conversation.

I began to think about this missing Book and my life if I can't locate it. What if Paul didn't keep it? Where do I go then? I can't walk up to Filpatrick and ask him to provide me the Book.

I know the men that gave me my unwelcome ride and threatened my life last night are part of the Russian mob. I could feel my friend, "Fear" slipping back into my thoughts. That was not a comfortable feeling. Too many people know where I live, drink and work. I am sure Sammy will show up at my office before long. Once they locate my office Jamie will be at risk.

The intercom began to buzz. Jamie said, "Phil it's Oscar for you." I thanked her and said, "Phil here." "Sir I have some times and dates of events Mrs. Robinson will be attending over the next week." I began writing down the information. I thanked him and ended the call.

I noticed there was one event this evening at eight p.m. but it was a black tie affair. It was easy to fore go that one. Even if I dressed in my best clothes I would stand out. She has a meeting Wednesday morning at ten a.m. in Manhattan. I will meet her then. I didn't like wasting Tuesday but Wednesday would be my best opportunity.

As I ended my call Sammy walked into my office. I greeted him and asked him to take a seat. I stepped out of my office and asked Jamie to pour a cup of coffee for our guest.

I returned and handed the coffee to Sammy. I said, "So now you know where I work. What else can I do for you?"

He sat there drinking his coffee. Your girl makes a good cup of coffee.

"Your dealings are with me and me only. Just remember that." He smiled then stood and walked out of the office.

Jamie came into my office and asked, "Who was that?"

"Jamie, pretend you didn't see anything. That man is the one that gave me my headache yesterday. Hopefully you will never see him again."

"He sure is big."

"Yes he is." Jamie returned to her desk.

Sammy coming to my office was very upsetting. These gangsters are hacking me off. I decided to see if Sammy was going to be following me all day. I told Jamie that I would be out of the office until early afternoon.

I drove into the City. With the traffic in the City if someone is following me it would be easier to determine and easier to shake them. As I drove I began to think about the day of the shooting. Paul and I located the Book on Coleman's yacht. Then Paul took the Book and told me to return home and wait for the call from the men holding Lisa.

How much time did Paul have between leaving me at the boat slip and arriving at my apartment? It took me about twenty minutes to drive home. I had been at home approximately thirty minutes before he arrived. So that would be fifty minutes.

Fifty minutes would have given Paul enough time to drive into the City and return to my place. He could have made it to the New York's Finest casino also. Where else?

I was getting into the City traffic and I was not paying attention to my backside. I began studying the cars behind me. After making a few turns and driving several blocks I parked and walked to a hotdog stand. I purchased two hotdogs and returned back to my car. I hadn't seen any suspicious cars. I began eating my hotdogs.

As I was finishing my first hotdog a man opened my car door next to the curb and stepped in. I looked at him and asked, "What do you think you're doing?"

He said, "Be calm we need to talk."

I positioned my uneaten hotdog on my knee and asked, "What do we need to talk about?"

"We need to talk about a little book that I need to locate."

"What little book and again who are you?"

"My name isn't important but you acting like an idiot could get you killed. Do you understand that?"

"Yes I understand. But I must tell you I have been threatened by so many people lately it is becoming meaningless. Do I make myself clear?"

"Finish your dog and then we are going to take a drive." I looked at the hotdog and then at the man. I wanted to take the hotdog I had just finished and give it to my new friend but that would mess up my front seat. Instead I threw the remaining hotdog out the window and said, "I'm finished what now?"

"Drive. I will direct you."

As I drove I continued checking my rearview mirror to see if Sammy was following me. It didn't appear that he was. My new friend instructed me to park behind one of the New York's Finest Restaurant.

This wasn't the one that Lisa and Ransom visited. He pulled a gun from his pocket and stepped out of my car. He motioned to me to step out. I followed him inside. Once inside the man said, "Head for the casino." He was known here because no one stopped him or assisted him to the casino.

We walked through the casino and into an office. My buddy had me sit and he walked off. This man was another big man. He looked like a professional football player, probably a guard or tackle. He had stayed in good shape. What is next? My head still hurts so I am going to be agreeable if I can. I don't need anymore pain.

My new friend returned and told me to follow him. We entered another office where there was a man behind a desk. He was well dressed. He reminded me of Paul Winford. He was young, tan and in good physical shape. He had rings on both hands. His fingers sparkled as the light bounced off of the diamonds in his rings.

He said, "My name is Franklin and I need you to assist me with a business matter." He was cooler than most of the thugs I have meet lately; he provided me his name.

I asked, "What can I assist you with?"

"I think you know?"

"A Book?"

"Yes a Book."

"Franklin, is it alright to call you Franklin?"

"Yes."

"Franklin, I am between a rock and a very hard place. You want to know about a Book and so do some other very insistent people that I have had the privilege of meeting lately.

"To be very honest if these people do not acquire the Book I am a corpse. I would also bet that if you don't acquire the Book a similar fate is in store for me?"

Franklin looked at me for several seconds. Then he said, "Do you have the Book?"

"No. Let me tell you the story."

He interrupted me. "Mister, do not get cute with me or your life will become miserable. I do not like a smart aleck. You need to treat me like the intelligent professional I am."

"I'm sorry but I have been knocked around more in the last couple of days than I have in my entire life and I am getting tired of it. Let me say I do not have the Book you are looking for. I am trying to locate it. I know if I don't locate it I'm dead and if I do locate it the group that doesn't get custody of it will kill me."

"Franklin, what would you do in my position?"

He looked at me and grinned. "I'm not sure sir."

"You don't know but you think I am a smart-aleck while I try to find a win-win situation."

"Do you know a man by the name of Andre? He is probably Russian."

"I know of his organization but not him personally?"

"Can you help me with Andre's organization if I locate the Book and give it to you?"

"Sir, we helped you stay alive during your last mess. We are sorry that we didn't do better follow up. We didn't expect instant retaliation. That is why your friend Mr. Winford isn't with us today. I must tell you the Book in question is very important to my boss. The information it contains could bring harm to some very important people if it falls into the wrong hands."

"The other group have given me until December Twenty-third to provide them the Book. I am willing to work with you but I will need your help.

Once we have the Book we will see that you are safe. Mr. Winford was our friend and I know he was your friend also."

"I do not need anymore predetermined schedules. My number one priority is to locate this Book. I have some thoughts as to where the Book may be but right now that is all that they are.

"If I have anything for you how do I contact you?"

"Call this telephone number anytime day or night. Someone will answer it and I will return your call."

"That is fair. I wrote down the telephone number."

"Is there anything else?"

"Only one small item. Do not cross me. I don't enjoy punishment but I enjoy being lied to even less. You may leave now."

I walked out of another crappy situation with all my parts. This is beginning to be ridiculous. Franklin did not tell me whom he was work-ing for but of course I did not ask either. I am getting gun shy when it comes to asking questions. It seems to hurt each time I do that.

Based on Franklin's location he has to be one of Filpatrick's men. Since Ragsdale is one of Filpatrick's boys he probably gave Franklin my name. I sure don't need his kind of help. If Ragsdale is going to continue providing my whereabouts to undesirable individuals I may have to find a way to silence him.

I never did determine if Sammy is following me. I don't think he is. Since his organization knows where I live and work they should sit back and wait for me to contact them.

This meeting tells me Paul kept the Book. But where did he stash it?" I wonder if he could have put it back on the Coleman's yacht. That would be a great hiding place. That would be something a very smart man would do.

I felt so good about that idea I decided to visit Captain Casey. I hoped he would be as nice to me without Paul as he was when Paul was with me. Before driving to the pier I called Jamie. When Jamie came on the line I asked her how her day was going. She said, "Fine. Alvin Wilson called and said the best time to catch him would be before eight a.m. tomorrow or after five p.m. today." I thanked her and told her I won't be returning to the office today. "I'll see you in the morning." I ended the call and returned to my car.

It was mid-afternoon when I parked at the pier. I walked up to Captain Casey's door and knocked. He invited me in. He told me how sorry he was to hear about Paul.

I asked him if I could have permission to board the Princess again. He said, "The Princess is not in her slip right now. She was towed to a maintenance facility."

"Do you think I could go to the maintenance facility and board her there?"

"Well I don't see why not. Let me make a call."

When he finished his call he provided me the location and the name of the supervisor at the Maintenance Facility." I thanked him and drove to the maintenance facility.

When I arrived at the facility it was buzzing with activity. I spotted the Princess. I walked into the office and introduced myself. The man in the office accompanied me to the Princess. He told me to be careful. I thanked him and climbed aboard.

I began my search in the sleeping spaces. I automatically went to the bed where we had located the Book originally. The tear was still in the mattress but no Book. No location caught my eye. I decided to take my time and revisit every inch of the lower deck before moving on.

An hour and a half later I hadn't found anything in the sleeping area. Maybe I am wrong. Paul may have taken it home.

I walked to the upper deck to continue my search. An hour later I still had not found anything. The supervisor that had given me permission to board the Princess returned. He indicated that in thirty minutes he would be closing for the day. He asked me what I was trying to locate. I told him a very valuable book. "I am employed by the Coleman's and the last time the book was seen it was on the yacht."

I asked the man if I could return tomorrow if needed. He said, "Sure, we open at seven a.m." By closing time I had not located the Book.

I returned to the office. Once there I told myself no drinking tonight. As I sat in the quietness, I asked myself, if the Book is not on the boat, where then? It could be at Paul's house but where else? I began thinking about the amount of time Paul had to stash the Book. It appeared that fifty minutes was the maximum time. It took me about twenty minutes to drive from the pier to my place. So that left thirty minutes for Paul to stash the Book somewhere.

Where is this conversion taking me? Could the Book have been left in his car? Was he in his car when he was killed? I needed to determine if Paul was killed in his car? I will look into that tomorrow.

Once I arrived at home it didn't take me anytime to fall asleep. When my enemy the alarm clock began its morning noise I felt pretty good. I was very hungry. I dressed and drove to the Newsstand and then onto the Coffee Shop.

As I was eating breakfast I began thinking about how I could determine whose car Paul was in when he was killed. I certainly didn't want to ask Tom Watson. The newspaper only talked about the people, location and that they were in a car. I finished breakfast and drove to the office. I was hopeful that December eighteen would be a better day.

When I entered the office, my little smiley face Jamie had the coffee made. We exchanged greetings and I walked into my office. All of a sudden I remembered I hadn't called Kitty yet. I need to remember to call her this evening if I am going to take her to dinner before Christmas.

As I sat drinking coffee my mind returned to the car Paul was in when he was killed. That car should still be in the police impound area. I should be able to drive down there and just ask which car Paul Winford died in.

Then Oscar came to mind. I am sure he could provide me with the type of car Paul drove? I decided to call him. As I prepared to place my call to Oscar a light came on in my mind. Paul had met me at the 42nd Street Men's Club. Someone had parked his car in the rear of the Club. From there we were together in my car.

When I left Paul at the pier he had no car. He had made a telephone call at Captain Casey's place once we located the Book. He had gone into another room to make the call. He told me he was updating Mr. Coleman. He may have been contacting the two men that were with him when he was killed.

Paul's car should still be parked at the 42nd Street Men's Club. I saw his car that morning but for the life of me I couldn't remember anything about it. If I can determine the type and color of Paul's car I can drive to the Club and confirm it is still there. Maybe this is the break I need?

20

I dialed Oscar's telephone number. I heard the little man say, "This is Oscar Williams, how may I assist you?"

"Oscar, this is Phil Storm. Do you know the type of car Paul Winford drove?

"No."

"I am looking into Paul's death. The Police have not located his car. Since I was with Paul most of the weekend I am going to retrace our steps and see if I can locate it but I first need to know the type of car he drove? Can you obtain that information?"

"I am sure I can."

"Will you let me know what you find?"

"Yes." I thanked Oscar and ended the conversation.

I felt finding Paul's car could be what keeps me alive.

Jamie buzzed me and said that Mrs. Robinson was on my line. I answered the telephone and greeted Mrs. Robinson. I said, "What an unexpected but pleasant call. What may I assist you with?"

"Good Day Mr. Storm. The reason for my call is because of a call I received from Oscar Williams. He informed me that you were asking about my social calendar. May I ask why you need that information?"

"Mrs. Robinson, I am looking into Paul Winford's death.

"I am sure you know about your sister, Lisa's experience. The horrible thing that happened to Paul took place while he was involved in rescuing your sister."

"Mr. Storm, I find your involvement in the Coleman's personal affairs something that is no longer needed."

"Madam, I have not said anything to your mother or father but I think Lisa's life is still at risk."

"What in the world are you talking about?"

"Your sister was involved with Eugene Ransom. We discussed this before. Well it came to my attention through helping Paul find Lisa that Mr. Ransom had something some very ugly people want. For your own safety that is all I am going to tell you.

If I need access to Paul's office in the City or his office in your parents home would you assist me?"

"Mr. Storm, this sounds like police business?"

"Yes Madam, but I don't think we should involve the police currently. Paul was killed because of a Book he had in possession. This Book is also what got Eugene Ransom killed and it could get your sister killed if I don't find it and turn it over to your friend, Filpatrick. It is that simple. The police are not aware of this Book." The organization that kidnapped Lisa wants the Book also. They have informed me that they are willing to leave your sister alone if I provide them with the Book but if I don't find the Book, my life and your sister's life are in jeopardy.

"Right now I am the middleman. I am trying to keep your sister out of the situation. I ask again. If I need into these offices will you help me?"

"Sir, you scare me. I want you out of our lives as soon as possible."

"Madam, I want off of the Coleman payroll as soon as possible also. If it's needed will you help me?"

"Yes."

"Thank you."

Jamie walked into my office. She asked, "Phil, I am going to lunch can I bring you anything?" I said, "Yes. Bring me a sandwich." She was off to lunch.

My telephone began ringing. I answered it and I heard, "Good Day Mr. Storm this is Oscar Williams."

"Thanks for returning my call so soon."

"Mr. Winford owned a 1945 Packard. It was solid white in color. Also Mr. Storm here is the license tag number. Will that provide you the information you need?"

"Yes, that is exactly what I need. Thank you."

I returned to the newspaper while waiting for Jamie to return with my sandwich. It wasn't long before she arrived.

Once I finished my sandwich I walked to Jamie's desk and told her I would be out of the office for awhile.

I drove to the 42nd Street Men's Club. I remembered that the parking lot was in the rear of the Club. On the left of the building was a street that lead to the rear of the building. I walked down the street to the parking lot. There sat a 1945 white Packard. I approached the car and tried to open the door. It was locked. Now what? As I stood beside the car I could sense someone watching me. I turned and there stood a man in a security uniform.

I approached him. I asked, "Sir, how are you today?"

"I am doing fine. Is there something I can help you with?"

"This is Paul Winford's car isn't it?

"Yes."

"I had a telephone conversation with Paul a few hours before his untimely death. We discussed a rare book of mine that I had loaned him. He informed me he had placed the book in his car so he would remember to return it. The man at the front desk told me his car was here so I thought I would retrieve my book but the car is locked. Is there anyway you could assist me in retrieving my book?"

"Who are you sir?"

"I am Phil Storm. I am a Private Investigator who worked with Mr. Winford on several Coleman family issues. Are you aware that Paul was employed by Robert Coleman?"

"Please wait here, I will return."

When the guard returned he had a folder in his hand. He confirmed that Mr. Winford was an attorney working for Mr. Robert Coleman.

"Is their anyway I can confirm your story?" I thought Oscar.

"If you take me to a telephone I can call one of Mr. Coleman's employees that will confirm who I am and why I am here."

"Come with me." He took me to a telephone. I dialed Oscar's number.

"Oscar I have located Mr. Winford's car but it is locked. Do you have a key?" The security guard heard every word I spoke to Oscar.

The Guard interrupted me and said, "Sir, if I can confirm that you have permission to enter the car I can provide Mr. Winford's car keys."

"Oscar, hold on a moment. So there is a key here?"

"Yes each member leaves a key for emergencies."

"So if the man on the telephone confirms I have the right to take the car you will provide the keys?

"Yes sir."

"Oscar, I am going to place a security guard at Mr. Winford's club on the telephone. He will want you to confirm who you are and your position with the Coleman family. Then he will need for you to confirm who I am. Then he will provide me the key to Paul's car. Will you discuss the issue with the guard?"

"Mr. Storm are you sure you should take his car?"

"Sure. The police will want to look it over."

"Fine let me speak to the guard." I handed the telephone to the guard. They talked for several minutes before he ended the telephone call.

The guard asked me to follow him. We walked in the rear entrance of the Club. There on the wall was a board with keys hanging from it. He retrieved a ring of keys. "These are Mr. Winford's keys. He handed them to me." I looked at the keys. There were four different keys.

"There is more than car keys here."

"I would guess his house keys are on the ring also."

"Do you want to take them?"

"Under the existing circumstance I can't see why it matters. Just leave them all together. When you take his car home you can place the keys in his house." I thanked him and walked out of the Club. That was just too easy. The car keys and the house keys.

I entered Paul's car and started it. I decided to drive it to the pier where The Princess is normally kept. There was private parking for owners there. I didn't think Captain Casey would mind.

As I pulled onto the street I noticed a man across the street in a car. I couldn't see his face because of the traffic. I need to determine if the person in the car is Sammy. Sure enough it was.

Now I have a problem. If I don't return to my car soon he will enter the Club looking for me. If he finds the friendly guard he will know that I left in Paul's car.

I decided to find a parking lot and leave Paul's car there until I can shake Sammy. I approached a parking lot and pulled in. The lot indicated it was open twenty-four hours a day.

Before I left the car I opened the glove compartment. I pulled out a little book lying on top of the other items there.

I opened it. It contained a list of men's names with dates next to them. Then next to the dates were the first names of women. Then there was a column indicating dollar amounts. Each man's name had several dates. Sometimes the woman's name would be the same for all of the entries of a specific man. The amount of money spent by these men took my breath. This is very expensive entertainment. I know this is the Book in demand.

I recognized some of the men's names. One was the former Mayor of New York City. I could see why Franklin didn't want this Book to fall into the hands of any one outside of Filpatrick's organization. The men in this Book would pay thousands of dollars to keep their names out of the press. This Book is worth a fortune. I thought, do I want to take the Book with me?

What if Sammy stops me and wants me to take a ride with him again? I decided to leave the book in the car for now.

I placed the Book under the carpet in the floorboard on the driver's side. That may be the first place someone would look but I knew it was better than just lying in the glove compartment.

I locked the car and walked out of the parking lot. I hailed a taxi and had the cabby take me a block past the Club. I walked to my car. Sammy was still sitting across the street.

I drove to the office. Once Sammy goes away I will return to Paul's car and drive it to the pier.

Sammy followed me to the office. I have the Book that is so wanted. I could feel my chest swell with pride. I knew my best chance of staying alive was to give the Book to Franklin. If the Coleman's side with Filpatrick I should do the same.

It was four-fifteen p.m. when I walked into the office. Jamie approached me and said, "Tom Watson was here looking for you."

"Did he say what he wanted?"

"The only thing he said was, "Tell Phil I can get him free headache pills."

"All I need is to have another person after me." I asked, "Am I to call him?"

"No. I was to pass on his comment to you. I told him that you would be back or you would call me before five p.m."

I will let Tom catch up with me. I'm not interested in anymore crap or questions. I thanked Jamie and told her to call it a day. I will be here until five p.m. She began cleaning the coffeepot and my cup.

I entered my office and realized I had forgotten about Sammy. I wonder if he is still outside. I decided to remain in the office until five thirty p.m. then I will walk to the bus stop close to the office and take a bus to the parking lot where I left Paul's car. If Sammy follows the bus I would ride it until I can lose him.

When I left the office I didn't see Sammy. The bus was almost empty. I walked to the last row of seats. I looked out of the bus's rear window.

It was so dirty I couldn't confirm if Sammy was following me. I changed buses. As I was waiting for my next bus I looked for Sammy but he was not in sight. I boarded the bus that would take me to Paul's car.

When I exited the bus I walked around the block before entering the lot. All seemed quiet. It was a cold walk but seeing the Christmas lights made it a nice walk. I paid the parking attendant and drove to the pier area.

Once at the pier I parked Paul's car in the general parking while I talked with Captain Casey.

With the Book in my coat pocket I approached the Captain's house and knocked on his door. When he came to the door he invited me in and wanted to know what brought me to his house. I asked him if I could park Paul's car in an owner's parking spot for a few days. He asked me why I had Paul's car. I said, "I had found it parked at his Club and since Paul's death was a homicide I wasn't sure what to do with it. In my line of work I don't get involved with the police any more than necessary. Maybe you could let the police know it is here.

Once I had parked the car I gave the Captain the keys and thanked him. Captain Casey said, "So you want me to call the police and let them know the car is here?" "Yes. What should I tell them?" "Tell them I dropped off Paul's car because I didn't know where else to take it." "Then just answer their questions." The Captain asked me how I was going to return to my car. I told him I would catch a bus. He said that he would drive me. I reminded him that it is in the Bronx. He indicated that wasn't a bad drive. We walked to his car and drove off.

It was six thirty p.m. when the Captain dropped me of at the office. Where can I stash the Book? The perfect place is the secret storage area behind the picture over the coffeepot.

When I removed the picture I could see that the space was nearly full of documents. With a little push I was able to slide it in beside the other documents. I replaced the picture and drove to Tennyson's.

I decided to visit Tennyson's and have a drink before dinner. When I entered Tennyson's I remembered my need to call Kitty but it was so noisy in the bar.

I approached Jerry, the bartender, and asked, "Is there a telephone in a more quite area?" He said, "Come with me." He walked me into an office behind the bar. He said make it short. I thanked him.

I dialed Kitty's number. She answered on the third ring. We

exchanged greetings then I asked her if I could take her to dinner either Friday or Saturday evening. She said, "Late Saturday afternoon would be fine."

"That is perfect. What would be a good time?"

"Maybe four thirty?"

"I'll be at your place at four thirty p.m." She indicated that she was looking forward to it. I ended the call.

I returned to the bar and ordered a drink. As I sat there it dawned on me that Saturday would be December twenty-two and the twenty-third is my deadline to provide the Book to Andre. I need to call Franklin and set up a meeting tomorrow. I wanted this issue over as soon as possible. Making life and death decisions with criminals was troubling me; I want it over.

When I finished my third drink I paid my tab and went to dinner. After dinner I drove home. Being full of food versus alcohol was a good feeling. As I approached my apartment door I saw Sammy.

I looked at him and said, "Don't you ever sleep?" He stood there looking at me. "If you can't talk, move and let me in my apartment. I'm tired." I pushed him and shut the door in his face. It felt good. I locked the door and began to prepare for bed.

I heard the telephone ringing. I looked at the clock. It was four thirty in the morning. I answered it and heard, "This is Tom Watson, Phil." I said to myself, what in the world does he want at this hour?

I said, "What's up Tom?"

"I am at the pier and I found Paul Winford's car. Do you know how it got here?" Crap can't he go home and sleep like most people do at four thirty a.m. He takes his job way too serious.

"Tom, I have been working for Robert Coleman. I found the car and I parked it there."

"Why didn't you call me?" I can't tell him I didn't want to so I'm stall for time.

"Phil, this is the last time I will call you regarding an ongoing police investigation. If you withhold information or evidence in the future you will be in police custody explaining yourself. This friend thing is over."

"I didn't want to create a problem for you but I owe my client as much privacy as possible."

Tom reiterated, "The next time I will not call you, the precinct will. Phil, what is the deal on Winford's car?"

"Tom, I was told that there was evidence in the car that would explain why Mr. Winford was killed. I searched the car but I didn't find anything. My source didn't indicate what the item was he just said it was in the car. As I said, I didn't find anything."

I thought, "That was close to the truth." Tom said, "Don't lie to me."

"Well Tom you either believe me or haul me in. I am very tired. What else can I do for you?"

"You aren't anything like Abe. Abe helped me he didn't lie to me. I think our conversations from now on should be official."

I felt bad but if I have burned a bridge it was necessary. I said, "Tom, I will not bother you anymore unless it is official." I ended the call.

I knew my night's sleep was over. It was Thursday, December twentieth.

I decided to drive to the Coffee Shop for an early breakfast. On the way I decided to see if the Newsstand was open. Just my luck no newspaper before six.

After breakfast I returned home. Since I still had on yesterday's clothes I needed to shower.

I left my place at six a.m. to get a morning paper. It was six-thirty a.m. when I arrived at the office. Everything was quiet. On the drive to the office I noticed there wasn't much traffic at this hour.

When I stepped out of my car it was so quiet I could hear my heart beating. The building that my office is in was pitch black and silent. The silence and black were very unsettling.

I remember being on the flight deck before sunrise. You could hear the waves hitting the ship. You could see the outline of the ship with the red lights around the flight deck. It made me think of Christmas.

I was thousands of miles from home but home was all I thought about. The darkness made me think that life is only memories and undetermined things to come. I was upset with the undetermined things to come.

I turned the office lights on, made the coffee and entered my office to read the newspaper. There was an article on the murder case Paul was involved in.

It indicated that the police investigation had determined that one of the men killed was an attorney that was employed by Mr. Robert Coleman, Chairman of CMI Corporation. It continued by indicating that the police had not determined the connection between Mr. Paul Winford and the other two men killed with him.

I felt so bad for Paul. He had everything going for him. I guess his desire to do whatever it took to serve the Coleman family and Filpatrick became too much. He could have let the Russians take Ransom's Book. It wouldn't have been any sweat off of his brow or would it? If he was serving two masters I guess that could have helped him make the decision he made but neither one of his masters were worth his life.

I poured a cup of coffee then scanned the rest of the paper. It was seven fifteen a.m. on December twentieth. Christmas was just around the corner. I had all my gifts purchased and I was looking forward to giving them to each person. I just needed to keep breathing for a few more days.

I began to think of Mr. Coleman. He never answered his own telephone calls. It was always someone else. He didn't seem to mix anything personal with business. It was all so nondescript. It appeared to me, "That as long as Mr. Coleman did not make it personal it wasn't. I felt sorry for him."

At seven fifty-five Jamie walked into the office. I greeted her and her very pretty smile.

I continue to marvel over the fact that she always has a smile and she seemed to be very happy. I can't understand why she doesn't have a man in her life. She seems so happy even though she is alone. I need a strong dose of happiness. I'm not real happy without a lady friend but I'm not very good at finding one or keeping one. Maybe someday I'll do better.

I told Jamie I had a ten a.m. meeting but would return to the office once it was completed.

Since I had not called Franklin in advance I was hopeful he would see me. I needed to determine what I was going to say to him. It was nine fifty-five a.m. when I arrived at the New York's Finest Restaurant. I pushed on the door. It was open so I entered. As soon as I was inside a man met me. I asked him if Franklin was available.

He said, "Yes he is in his office."

"Would you ask him if he has time to see Phil Storm?" The man walked off.

In what seemed to be forever the man returned. He said, "Mr. French was busy but he can see you in about twenty minutes."

"Can I wait here or should I leave and return later?"

"If you would like to wait here, it will be fine. I can bring you some coffee if you would like?"

"That would be good." I realized this young man was just an employee.

I was sitting quietly drinking my coffee when the young man returned and said, "Mr. French will see you now."

As I entered Franklin's office he was sitting behind his desk doing all he could to look busy and intelligent. I walked up to him and we exchanged greetings. I sat down as he said, "What is it I can do for you today Mr. Storm?" I was impressed with Franklin; he remembered my name.

"Franklin, I want to discuss this elusive Book? If this Book is delivered to you will you provide protection?"

Franklin said without hesitation, "Yes. You can bank on it. This is a very important Book."

"I mentioned to you that there was another group interested in the Book?"

"Yes you mentioned that."

"I really believe if that group doesn't receive this Book I will be in harms way."

Franklin said, "I am aware of a big dumb man following you from time to time over the last few days. I am also quite aware of his organization. I made sure the big man did not follow you here today. I would imagine he is quite frustrated by being derailed this morning. Did you know he was following you this morning?"

"No, I didn't."

"I will guarantee support and protection."

"How much lead time will you need to have your protection team in place?"

"Phil, if you indicated that you would meet with me at ten a.m. tomorrow morning I would schedule a meeting with Mr. Andre and his organization at ten tomorrow morning. This would guarantee that your delivery would be made without any interruptions and it would also guarantee there wouldn't be any retaliation. Do you think this sounds acceptable?"

"Very acceptable."

"Mr. Storm, can we schedule a meeting for tomorrow morning at ten o'clock?"

I looked at Franklin and said, "Tell me why I should believe you?"

"Because I have given you my word. In my business my word is my most important asset. Break your word and you are out of business.

Mr. Storm, how can I be sure you will meet with me tomorrow at ten o'clock and provide the Book?"

"Franklin, I work on the same principle. If I can't be trusted who will hire me? I'll see you at ten in the morning."

I left the restaurant and returned to my car. It was eleven thirty a.m. I felt that Jamie would be at lunch so I decided to stop for a sandwich before returning to the office.

Tomorrow is Friday. I have mixed emotions about the day. I am placing a lot of trust in Franklin. Is it the best decision?

21

I parked my car and walked up the stairs to the office. There was Jamie reading a book. Someday I will have enough clients to keep her busy.

"Any messages?"

She marked the page in her book and said, "Alvin and Mrs. Robinson called. Mrs. Robinson wanted to know if you were going to need her assistance. She is leaving the country after the holidays. I told her to call Mrs. Robinson tomorrow and inform her I will not need her assistance."

I placed a call to Alvin. Mary indicated he was not available but he would like to meet for a drink after five p.m. Friday.

"Mary, where does he want to meet?"

"He was going to leave that decision to you."

"Have him meet me at Tennyson's."

"I will tell him." That will work out fine. I will have lunch with the ladies and drinks with Alvin.

I hope the day is uneventful. It will only take a few minutes to deliver the Book to Franklin. Then I will be ready to enjoy my Christmas lunch. I have eaten twice today and I feel very good. I decided to stay away from the drinks tonight. I will check the entertainment section of the newspaper and see what movies are showing. I noticed that *"The Lost Weekend"* was showing. It has received very good reviews.

When the clock struck five p.m. I told Jamie to have a great evening and I would see her in the morning. I told her the only thing on the calendar tomorrow was a ten a.m. meeting. Then the rest of the day is for our Christmas lunch. She gave me one of her pretty little smiles and said, "Phil have a good evening." I took her coat from the coat rack and laid it over her shoulders. She placed her arms in it and disappeared into the night.

The next showing of the *Lost Weekend* didn't begin until six ten p.m. I decided to drive to the theatre from the office.

As I sat at my desk without a thought going through my mind I looked up and who did my wondering eyes see; again it wasn't Santa and his eight little reindeer. It was Sammy and Andre walking into my office. I stood and said, "Sit down boys." Andre sat but Sammy stood by the door with his hand in his coat pocket. I knew he was trying to scare me.

I said, "What do I owe this visit to? I thought you were going to give me until December twenty-third?"

"That is your drop dead date. I want to discuss what happened earlier today. It appears that you have someone running interference for you. Do you care to explain?"

"What are you talking about?" I could see Andre was upset with me.

"I told you about wise guys. Where did you go when you left your office this morning?"

"I went to my mother's place to finalize her Christmas plans. My mother works nights and goes to bed in the early afternoon. So morning is the only time I can visit with her." Man was I becoming a professional liar.

Andre said, "If you are messing with me you are dead. Someone is following you and it is not just Sammy. Now who is it?"

I sat quietly. Andre had caught me without a good response. I will tell Andre that the security guard at Ransom's apartment told the police about me being in his suite and they consider me a suspect in his murder.

I looked at Andre and said, "It is probably the cops."

"There wasn't any uniforms and they didn't try to stop Sammy they just detained him long enough for you to get out of sight. One more time Mr. Storm, who was following you?"

"The word on the street has it that the cops have set up a Special Organized Crime Taskforce. They are looking into Ransom's murder and the other two murders that happened last Sunday. Maybe it was the detectives assigned to that Taskforce. If it isn't the cops then I do not know who it is?"

Andre stood and said, "I will see you Sunday!" Then they left as quickly as they arrived. I looked at my watch; it was five thirty p.m. I still had time to make the movie. As I walked to my car I thought, Franklin better be the proper scumbag to trust with my life.

I enjoyed the movie. I had worked up an appetite. I drove to a restaurant just two blocks from my place.

As I entered the restaurant there was a lady with tears in her eyes talking to a waitress. I found a booth close to where the two ladies were talking. The lady was dressed in very worn clothes. The waitress was saying, "Miss, it will cost more money than you have. I am only a waitress. I can't give food away. I am very sorry."

The woman looked down and began to walk away. I said to her, "Just a minute Miss." She stopped and looked at me. "Would you sit down and tell me what you and the waitress were discussing?" The woman was beginning to cry again. "Sit down for a minute." She sat. I reached for a napkin and handed it to her. She began to dry her eyes. "What's going on?"

She looked down at the floor and said, "I don't have enough money"—then she began to cry hard.

I stood and walked over to the waitress and asked, "What does she need?"

"The woman wants to buy four meals. She wants me to wrap them up so she can take them home. She has three children. I told her she didn't have enough money for four meals."

I asked the waitress, "How much did she need?"

"She needs three dollars."

"Get her whatever she wants, as I laid a ten-dollar bill on the counter."

"Sir, are you sure?"

"I am positive. And make sure there is dessert for everyone also." The waitress turned in the lady's order.

I returned to my booth. The woman had quit crying. I said, "Miss the waitress has turned in your order."

"Sir, is there anything I can do to repay you?

"Yes there is lady. You can pay me in full if you will take this twenty-dollar bill and have a Merry Christmas. Lady, that is all I want."

The waitress brought the food over and handed it to the lady. She was still sitting in my booth with the twenty-dollar bill wadded up in her hand. She looked at the food then at me. She began to cry again. I said, "Lady quit that crying. Your face will freeze when you go outside."

She wiped her face and said, "God Bless you sir." Then she picked up the food and left the restaurant.

The waitress took my order and handed me the change from the ten-dollar bill. I picked it up and handed it back to the waitress. I said,

"This is yours. Get my order turned in I am starving." The waitress walked away.

I ate in silence. As I was driving home the woman at the restaurant returned to my mind. She was the reason I ate at this particular restaurant tonight.

I slept like a baby. I prepared for the day. Will the bad luck that seems to surround this Book end today?

After a stop at the Newsstand, it was on to the Coffee Shop.

My stomach didn't handle breakfast very well. Does Franklin have the muscle needed to close Andre's mouth?

As I entered the office my telephone was ringing. I picked up the receiver. I heard, "Mr. Storm, this is Franklin French."

Crap, what now? "What's on your mind, Franklin?"

"I wanted to inform you that the police picked Andre up this morning. They want to talk with him regarding Eugene Ransom's murder."

"What does that mean to me?"

"It will slow down my visit with Andre and his group. If they release him we will take the action then. If he is booked we will wait. His associates aren't going to do anything without him. I have friends keeping their eyes on him and the movements of his people while he is away."

"Thanks. I'll see you at ten a.m." With that I ended our conversation. That conversation reminded me that I needed to remove the book from storage. I placed it in my suit coat pocket.

I was pouring a cup of coffee as Jamie came bouncing in. She looked especially pretty today. She had on a red dress and the same color shoes. She had on a very pretty necklace with matching earrings. She was really ready for lunch. "I reminded her of my ten a.m. meeting."

As I was driving to my meeting I had a feeling that someone was following me. I'm not sure whether it is paranoia or fear but I can sense it. As I drove I began watching my rearview mirror. When I made my first right turn I checked my rearview mirror. No one turned behind me. As I made a left turn at the next corner there was a car several car links behind me. It looked like a DeSoto. It was light blue. I turned the corner and drove a full block. The DeSoto was not in sight. Being involved with the mob is making me crazy.

I arrived at the restaurant at nine forty-five a.m. When I entered a man approached me. I told him I had a ten o'clock appointment with Mr. French. He said, "I'll be right back."

The man returned and escorted me to Franklin's office.

Franklin said, "How are you Mr. Storm?"

"I'm fine." I reached into my coat pocket and handed Franklin the Book.

Franklin spent several minutes looking at it. Then he said, "Mr. Storm, I will be right back." He left his office through the back door.

When he returned he said, "Sir our business is completed. I thank you and my boss thanks you. We will be watching over you until we feel all is safe for you."

"Thanks."

"I hope you have a very Merry Christmas."

I found myself saying, "I hope you have a Merry Christmas also."

As I returned to my car I thought, *my Christmas present from him is an ongoing life*. I put my life on the line for him today and I hope he will hold up his end of the bargain.

It was ten forty a.m. when I parked my car and entered the office. There stood Jamie. She looked good in red. She said, "Mary from Mr. Wilson's office called. She wanted to tell you that Alvin will meet you at five thirty p.m. at Tennyson's Club. I thanked her.

Jamie and I spent the remainder of the morning talking.

Miss Emerald interrupted us when she arrived. She had on a very pretty black dress. She looked very nice. I said, "Madam you look very nice today."

As we were walking to my car I asked Miss Emerald, "May I call you Olivia?"

"Yes. That is fine."

"From now on I want you to call me Phil. Mr. Storm is too formal."

She said, "Thank you Phil."

I had selected a very nice restaurant. It had atmosphere. It didn't have a counter where people ate and it didn't have booths. Everyone ate at nice tables.

It was eleven fifty a.m. when we arrived at the restaurant. We were seated immediately. The ladies both indicated that they were very pleased with my selection.

As we ate I found it interesting how talkative Miss Emerald was.

When she talked she always looked at Jamie. She never looked me straight in the eye.

She told us that her mother, sister and brother-in-law lived in Queens. Her sister had two children. She indicated that the family met at her sister's home for Christmas.

She told us it was a family tradition for them to meet at her sister's home to decorate the family Christmas tree, then they met on Christmas Eve to attend church service and then Christmas day to open gifts and have dinner.

I was so surprised how much Miss Emerald talked. Jamie hung on every word. The food was very good and I really enjoyed the laughter and listening to the ladies talk. It was like having a family.

Once we had finished dessert I pulled out the envelopes. I handed each lady one. "Before you open the envelopes I want to tell you how much I have enjoyed getting to know both of you. I wish the reason that brought us closer had been different. I miss Abe. I want you both to know I consider us a team. I wish both of you a very Merry Christmas and a wonderful 1946. Now you can open the envelope."

They thanked me for the very nice lunch and the gift.

"You both are welcome. Now the next part of the gift is that you both can take the afternoon off."

I returned the ladies to the office so they could catch their buses.

Once the car was parked outside the office Miss Emerald thanked me again. She shook my hand and wished me a Merry Christmas and a Happy New Year before walking off to the bus stop. Jamie said, "Phil, I will see you Monday, have a good weekend." Then off she scurried to the bus stop.

I entered the office. This has been my best Christmas in many years. I don't have anything to do until I meet Alvin. I reread the newspaper. Then I opened my desk drawer and pulled out a deck of cards. I played a few hands of solitaire to pass the time.

I was going cross-eyed looking at the cards so I returned them to my desk drawer. As I sat I began to notice how quiet it.

Then the telephone rang. I thought it would be Alvin about tonight. But to my surprise it was Franklin. He said, "Phil, I wanted to tell you that the police released Andre. I want you to call me at eight p.m. tonight."

"Franklin, what is the eight p.m. telephone call about?"

"Just consider it a confirmation call."

"Fine I will call you at eight." Franklin ended the conversation.

So now that the police have released Andre can I expect another visit from big Sammy? This is still Friday and at Andre's surprise visit to my office he said he would see me Sunday. Crap this scumbag is trying to ruin my Christmas. I looked at my watch it was three forty p.m. I decided to leave the office and go to Tennyson's. At least at Tennyson's I won't get anymore bad news.

I stood and walked out into the cold December day. It was four fifty p.m. when I arrived at Tennyson's. There was a large crowd. I approached the bar and took a seat. I wished Jerry a Merry Christmas and asked for a scotch and water. Jerry returned the greeting.

Even with the large crowd I was very much alone. I couldn't get Andre off of my mind. Would I see him again?

22

I looked up and spotted Alvin entering the door. I stood, shook his hand and wished him a Merry Christmas. He had a big smile on his face as he took my hand and wished me a Merry Christmas. I ordered him a drink and we sat down.

Alvin said, "It is good to see you Phil. I have something I want to discuss with you. That is if you don't mind a little business discussion before pleasure?"

I said, "What's on your mind Alvin?"

"Yesterday I was approached by a man that would like to hire me to look into a matter involving his business. This person is Mr. Terrance Nance Wilson. He is the President of Executive Furniture and Accessories. His Company sells furniture and accessories to commercial clients. Does this company ring a bell, Phil?"

I sat there for a few seconds thinking then I turned to Alvin and said, "No. Nothing right off. Should it?"

"Phil, it is a subsidiary of the CMI Corporation. Now does it have any meaning?"

"Now that you connect it to CMI Corporation I remember hearing of him. I know his name and the company's name, nothing more. How did you connect me to the CMI Corporation? I don't remember us talking about it?"

"Phil, I have been a PI for eighteen years. To cut through it Phil, I was in contact with a man named Johnson from a PI Firm in Boston regarding a person in my current case. While we were talking he mentioned your name. Then one thing led to another and he told me you and he had worked on a case for the Coleman family."

"Yes, Johnson helped me. Alvin, where is all of this going?"

"I am spread very thin these days. I told Mr. Wilson that I would let him know on Monday if I could handle his case. My question to you is would you have time to work this case for me? It would be my case but you would do the legwork. What do you think?"

"Can you provide any details on the case?"

"In my initial meeting with Mr. Wilson he indicated that the furniture his company is selling to a local Hotel is not being delivered to the Hotel. Then he indicated his situation wasn't as clear-cut as that statement sounds. If it was he would turn the situation over to the police.

"Mr. Wilson indicated that his merchandise is loaded on his delivery truck at his warehouse and the customer receives merchandise but it is not the furniture that leaves Mr. Wilson's warehouse. His issue is, "What is happening to the furniture that leaves his warehouse and where is the furniture that is delivered to the hotel coming from?"

"Alvin, are you intentionally trying to confuse me?"

"Phil, it is hard to follow but the furniture that is delivered to the hotel looks just like Mr. Wilson's furniture but it is of inferior quality. Mr. Wilson said he has no idea how long this has been going on.

"The furniture switch was discovered when Mr. Wilson's Vice President of Merchandise Sales visited the customer. The quality of the furniture was not in question. The Vice President was there to ensure the customer was satisfied with the furniture he was receiving.

"In one of the rooms the Vice-President picked up the cushion from the sofa. As she held the cushion it felt fine but when she turned it over there wasn't a vendor tag.

"She quietly placed the cushion down and inspected a nightstand. It appeared much lighter in weight than she remembered. She removed the drawers from the dresser. They were also very light and she noticed that the drawers were glued together versus being nailed together.

"When she returned to her showroom she compared their merchandise with what she had seen in the hotel. She knew something was going on so she reported her finding to Mr. Wilson and he called me.

I said, "Yes, I'll do the legwork for you. Now let's just have a few drinks and consider dinner later."

"That is fine with me."

I looked at my watch and it was seven fifty-five p.m. I told Alvin I had to make a telephone call. I asked Jerry if I could use the telephone in the back office. He said, "Yes." I walked to the office and dialed Franklin's number. The telephone rang. Then I heard, "This is Mr. French's line, Sue speaking."

"This is Phil Storm. Mr. French asked me to call him at eight o'clock this evening. Is he available?"

"Just one minute."

Then I heard, "Phil, this is Franklin."

"What's going on Franklin?"

"I want to inform you that you will not be hearing from Andre anymore."

"That sure sounds great. Thank you Franklin."

I said, "Good night and returned to the bar."

After several drinks and too many war stories we waddled out of Tennyson's. It was really getting cold. We decided to take a cab to a restaurant. We were hopeful that after eating we could find our way home.

As we ate I could not stay away from the pending case. I said, "We need to determine if this is isolated to this customer or if it is affecting other customers. This will be interesting."

"Phil we'll have time to discuss this later." We finished our meal without further conversation.

After dinner we hailed a taxi and returned to Tennyson's. It was early Saturday morning. I said, "Alvin, I have never asked. Are you married?"

"Would I be out this late with you at Christmas time if I was? No I am not currently married. I was once but that has been several years ago. I'll call you Monday to inform you the status of the Wilson case." We wished each other a Merry Christmas and went our separate ways.

I woke up at eleven a.m. Saturday morning. I felt like I needed to drink a gallon of water. I don't understand how I enjoy drinking but can't stand waking up afterwards. Oh well, I'll take a shower and drink some coffee.

Since it was noon by the time I was dressed a late breakfast sounded good. I was looking forward to having dinner with Kitty this evening. I stopped at the Newsstand on the way to the restaurant.

While eating I found an article on page three regarding the on-going investigation into the death of Eugene Ransom. The article indicated that the police had interviewed an Andre Zgersky. Mr. Zgersky has ties to organized crime. No charges were filed.

There was nothing regarding the murders of Paul and the other men killed with him nor of the two men murdered outside the Wharf Bar. I wondered why. I wasn't going to call Tom Watson and ask him.

After breakfast I returned home. I put Kitty's Christmas present in my coat pocket so I would not forget it.

I arrived at Kitty's house at four p.m. sharp. Kitty met me at the front door. As I entered her house I could see her Christmas tree. I said, "I like your Christmas tree."

"Thanks. Christmas isn't Christmas without a tree."

"Madam you look beautiful." I couldn't believe I had said that. My expression told her I had shocked myself as much as my comment had shocked her. I stood there with a dumb look on my face.

"Kitty, I have something for you and I would like for you to open it before we leave. I reached into my coat pocket and placed the present in her hand.

"Phil, I didn't buy you anything, you shouldn't have."

She slowly removed the wrapping paper. Then she opened the box. It was like watching a queen opening the royal jewels. I could tell without saying anything dumb that she was pleased with the necklace. She said, "Phil, it is beautiful." Man there was that word again. I just smiled. She asked me to fasten it around her neck. "How does it look?"

"It looks just right."

"Thanks. I have always wanted a necklace like this."

"I'm hungry. Let's go to dinner." Off we drove.

I told her that I had found a restaurant in Scarsdale I wanted to try and asked her if it sounded good to her. She said, "Well Phil if it is in Scarsdale I'm sure I will like it but it will be expensive."

"Kitty it is Christmas."

It was after five p.m. when we arrived at the restaurant. We were seated immediately. It was an elegant place. "Phil, this place is a splendid choice. I feel like a bootlegger's wife." I knew what she meant. In the 1930's bootleggers were the only ones with enough money to come to a place like this.

"I'm glad you like it."

We sat quietly as we ate. I think the reason we didn't talk was we wanted to absorb the elegance we were in. To break the silence I said, "How is your food?"

"It is delicious."

"Once we finish our meal would you like to drive around Scarsdale and look at the Christmas lights before we drive home?"

"That would be very nice."

Once we finished eating Kitty said, "I will remember this place forever. I have never eaten in a place so elegant. Thanks for bringing me here Phil." I'm glad you liked it."

Thanks for coming with me. Let's go do the town."

As we drove through the town it was easy to see the wealth in Scarsdale. After about an hour of looking at fabulous homes covered in Christmas lights I drove Kitty home.

It was eight p.m. when we arrived at Kitty's house. I stepped out of the car and walked to Kitty's side of the car and opened her door. This good night thing was always difficult for me. I never knew if I should ask to come in or just let the woman determine that.

As we walked to her door she said, "Phil, would you like to come in and help me wrap Christmas presents? I haven't wrapped any of my gifts."

"Sure that would be nice but I must tell you I'm all thumbs when it comes to wrapping presents. Your gift was wrapped nicely because I had it wrapped at the store."

"Well that's okay I am sure you will do fine." As we began wrapping the presents she told me whom each present was for and why she selected the specific gift for them. It was fun helping her. She gave me wrapping lessons and laughed when the lesson didn't help the look of the present.

We talked and laughed until nine thirty p.m. When the last present was wrapped I said, "Lady, I have had a wonderful time. Thanks for letting me help you wrap your gifts. Kitty, I haven't laughed so much in a long time. I want to thank you for a very special night. It is getting late I should leave now."

I stood and was putting my coat on as she approached me. She placed her hand on my shoulder and kissed me gently on the cheek. At that moment I realized how good it felt having a woman kiss me even if it was only on the cheek."

"Thanks for the necklace." I left.

I began my drive home thinking about Kitty's kiss. It reminded me of what I am missing. Being alone is getting old. I didn't want to grow old alone. The evening was great. I couldn't ruin this wonderful evening by going to a place like Tennyson's. I decided to go home and get a good night's sleep.

Sunday was a lazy day. I began thinking about the new case. I decided to jot down some questions for the meeting. I drove to the office.

Once at the office I removed the Coleman family pictures and took a look at Terrance Nance Wilson. He was probably thirty-five years old. Tall, brown hair, slim, and in good physical shape.

I began reviewing the brief amount of information I had on this new case. So the furniture that is loaded at Wilson's warehouse is not the same furniture that is delivered to his customer.

I began my list with, "How many warehouses does Executive have in the New York City area? How many customers are supplied merchandise from each warehouse?

Does Executive buy direct from factories or are their wholesale companies involved? Who is in charge of the loading and delivery of the merchandise? How long has this person worked for Executive? How many employees work for that person?

If I walked into the hotel where the imitation furniture is being taken how would I identify it? Does the Vice President that noticed the difference in the furniture have any idea what company made the imitation furniture? I decided that was enough questions for the initial meeting.

With my list completed I left the office. There were three movie theatres between my office and my home. I decided to see what was playing. As I approached the first theatre I stopped. The Humphrey Bogart movie *"To Have and Have Not" was* playing. I found a parking spot and went in.

It was a great movie. Lauren Bacall is a beautiful woman. I could watch that movie again just to look at her. Even with the popcorn I had worked up an appetite.

I could see a restaurant three doors down from the movie theatre. I walked to it. I noticed a Sunday paper lying on the front counter so I sat down and placed my order.

I began reading the newspaper. On page two there was an article about the Organized Crime Unit of the police department.

It said that this unit was made up of the best detectives from each of the five boroughs. It indicated they were working on three murder cases. The article indicated that the killing of a prominent attorney and two other men was at the top of their list.

It led me to believe that Tom Watson was a very busy man this holiday season.

I finished my meal and drove to Tennyson's. Going home at this hour would mean staring at the walls until I became sleepy. I told myself

I would only sip the drinks. I didn't want to wake up Monday morning with a hangover.

To my amazement Tennyson's was packed. The Christmas spirit filled the place. The jukebox was playing Christmas music. Gene Autry was singing "Jingle Bells" when I walked in. It was a good song by anyone, but Gene did it the best. As the Christmas music blared I lost track of the number of drinks I had downed.

I left Tennyson's with a glow. I had enjoyed the Christmas music and singing with it. I looked forward to Monday. It would be Christmas Eve.

My friend the alarm clock began singing at six a.m. Monday morning. I started the coffee and then jumped in the shower.

It was seven thirty a.m. when I arrived at the office. I started the coffee and returned to the newspaper.

The paper listed the big names in music in 1945. It had Gene Autry, Bing Crosby, Judy Garland, King Cole Trio, Glenn Miller and Frank Sinatra. I was glad to read something in the newspaper besides bad news.

The paper was full of Christmas stories. It had an article written by Franklin Delano Roosevelt about his favorite Christmas. It was as if he was still with us. A great article. I was getting excited for the season and the day. I laid the paper down and went to pour a cup of coffee.

After I filled my coffee cup I focused on another article in the news. It was about all of the returning veterans. It said since so many veterans were coming home for Christmas the train and bus services were overloaded. The International News Service called it the worst continental traffic jam in history. I felt so sorry for them. I know how nice it is to be home.

I looked up and there was Jamie just bouncing with energy and that smile that made the day worthwhile. I stepped out of my office and said, "Merry Christmas." She said without losing her smile, "Merry Christmas to you Phil."

I asked, "How was your weekend?"

"It was great. I helped my sister prepare things for Tuesday's dinner and gift opening. Her children are so excited. How was your weekend?"

"It was good. Kitty and I had dinner Saturday. Sunday I just loafed."

"We may have another case. I will be working with Alvin. It is his case but since he is so busy he has asked me to work it for him. Another interesting item about the case is it involves the Coleman family."

"That is wild."

"The case will involve Mr. Terrance Wilson. He is the president of the Executive Furniture and Accessories Company, which is one of the CMI companies. He is married to one of the Coleman daughters. Alvin and I are to meet with him today to confirm the job." I poured a cup of coffee and returned to my desk.

I was sitting at my desk drinking coffee and reviewing the newspaper when the telephone began to ring. Jamie picked it and then buzzed me and said, "It is Alvin Wilson." I greeted Alvin with a good morning, and he returned the good morning.

Then he said, "Phil, Mr. Wilson wants to meet at four-thirty p.m. at a suitable meeting place between the City and Scarsdale. If you don't mind I thought we could meet in your office."

"That will be fine."

When I ended my call I waved at Jamie. She walked into my office. "We are closing the office at noon today." "Thanks Phil."

Once Jamie had returned to her desk I began thinking how nice it will be working with Alvin. It would be like having Abe back.

At noon Jamie returned to my office and asked, "Do you want me to leave the coffee on for you?"

"No. I am going to be leaving the office until four p.m. At four-thirty p.m. Alvin and I are meeting here with Mr. Wilson."

Jamie said, "So you have to work late on Christmas Eve?"

"It will be worth it. Besides I have my Christmas shopping completed and I don't have to arrive at my mother's until two o'clock tomorrow afternoon." I stood and wished her a Merry Christmas.

She leaned forward and gave me a hug and a kiss on the cheek. Just like with Kitty I was frozen in place momentarily as she hugged me. I could feel the warmth of her body. I couldn't think of anything to say so I smiled at her and said thanks. She turned and left the office.

I decided to have lunch and then made a trip to the bank. The streets were full of people and they were all in a hurry. I felt like walking fast and looking worried just to fit in. But I didn't have a reason to hurry.

When I arrived at the bank it was quite obvious I had made a mistake. The teller windows all had lines. It took me fifteen minutes to have my turn with a teller. I then returned to the office to wait for the meeting with Alvin and Mr. Wilson.

I opened my desk drawer and removed my deck of cards. I began playing solitaire.

At four fifteen I put my cards away and made coffee. I looked under the table that held the coffeepot and found two cups. I had just filled my coffee cup when Alvin and Mr. Wilson arrived.

Alvin and I exchanged greetings. Then Alvin introduced me to Mr. Wilson. I walked to Jamie's desk and moved her chair into my office. I felt like a bum only having one guest chair. Here is the President of a very large company and I slide in a secretary chair for him to sit in.

I asked Mr. Wilson and Alvin to be seated. Mr. Wilson pulled two business cards out of a small container. He said, "On the back of the cards is a telephone number that can be used to reach me twenty-four hours a day. It is critical that this number remains confidential."

"Mr. Wilson all information we share will remain confidential."

"When it is necessary for us to meet in the future we will meet at the 42nd Street Men's Club. Do you know its location?"

"Yes sir."

Mr. Wilson reviewed the case information he had provided Alvin at their initial meeting. Then I began asking my questions.

"If I were to check into a room at the hotel where the imitation furniture is being delivered how will I know the difference between it and your furniture?"

"You will need to visit our Manhattan store and review the construction of our product. Once you have accomplished that it will be easy to determine the difference."

"Does the Vice President that noticed this difference in quality have any thoughts where the furniture is coming from?"

"No."

I asked for the address of the warehouse where the furniture is being loaded. That will be where I start. I will need the name and telephone number of someone that can provide me with a schedule of upcoming deliveries to the hotel. I will watch the loading and follow the truck to its destination.

I looked at Alvin and said, "Any questions?" He said, "No."

I said, "Mr. Wilson, would it be possible to meet with your Vice President that uncovered the issue?

"Yes. I will arrange it. I will talk with her on Wednesday and have her contact you."

I provided Mr. Wilson my work and home telephone numbers. I said, "My office telephone is answered from eight a.m. until five p.m. Who will supply me with the delivery schedule?"

"My Vice President of Merchandise Sales. Her name is Donna Turner. She is the person that will call you on Wednesday."

"Mr. Wilson, I wish you and your family a very Merry Christmas." He stood and wished both Alvin and I a Merry Christmas and left.

Alvin said, "I have a Christmas Eve event I have to attend." He followed Mr. Wilson out of the office.

I turned off the coffeepot. It is five-thirty p.m. Christmas Eve, what now? I stood in front of Jamie's desk and looked at the telephone. It was as silent as my thoughts. What now? This Christmas season has proven that one is the loneliest number.

I decided to drive to Tennyson's for awhile. Tennyson's was nearly empty. Jerry, the Bartender, wasn't even there. I downed a couple of drinks then it was off to eat alone. After dinner there wasn't anywhere to go but home.

It was eight a. m. Christmas morning when I started my day. I showered, dressed and drove to the Newsstand and then on to the Coffee Shop for breakfast.

When I arrived at the Coffee Shop I was one of three customers. I sat down, ordered breakfast and began reading the newspaper.

The headlines read, "The World is at Peace." As I sat reading the paper it was hard to believe that the War had only been over a couple of months. Just nine short months ago I was on the USS Franklin and it was totally engulfed in flames. I know that there are 724 men that will not be home for Christmas, 1945. I am one of the lucky ones that survived. So many men and women died in the War.

Once I finished breakfast I couldn't stand the thought of returning home. I took my newspaper and drove to the office.

As I sat in my chair I found it nearly impossible to concentrate. I didn't want to think about my life so I began to think about Kitty, Jamie and even Olivia. Those thoughts didn't last long. I removed the cards from my desk drawer and begun playing solitaire.

I left the office at one fifteen p.m. When I arrived at my mother's apartment I found it bursting at the seams with people. There were several ladies and a few children. Mother began introducing me to her friends. She pointed me to a chair and handed me a present.

She asked me to open it. I opened it and was trying to determine what it was when she said, "Phil, it is a paperweight for your office." Along with the paperweight was a package of handkerchiefs. I stood and thanked her for the gifts.

"Open your gift." She began tearing the paper. When she opened the card the money fell out. She picked it up and tried to hand it to me. I said, "Mom, this is part of your present. I didn't know what to buy you so I want you to please yourself."

She turned to her friends and said, "Would you look at what my son gave me." She placed the money back inside the card and began looking at the handkerchiefs. Then she gave me a hug.

At two fifteen all but three of mom's friends had left. The remaining ladies began placing Christmas dinner on the table. We all took a seat. My mother said a prayer and we began eating. The meal was very good. I didn't have to say much. The ladies kept the conversation going without me.

While the ladies cleared the table I sat on the sofa. I thought to myself what a nice day. I felt stuffed and in a warm room. Those two items together told me not to close my eyes or I would fall asleep.

Once mother and her friends had finished cleaning they sat around the kitchen table. I walked over to the table and thanked mother for my presents and told her that I was leaving. I told her that the meal was great and it was nice to meet her friends. I smiled at the ladies and shook their hands. She stood, hugged me and thanked me again for her gifts.

It was five p.m. when I arrived at home. I took off my coat and poured myself a drink.

It had been a very good day. I am looking forward to tomorrow and the new case. My future is looking bright.

23

I came out of a sound sleep and my bed at the same time. I couldn't determine what was happening. As a light came on I could see three men. Two of them were holding me. The third man was standing in front of me.

I looked at him and asked, "What are you doing here?"

He said, "I've been told you have something I need to retrieve." I thought who is this man?

I said, "Who are you? What do you want?"

"Who I am isn't important but what I want is if you want to be alive in 1946."

I asked, "Can I put my slacks on?" He motioned to the two men holding me to move back. I slowly reached for my slacks and pulled them on.

As I looked into the eyes of this man I saw anger and hate. He was a large muscular man. I could see tattoos on his knuckles. On his right knuckles were the letters H.A.T.E and on his left was the word K.I.L.L.

While loose I sat on the bed and put on my socks and shoes. I then stood and put on my shirt. I knew I was going somewhere. All I could think about was Franklin's call. Andre is gone forever. If that is so then who are these men? The man in front of me said, "Mr. Storm, get your coat we are going for a ride."

"Where are we going?"

"You will see when we arrive."

My mood changed from frustrated to angry. These muddle-headed gangsters pulled me out of bed, made me dress before a shower and didn't offer me coffee. The men on each side of me took my arms again and began dragging me. I pulled loose and told them to, "Keep their hands off of me." The man on my left reached out to grab me again. I hit him in the face and knocked him to the floor.

My next memory was the floorboard of a car. Waking up in the floorboard of a car is getting to be too common. I felt the back of my neck. It hurt all the way down my back. When I pulled my hand off my neck it was covered in blood. I eased my hand up the back of my head. It was gashed close to my neck.

I looked up slowly. There wasn't anyone in the backseat. I'm not sure why all of these dim-witted delivery boys have to go for the head with their gun.

When the car stopped the backdoors opened and my two buddies began pulling me out of the car. They were enjoying knocking me around. Once they had me out of the car they let go. I fell to the ground in a blob. I could not control my legs.

I knew I was still alive because I could feel the cold December morning. After a few seconds I was able to pull myself to my knees. With a hand from my bodyguards I was able to stand. As I staggered toward the building it looked familiar. It is the building where I had met Andre. Crap, not again. I guess you can't trust any crooks. Franklin let me down once he had what he wanted.

Once inside the building I was pushed down in the chair I had occupied before. Then my buddies moved behind me. I thought, I don't have anything to bargain with this time.

I changed my thoughts from what to do, to who in the world is this? A man walked into the room. He looked awful. He had a large reddish spot covering half of his face. He had grayish hair. He was six foot tall with a large stomach and oversized feet. He had three fingers missing from his left hand. Then he smiled, showing three gold teeth in his front upper.

As he stood before me I felt that this man is bad news. Then he spoke. "Dead man do you know what day it is?"

"It's Wednesday."

Mr. Goldtooth said, "Yes it is Wednesday. Weren't you told to be here last Sunday with a gift? Where is the gift?"

"Who are you and what is it you want from me?"

Mr. Goldtooth walked over to me and said, "I'm someone that you will never forget." He walked behind me and put his hands on the back of my chair. I fell to the floor as he pulled the chair out from under me.

"I am someone that will get under your skin and I mean under your skin." I was afraid I knew what he met. "If you want to continue playing dumb I will introduce myself to you."

I asked, "If I had been here last Sunday who was I to meet?" Instead of answering my question he kicked me in the ribs. The pain took my breath.

He said, "Where is the Book? You know what I am talking about. This Book is very important to my boss. I assured him I would obtain it and I will. Now you have a decision to make. Will you leave here today or will you die here?"

I said, "Can I have something to drink?"

I remember being picked up. Then my face went numb. I remember thinking about Kitty and last Saturday night. I felt my face. It was odd I was touching it but there wasn't any feeling. Then I felt a large lump just under my left eye. As I went down my face I found two holes where there used to be teeth. I didn't think that was a good sign.

As I lay on the floor I understood the meaning of the word hate. Real hate. I wanted to pull this man's gold teeth out, rub his reddish spot with sandpaper and break his ribs one at a time.

My thoughts were interrupted when my friends picked me up and carried me into a small room. The room didn't have any windows or furniture. I was placed on the floor. Mr. Goldtooth came to the door and said, "You will tell me what I want to know now or later."

I pulled myself up against the wall and just stared at him. I wasn't sure if I was seeing him or just remembering what he looked like. Then I realized he was real as he kicked me in the stomach. It felt like white heat. It made me sick and everything came up Mr. Goldtooth turned off the light and shut the door.

As I lay on the floor I thought about the day the Franklin was bombed and the Franklin Feeling. I was hoping the magic of the Franklin Feeling would help me survive this mess because without that type of support I am a dead man.

I couldn't move nor handle much more physical abuse. I needed to determine if I could stand. I made it to my knees and crawled to the wall where the door was. I found the door and reached for the doorknob. It would not turn. The door was locked; as I felt it I determined it was metal. So breaking it wouldn't happen.

I crawled away from the door. My ribs were beginning to hurt more with each breath and every time I took a deep breath the pain took my breath. I had to remain calm and breathe easy.

Well, if I can't take deep breaths I sure can't stand and run. Crap, I can't just lay here.

Minutes turned into hours, at least it seemed like hours. I decided to try and stand again. I very gently pulled myself to my knees. I had to hold my ribs with my right hand when I moved. I was able to pull myself up and take a few steps. I slowly walked across the room to the door. I began to feel weak so I sat down. Being able to stand and walk a few steps felt good.

As I was feeling good about my mobility the door opened and the light came on. I was blinded. Once my eyes focused I saw my big ugly friend standing in the doorway. He said, "You smell. I want you to come with me. We have someone we want you to meet." I stood very slowly. Mr. Goldtooth pointed to the men that had brought me in the room and said, "Take him and let him wash off that smell. Then bring him to me."

One of the men started to grab me. I said, "I'll do it on my own. I knew they would make it hurt more. I slowly walked into a room with a sink. There was a washcloth and two towels. I took the washcloth in my left hand and began to wash my face. It hurt to push on my face but the cool water felt good. Once I washed my face and arms I began to wash the mess off of my slacks.

Then I bent down slowly and got a drink of water. I am glad there isn't a mirror over the sink. I don't want to see my face. Then one of the men said, "Okay, let's go."

One of the men walked in front of me while the other two were behind me. The man in front led me back into the room where I began my meeting. Then I looked up and said in more pain than I thought a man could feel, "What are you doing?"

Mr. Goldtooth said, "I thought you needed someone to jog your memory." There stood Jamie.

She began walking toward me. Mr. Goldtooth stopped her. Then she said, "Phil, Oh Phil! What is going on?" I could tell by the look on her face I didn't look pretty.

I said, "You had no right bringing her here. Return her to where you found her. You do that right now or you'll get nothing from me."

Goldtooth put his hands around Jamie's waist and said, "Me, and this little beauty may have fun before the day is over." The look on Jamie's face was one of intense fear.

"Take your hands off of her if you want my help."

"Well it's about time you said those magic words."

I said, "Okay, I'll help you but keep your hands off of her."

Goldtooth smiled and said, "You will help me no matter what I do with this young beauty. When I have my merchandise I will set her free. You realize I said her. I haven't decided what will happen to you."

"I'll have to return to my office to retrieve what you want."

"Jamie is to join me. Once I have given your men the Book I want her left there. I will return."

"You are not making the rules, I am. She will stay here until you return."

"I am not leaving her alone with you for a minute."

Goldtooth looked at his men and said, "Take him back to the room I'll be there in a few minutes. It appears he needs some more convincing. I need sometime alone with sweetie."

"No just a minute. You are in charge. I will get your merchandise. Will you promise me that you will release her once you have the merchandise?"

I don't know why I asked him that question. He would agree and it would be a lie. I had to come up with away to retrieve the gun taped to the underside of the top drawer of my desk.

I looked at Jamie and said, "I'm sorry. I'll be back."

All three of the men escorted me to their car. As we drove I knew the only chance to save Jamie and me was to retrieve that gun.

When we arrive at the office I will tell the men that the Book is taped to the underside of my desk. Once I pull the gun loose I will fire through the desk. That should get their attention.

Since there were three of them nothing is going to be easy.

When we arrived at the office I could tell they had been there. The door to the office was open and it had been ransacked.

I could see that all of the drawers in my desk were pulled out.

I approached my desk and for the first time one of the men said, "It's not in your desk. We went though it when we were here to get the girl."

"It is there. I taped it to the underside of the desk just above the top drawer." I could tell that got their attention.

As I knelt behind my desk I could see someone at the office door. It was Alvin. I couldn't believe it but there he stood. As I reached my hand under my desk Alvin said, "All of you drop your guns." All three men turned at the same time. Only one of the men had his gun in his hand. As the other two reached for their guns Alvin fired at the man with the gun. He fell to the floor. The other two men placed their hands over their head. The one on the floor wasn't moving.

Alvin told the other two men to drop to their knees with their hands behind them.

He reached into his coat pocket and pulled out a pair of handcuffs. He handcuffed them together. He said, "Phil, you don't look so good."

"Alvin, you look great."

Alvin asked, "Are you okay. I told him I was fine but Jamie is being held by another man. Alvin asked me if I could take him to where Jamie is being held. I told him I thought so but I wasn't sure. He said, "Well take our friends with us they will show us the way or they will get a bullet. The two men never moved or said a word."

Alvin placed his gun against the face of one of the men and said, "You'll show me the way or you can join your buddy on the floor.

The man didn't say anything. Alvin cocked his gun and placed it back on the man's face. The man said "Yes I'll show you."

I said, "Alvin, how did you find out about this mess?"

"When you didn't show up for work Jamie called your home. You didn't answer so she called me. I drove by your place and found the door wide open and no Phil. I then drove to your office and found the door was wide open and no Jamie. Since I didn't know where to go from there I waited in my car hoping someone would return to the office. And as we know that is what happened."

"Alvin, I owe you big time. We need to get Jamie as soon as possible. We will leave this man on the floor and lock the office door."

I asked Alvin for one of the guns. He looked at me and said, "Phil, you can barely stand let alone handle a gun."

"I need to have a gun. We can't give the man holding Jamie any slack. We will have to kill him." He handed me a gun.

We led the two men to Alvin's car.

As we were returning to the building I knew the Franklin Feeling had pulled me though another very bad day. I am a living example of how the spirits and kinship of former shipmates assist you through life.

When we arrived in front of the building I let the two men out of the car. Alvin looked at them and said, "Both of you can live or die today. If you want to live just do what I ask."

When we reached the door Alvin moved up and opened it. There wasn't anyone in the big room.

I told Alvin to take the hall to the right and I will lead these two men down the hall to the left. As I walked down the hall there were gunshots. I moved toward the noise.

Then I saw Jamie bent over sick at her stomach. She had her hands over her ears. As she straightened up and wiped her face she came running toward me. As she approached me she reached out and threw her arms around me and began crying. The pain from my ribs took my breath but her holding me made the pain secondary.

She kissed me and then in a broken voice she said, "I was terrified of that man. He said some very sickening things to me. I didn't think I would ever see you again. I was terrified."

"Are you all right?"

"Yes but I was scared to death."

"Did he hurt you?"

"No. But I think he would have if you had been gone much longer?"

At that moment I realized she was still hugging me. With her body next to mine I was spellbound. I could still taste her kiss. What felt the best was she had come to me for comfort. What a moment.

Alvin came walking down the hall. He said, "It's over."

"Alvin, I would like to believe that but I am not sure it will ever be over." Alvin approached the two men and removed their handcuffs. He took their guns and pushed them out the door.

"Alvin, we'll need a ride home."

Jamie eased her grip on me and said, "Phil, you need to see a doctor." I told her I wanted to clean up first.

Then I remembered the body on the office floor. I turned to Alvin and said, "Drop me off at the office before you take Jamie home.

"Sure I remember we have some unfinished business there."

I stepped into the backseat with Jamie. She sat with her arms around me all the way to the office. I knew it was going to be very lonely when she let go.

When we arrived at the office I pushed her hair out of her eyes and said, "I am sorry for getting you involved in this horrible mess." She placed her hands on my cheeks and said, "Aren't we okay now?"

"Yes. We are okay now." Alvin helped me out of the car and then drove Jamie home.

I very slowly walked up the stairs to the office. I knew we had to clean up the blood. I found a bucket and some rags in the janitor's storage room. I placed water in the bucket and began cleaning up the mess.

It was getting dark. I thought we could load this body in my car and take it to the building where Goldtooth's body is. My mouth was hurting. I needed to see a doctor but I had to take care of this mess first.

I had the blood cleaned up by the time Alvin returned. I asked him what he thought about taking this body to the building where Goldtooth's body is. Alvin said, "We can stop there. If there isn't anyone around we'll leave it there."

"Alvin, I am not sure how much help I will be moving this man's body down stairs. But I'll try.

My car is a four-door so we'll load the body in it." I handed Alvin my keys. He pulled my car directly below the stairs leading into my office. Then we lifted the body and carried it to my car. Alvin told me to get in the car and wait for him. He returned to my office.

In a few minutes he returned to the car. He said, "I wanted to make sure that there wasn't a blood trail down the stairs." Alvin returned to Goldtooth's resting place. When we arrived Alvin entered and determined no one was home except for Goldtooth's body. We carried the other body in and laid it next to Mr. Goldtooth.

Alvin had all three guns. He went into the bathroom and cleaned each gun. Then he threw the guns on the floor and we left.

As we were driving to my place I told Alvin about the part of the day he had missed. All he said was, "Phil, you are very lucky to be alive."

When we arrived at my place I thanked Alvin for everything. He said, "Phil, some of these places look like they need a doctor's touch."

"Alvin, I don't think I will be able to shift gears. If I go to a doctor you'll have to drive."

"Clean up and I'll take you to the doctor."

"Alvin I think this has been the longest day of my life. I know it is the most painful."

On the way to the emergency room I asked Alvin if Jamie had seen him kill Mr. Goldtooth. He indicated she had. I said, "That had to be horrible for her."

"To tell you the truth I think she was rather glad it happened. She was afraid of that man."

Once we arrived at the hospital emergency room I asked Alvin if he would call Mr. Wilson and asked him if we can delay the start of his case until Monday. "I think Jamie and I need some healing time."

Alvin indicated he would take care of that.

He asked me if I had Jamie's home telephone number. I said, "Yes." He said that he would call her and tell her to rest and return to the office on Monday morning.

A nurse escorted me to a room to await the doctor. In a few minutes a doctor arrived. He took one look at me and said, "Do you feel as bad as you look?"

"Yes sir I do. I hurt all over."

He looked at my face and the back of my head. He indicated the back of my head would require stitches and so would my mouth. He x-rayed my ribs. He indicated that I had two badly bruised ribs on my left side. I would have to be taped up and he suggested I stay off my feet for several days if possible. He stitched my head and mouth. Then he taped my ribs. He gave me a prescription for pain medicine.

He provided me the name of a dentist and recommended I contact him soon. I thanked him.

When I returned to the emergency room lobby I found Alvin sleeping like a baby.

I felt bad about waking him. I touched his arm. He looked up at me and said, "It has been a long day. I spoke to Jamie. She said she was doing fine. I told her she should be careful whom she told about her day. She was glad to hear you were seeing a doctor. She is worried about you."

"Alvin, thank you for everything you have done for me today."

He asked, "Do you have any prescriptions that we should fill before I take you home?"

"Yes I have one for pain."

"Alvin, I bet you regret getting involved with me?"

"Phil, when we have some time I will tell you about some of my scary cases and how others helped me. This type of situation comes with the job. We both will live to fight another day. Let's get you home."

I was glad to be home but I was also afraid to be here. The lock on my front door was torn off. The door would close but not lock. I took two of the pain pills and went to bed.

• • •

It was three-thirty Thursday afternoon when I awoke. I hurt everywhere. I stood and made my way to the kitchen and took two of the pain pills. I didn't know pain until the water hit my mouth. The pain almost made me sick. I sat down.

My head was splitting and my ribs were pounding against my skin. Mixed in with the pounding and the pain was a feeling of hunger. I stood again. This time the standing wasn't as bad.

I dressed and walked to a neighborhood restaurant. I ordered soup. I asked the waitress to put the soup in a glass and bring me a straw. After the second glass of soup I could tell this would work. I drank four glasses.

Then I returned to my place and called the dentist that was recommended by the emergency room doctor. There was no answer. Then I looked at the clock. It was five minutes after five p.m. I had forgotten that it was three thirty when I woke up. Oh will I well try tomorrow. My mouth and my head were beginning to hurt again. I knew it was time to take two more pain pills.

My telephone began to ring. I very slowly reached for it. When I placed it to my ear I heard Alvin's voice, "How are you Phil?"

"I am doing pretty good." I told him how long I had slept and what I had eaten.

Alvin told me he had talked with Mr. Wilson and his Vice President will call me Monday with the delivery schedules. Alvin indicated that he had spoken to Jamie and she is doing fine. "She asked about you. She wanted to call you but she didn't want to wake you."

I asked him if he had read a newspaper today. He indicated he had but there wasn't anything that indicated our friends had been found.

"There was one item in the newspaper that will interest you. You know that Andre you told me about?"

"Sure."

"The DA wants to speak with him again but he cannot be located. The article indicated he hadn't been seen at his residence for several days. That was determined by the mail in his mailbox. The police have issued a warrant for his arrest. The DA has a witness that places Andre with Eugene Ransom the night he was murdered." I found that very interesting.

Andre must have headed for the hills when the police released him. I thanked Alvin for the update.

I decided to call Jamie. I dialed her number. When she answered I told her it was Mr. Toothless and asked her how she was doing. Her answer came without the normal sound of happiness. She told me she was fine.

I told her I was feeling better. I told her of my diet of soup through a straw. Again no laugh.

Jamie may have said she is doing fine but I can tell by the sound she wasn't. I told her that I wanted to apologize for putting her through this horrible situation. I am very sorry. "Phil you told me that I am your partner. Is that true?"

"It sure is lady."

"Then you don't have to apologize for anything."

She indicated she was glad that I had called and asked me to take it easy this weekend.

"I am looking forward to seeing you Monday." I ended the call.

I wanted to read the newspaper but driving was out of the question. Maybe there will be a newspaper at the restaurant.

I returned to the restaurant. I asked a waitress if there was a newspaper. She walked to the counter and handed it to me. She asked, "Is there anything I can get you?"

"Coffee."

"Do you want a straw?"

As I looked at her I realized it was the waitress that had brought me my soup earlier. I said, "Yes. Thanks for asking."

I found the article about Andre. It stated that a witness had come forward placing Andre with Ransom on the night of his murder. It didn't give the name of the witness. I wondered why Andre wasn't involved with my visit to the warehouse?

The Eugene Ransom murder made me think of Lisa Coleman. I hoped that she was recovering from our near death experience. I wondered if this witness was Lisa? I will keep my eyes on the newspaper and see if her name appears.

I placed the straw in the coffee and took a drink. It hurt but it tasted so good. I waved at the waitress. When she approached my booth I said, "Would you bring me a glass of tomato soup?"

She said, "Coming right up." The soup was good.

On my walk home I realized how lucky I am. Even if I walk funny and look funny I am still alive.

Once home I took more pain medicine and went to bed.

Friday morning reminded me how stiff and sore I was. The doctor told me I could bathe but no showers.

So once I had taken a bath and dressed I called the dentist to schedule an appointment. I told his assistant that I had lost two front teeth and needed to see a dentist. She indicated that the dentist could see me at two thirty p.m. today. I ended the call and began to think about food.

I thought what type of breakfast food could I drink through a straw? I wasn't fond of oatmeal but with enough milk in it I felt it would come through a straw.

Since my side was still very tender I decided not to drive to the Coffee Shop. I returned to the restaurant I visited yesterday. There wasn't a newsstand between my place and the restaurant but maybe there would be a paper at the restaurant.

As I entered the restaurant I spotted a newspaper on the counter. I picked it up on my way to a booth. I ordered coffee and oatmeal. I asked the waitress to bring me a glass of milk and a straw. While I waited for my breakfast I began reviewing the newspaper.

There wasn't anything in the paper about bodies being found in a building near Harlem. There wasn't anything new about the Ransom murder either.

When breakfast came I cooled the oatmeal with milk. My mouth is very sensitive to both hot and cold. I was hungry and the oatmeal tasted good. By the time I finished the oatmeal my coffee was cool enough to drink. Breakfast was very good.

Breakfast had given me energy. I decided to see if my ribs would let me drive.

I opened the door and slid into the driver's seat. I placed my left foot on the clutch and shifted through the gears. There wasn't much pain. The real test would be to start the car and pull into traffic.

My first turn was to the right. Dang that turn took my breath but I made it. Now I had to try a left turn. To my surprise the left turn hurt less. At least I could stand to shift gears. So driving is possible. I returned to my parking place.

Then I returned home and called Alvin. Mary answered and indicated Alvin was out on the office. I asked her to advise him that Phil had called and he is doing much better today. She indicated that she would convey my message as soon as Alvin returned to the office. I kicked my shoes off and stretched out on my bed.

At twelve thirty I sat up in bed and realized that I was hungry again. This liquid diet requires me to eat more than three times a day. I was feeling better with each meal.

I arrived at the dentist's office at two fifteen p.m. and after filling out some forms I was taken to a dental chair to wait for the dentist. As the dentist looked in my mouth he said, "Mister you have some real damage." He asked me how it happened.

"Well let's say it was a dispute and I lost."

The dentist didn't say a word.

He continued looking in my mouth. After a few minutes he asked, "Do you have any pain medicine?"

"Yes the doctor that placed the stitches in my mouth provided me with a prescription."

"Right now there isn't anything I can do. We need to let your mouth heal. When the stitches are removed make an appointment with me and we will look at making you a partial or a fixed bridge. Just continue taking your pain medicine as needed." I thanked the dentist and walked to the front desk to pay for my visit.

After leaving the dentist office I was hungry again. This trip to the restaurant was daring. I asked for some crackers. I broke them up and placed them in the soup. I chewed them very slowly.

On my walk home I remembered that I still couldn't lock my front door. When I arrived at home I called a furniture repairman to see if he could fix or replace my door. He indicated he would come by my place today and take a look at what repairs would be needed. I provided him my address.

When the repairman arrived it didn't take him long to determine that I would needed a new door. He told me he would return at eight a.m. tomorrow and replace the door. So one more night without being able to lock my door.

Saturday morning my alarm clock began its tortuous yell at seven thirty a.m. I wanted to be awake and dressed when the repairman arrived. Once my door was replaced I drove to the office. The men that took

Jamie had ransacked the office. I didn't want Jamie to be faced with the mess on Monday morning.

It was eleven a.m. when I arrived at the office. I entered and began picking things up. Since all of the drawers from my desk were on the floor I looked to see if my gun was still taped to the underside of my desk just above the top drawer. It was. I decided to put it in my coat pocket. I didn't want to take another beating without at least trying to protect myself. Once the office was straightened up I left.

The rest of Saturday and Sunday were just easy going. I just ate and rested.

24

I arrived at the office at seven a.m. this beautiful Monday morning. I was happy to return to work but I found it difficult to believe that this was the last day of 1945.

I placed a call to Alvin and informed him I was in the office and ready for the day. He reminded me that Ms. Donna Turner from Executive Furniture would be calling me this morning.

I informed him I was looking forward to getting the case underway. Alvin suggested that we establish a day and time each week to discuss the Executive Furniture case. I suggested each Wednesday at seven a.m. Alvin agreed."

It was seven fifty a.m. when Jamie entered the office. As usual she had a smile on the face but the smile wasn't as radiant as normal.

I stood and said, "Good Morning. Are you ready for the day?"

"Phil I am ready for the day. Are you?"

"I'm fine but it will be awhile before I do much smiling."

I told Jamie that a lady by the name of Donna Turner would be calling me. She will be our initial contact on the Executive Furniture case. I returned to my office.

The telephone rang and my intercom buzzed. Jamie said, "It's Ms. Turner." I thanked her and answered the telephone.

Ms. Turner and I exchanged greetings. Then she said, "I have our delivery schedule and the names of the employees that will be making the deliveries to the hotel over the next four days." I thanked her and jotted down the information.

As I reviewed the delivery schedule I noticed that the same two men were making all of the deliveries to the hotel in question. I asked, "Why are the same two men used to make all of the deliveries to the hotel in question?"

"I'm not sure. Is that important?"

"It may be. If the same two men are always assigned to make deliveries to the Hotel it probably means that the warehouse supervisor is involved. As you provide me additional schedules we will see if the same men are involved."

I asked Ms. Turner for the address of the Manhattan warehouse where the furniture is loaded and the address of the hotel the furniture is taken to. Then I asked her if this was the only crew working out of this warehouse. She said, "No."

"How will I identify this crew?"

"Truck Number Five is assigned to them. You will see the Number Five on both doors of the truck." I thanked her for the information and advised her I would begin surveillance this afternoon. I walked out to Jamie's desk and told her that I was going to lunch. Then after lunch I am going to begin my surveillance of Mr. Wilson's deliverymen.

I grabbed my coat and walked out into the bitter cold day.

When I arrived at the restaurant it was crowded. I ordered tomato soup and crackers. Today my mouth wasn't as sensitive to the hot soup. I downed three large glasses.

After lunch I drove to the Executive Furniture warehouse. I circled the warehouse and located the loading dock. I parked across the street from the loading dock. I had a good view of the trucks being loaded. I located truck number five. It was parked in the loading area.

I looked at my watch. It was twelve-fifteen p.m. I figured the deliverymen were at lunch. There was a magazine shop a few feet from where I parked. I walked into it and purchased a newspaper. I returned to my car and began scanning the paper.

The first article that caught my eye was the article that indicated the police were still looking for Andre Zgersky. It indicated that he was now considered a very important individual in the Eugene Ransom murder case.

The next article indicated that the Organized Crime Unit was investigating a double homicide. Two men without any identification were found dead side by side in a building in Harlem. This building is linked to the Russian Mafia. The killings did not appear to be mob hits. It was thought one of the bodies had been murdered elsewhere and deposited in the building. Tom Watson and his team are smart policemen.

I looked up from the newspaper and saw a man stepping into truck number five. He began backing up to the loading dock. I couldn't see his face from my position. I wish I had my binoculars. Once the truck was against the loading dock the driver stepped out and was met by another man. They stood beside the truck talking. Men on the loading dock began loading their truck.

Once the truck was loaded the driver and his helper entered the truck and drove off. I started my car and pulled in behind them.

I stayed a few car links behind them. As they turned the corner it was clear that we were not going in the direction of the Hotel. They were heading in the opposite direction. After a few miles it appeared they were driving toward the New Jersey state line.

Just across the New Jersey line they turned into a commercial warehouse complex. Since there wasn't much traffic I dropped off.

I saw the truck stop at the loading dock of Building Number 39.

The driver stepped out of the truck and entered the warehouse. Then the loading dock doors opened. I had to stay so far away I could not see inside the building. The men that opened the loading dock doors began to unload the truck.

Once the truck was unloaded the men began reloading the truck with the imitation furniture. So the switch takes place here.

Minutes after the truck was reloaded it drove away. They have this unloading and reloading down to a science. I am impressed. The truck then drove directly to the Hotel's loading dock. A crew at the Hotel unloaded the furniture. The two deliverymen had a good racket. All they do is drive. They don't have to lay a finger on the loading or unloading. Once the truck was unloaded it returned to the Executive Furniture warehouse.

I returned to my parking spot across the street from the loading dock. I could see truck number five backing up to the loading dock again.

It wasn't long before the truck drove off again. It was the same routine. They drove directly to the New Jersey Warehouse Complex stopping at Warehouse Building Number 39.

Again the same procedure was followed. This time I parked and walked to the Hotel loading dock.

Once the truck was unloaded I watched the hotel workmen begin to move the furniture onto the hotel receiving area. There was a side door into the hotel receiving area so I opened it and walked in.

The furniture that had just been delivered was being moved with a forklift to an elevator. I watched the elevator stop on the sixteenth floor. I walked through the receiving area and located a hotel elevator. When I arrived on the sixteenth floor I could see the men unloading the sofa into room sixteen forty-two. That was all I needed to know for now.

I left the Hotel and found a telephone. I called Jamie and asked how her day has been. She indicated it has been a good day. Franklin called and wants to speak with you. I immediately felt my coat packet to make sure my gun was there. Then I thanked Jamie for the information and ended the call.

I then placed a call to Ms. Turner. A lady by the name of Paula answered the telephone. I introduced myself and asked to speak to Ms. Turner. Paula informed me that she wouldn't be available until five p.m. I told her I would call her at five fifteen. Paula indicated that she would convey my message.

I had no desire to call Franklin. As far as I am concerned he doesn't have anything to say to me that would make me feel better. I put Franklin's message in the trash and went to dinner.

I finished drinking my meal at five fifteen p.m. I found a telephone and called Ms. Turner. Paula answered again. I said, "This Phil Storm, is Ms. Turner available?"

"Yes I will transfer the call." Ms. Turner came on the line.

After exchanging greetings I told her I would like to meet with her. She asked me where I was. I told her I was at a restaurant close to her Mid-Town Warehouse. She asked if I could come to her office now. I said, "Yes." She asked me if I knew the location of their Corporate Offices. "Yes." She then indicated that her office was on the sixth floor and she would meet me at the elevator. "I'm on my way."

When I exited the elevator on the sixth floor there was the desk where the lady sat that had given me Mr. Johnson's name. Since it was after five p.m. no one was there.

I sat down. In a few minutes a very pretty young lady came walking up to me. She said, "Are you Mr. Storm?"

"Yes, I'm Phil Storm."

"Phil, I am Donna Turner." We exchanged greetings.

She said, "Phil, I apologize for asking but what happened to you?" I stood there thinking what would be a good answer to that question. I decided something close to the truth was in order.

"Ms. Turner, sometimes the investigation business isn't a friendly profession."

I felt that would end the question. But to my surprise she said, "You mean someone involved in one of your cases did that?"

"It would be better to say someone my case involved me with did this."

I could tell by looking that she wanted to hear more but since she only thought it and didn't say it I kept my mouth closed.

As we walked to her office I thought she has made the big time very young. I would say she is in her late twenties or thirty at the oldest and already a Vice President. She was a very pretty lady. She had long hair that touched her shoulders. I would say its color is strawberry blonde. She's about five foot three inches tall and thin. Maybe a hundred pounds. It looked like she had green eyes but I only had a quick glance. I was to busy keeping all of her in focus to be positive about her eye color.

As we entered her office she said, "Phil, please call me Donna."

"Thank you."

"How long have you been in the investigation field?"

"Only a short time but I had a great teacher."

"Let me tell you what I have so far. I watched truck number five being loaded. Then the truck drove directly to a commercial storage complex in New Jersey. Once there several men unloaded your furniture and loaded the imitation furniture. Then your deliverymen drove directly to your client's Hotel and his employees unloaded it. Then your deliverymen returned to your warehouse. The second trip was exactly the same.

Donna said, "What's next?"

"I need to continue watching your deliverymen for a few more days to determine if their routine is the same everyday. Eventually I will need to get inside the New Jersey warehouse. I will also need to determine who is leasing the space in the New Jersey warehouse.

"I need to determine the origin of the imitation merchandise. I may need to get some background on the Hotel owner. What can you tell me about him?"

"I don't know much about him."

"We can leave it that way for now. I will let you know if I need detailed information on him."

"What can I do to assist you?"

"Show me how I determine the differences between your furniture and the imitation furniture?"

"We can drive to our Midtown warehouse's showroom now if you would like. I can show you how to determine the differences in the furniture."

"Are you sure you want to do it now? It's six-thirty p.m. on New Year's Eve."

"Now is as good a time as any. The showroom is closed and there is only a small crew that works in the evenings."

"It's fine with me."

"I'll drive. There's no reason to take two cars." I agreed.

On the drive to the warehouse Donna told me her life's story. She was a talker. She was born and raised in Westchester County, New York. She attended college in Vermont. When she completed college she returned to New York and began her career with Executive Furniture and Accessories as a Salesperson. Then as she put it, the rest is history.

I asked her what type of man Mr. Wilson was to work for. She told me he was very nice and very smart. She had known him most of her live. He and his wife are close friends of my parents. There it is again. Money loves money or those with money stick together. She loved talking so much that she never once asked me about my life and I was glad.

When we arrived at the warehouse she unlocked the showroom. She began showing me the fine details of their furniture and how to recognize the imitation furniture. I was sure that I could recognize the differences. We exited the showroom.

On the return trip to her office she continued the story of her life, both business and personal. She was a very pretty lady but her non-stop talking was a turn off to me.

As I stepped out of Donna's car I said, "Will you update Mr. Wilson on the case?"

"Yes." I could tell that was very important to her.

This had been a full day. My ribs were beginning to hurt. I drove home to take some pain medicine and go to bed. I plan on spending New Year's Eve sound asleep if possible.

It was nice to wake up without any agenda. Here it was January 1st, 1946 and I was feeling better. Tuesday was a very pleasant day of rest.

My friend the alarm clock let me know it was six a.m. on what I hoped would be a good Wednesday. I am beginning to dislike baths. Hopefully it won't be much longer before my body is back to normal.

As I was dressing it dawned on me that today was Wednesday. Alvin would be expecting my call at seven a.m. I looked at my watch. It was six twenty-five a.m.

As I was unlocking the office door I could hear my telephone ringing. I picked up the receiver and said, "Phil Storm here."

I heard the man say, "This is Franklin."

"What's up Franklin?"

"Are you alright?"

"If you mean am I still alive then yes I am. But if you notice two of my teeth missing, some banged up ribs and other cuts and bruises then I am not alright."

"So it was you?"

"Is this crap ever going to end? I am sick and tired of having to look over my shoulder. How many more times am I going to have to tell unpleasant people that I do not have what they think I have?"

Franklin then said, "It's over. I know I told you that once before but believe me it is over. Phil, my boss has personally put the word out. No more bad times for you?"

"Why doesn't that make me feel better? Who is this boss?"

"That information you don't need. The only information you do need is that you will not have any further trouble from your international friends."

I should say thanks and end the call but I couldn't resist.

"Thanks Franklin but only time will tell if your word is good."

Franklin yelled into the telephone, "Never doubt my word. It's over because I say it is over." I wasn't going to argue with him anymore.

"I'm sorry Franklin. Thanks for the information." He slammed the telephone in my ear. I probably shouldn't completely alienate him. My big mouth is too big sometimes.

And I was hoping for a good Wednesday. I dialed Alvin's telephone number. I was a little late because of Franklin. On the third ring Alvin answered his telephone. He said, "I was beginning to think you weren't going to call."

"I'm sorry but as soon as I walked into my office my telephone was ringing. It was the man I told you about that works for Filpatrick. I'll give you that update later.

"Now about the case. I know where the furniture exchange is taking place and who is making the physical switch on Wilson's side. Since

Wilson's deliverymen are so calm when the make their switch I am sure their boss is involved. I'm going to the Warehouse Complex and try to determine who is leasing Building Number 39. Ms. Turner gave me a demonstration of the difference between Wilson's furniture and the imitation furniture. It is easy to tell the difference. She indicated she would update Mr. Wilson."

"It all sounds good. Please be careful while trying to obtain the name of the lessee. Banged up ribs will hurt worse if they are beat on a second time."

"I am not going to do anything dumb. I'll be careful and I will keep you informed." We ended our call.

As I was making coffee I thought of Ragsdale. "Would he know about the furniture switch? He seems to be in the know about a lot of Filpatrick's illegal activities. I decided not to involve him. He might get me beat on again.

My thoughts were interrupted when I looked up and saw Jamie walking into the office.

I said, "Jamie, come here and tell me about your Christmas." She walked into my office and sat down. "It was very nice. I stayed at my sister's house on Christmas Eve. We made cookies, listened to Christmas music on the radio and had a nice dinner. The girls were so full of excitement it was ten thirty that evening before the last one fell a sleep. The girls woke up at five fifteen Christmas morning. We opened presents and had breakfast. They spent the rest of the day playing with their new toys. It was a very good Christmas." I told her about my day with my mom and her friends. It was nice to sit and talk. Then Jamie returned to her desk.

Christmas seemed so long ago. I hope that 1946 will be a good year for my business and my personal life. It was time to determine what is in New Jersey Warehouse Building 39 and who is leasing it.

25

As I walked out of the office I noticed the wind gusts were very strong. The temperature was frigid and it was beginning to snow. The day had a hint of darkness. The clouds were dark gray with a hint of black. It wasn't going to be a fun day to be out and about.

When I arrived at the warehouse complex I drove in front of Warehouse Building Number 39. There wasn't any noticeable activity. There was one car parked in front. I began to drive through the complex looking for address information.

I noticed a man stepping out of a car in front of one of the buildings. I pulled up beside him and rolled my window down and asked, "Sir if I wanted to lease one of these buildings who would I contact?"

The man turned towards me and said, "If you will come into my office I'll tell you. I am freezing out here."

I parked and walked into Warehouse Building Number 22. The man was waiting just inside the door. I followed him to his office. He took off his coat and hat then asked me if I had time for coffee. I said, "No, but thank you." He handed me a piece of paper and said, "This is the Leasing Company's name, address and telephone number." I thanked him and returned to car.

Once in my car I thought, "Now, that I have the name and address of the leasing company how can I determine the name of the person leasing Warehouse Building Number 39? I decided to drive to the Leasing Company and tell them I was interested in leasing some warehouse space and see where that leads me.

I arrived at the Leasing Company at eleven fifteen a.m. It was beginning to snow hard. The way the wind was blowing it appeared that we might have a great northerner. I didn't look forward to that.

Once in the building there was a sign directing me to the leasing office. I walked up to a young man sitting behind a desk. He looked up and asked, "Is there something I can assist you with today?"

"I am interested in leasing some warehouse space. Is there space available at this address? I handed him the note I had received from the man in Warehouse Building Number 22. He looked at the address and then he pulled a plat out of a filing cabinet and spread it across his desk.

The plat indicated that each warehouse building had a total storage capacity of 25,000 square feet. I noticed each warehouse building had four loading docks and four offices. The offices and loading docks were located in the front, back and on each side. I asked the young man, "Can you lease just part of a building?"

"Yes, we can separate each building into four sections of approximately 6,000 square feet each. Each section has its own loading dock and office area. How much storage space do you need?"

"6,000 square feet would be sufficient."

Then he pulled out another plat that had all of the warehouse buildings on it. Some buildings were all the same color and other buildings were in four different colors. I focused on Building Number 39. It was all in gray. I asked, "What indicates vacant space?"

"The white areas are vacant space." I looked at the plat. I could see that Building Number 36 and 37 had vacant space.

After another look at the plat I noticed that Building Number 49 sat behind 39 and it had open space on the end right across from Building Number 39. "What is the monthly fee for 6,000 square feet?"

The young man said, "The lease fee is three hundred dollars a month. You will have to pay the first month and last month rental fee when you sign a lease."

"Can I see the space?"

The young man said, "Of course. Is there a particular space you would like to see?"

"Let's look at the space in Building Number 49."

"When would you like to look at the space?"

"Could we drive over there today?" The young man looked at me and I knew he didn't want to get out in the cold weather.

"Hold the space in Building Number 49. I will contact the people I am in business with and give them the location and price of the space. If they agree with the location and price I will return to look at the space and sign a lease agreement."

The young man looked relieved. He said, "That will be acceptable."

I asked the young man if there was a telephone I could use to call Manhattan. He took me to an empty office.

"How do I pay you for a long distance call?"

"This telephone is used by customers or potential customers at no charge." I thanked him and dialed the office.

It was one fifteen p.m. I said, "Jamie, it is Phil. What's going on?"

"All is quiet."

"Is it snowing in the City?"

"It is coming down very hard."

"Lock the door and go home. We'll start again tomorrow. I am in New Jersey and I do not plan on returning to the office today." Jamie thanked me and I ended the call.

I returned to the young man's office and thanked him. Once outside I could tell the snow was falling much harder and with the gusting wind it was becoming more difficult to see. The flakes were large and wet. I disliked driving in this weather. The closer I came to the City the slower the traffic was moving. I decided to drive home, park my car and walk to my neighborhood restaurant for dinner.

When walking to the restaurant I noticed that the snow was beginning to stick to the sidewalks. Once I entered the restaurant I noticed a newspaper lying on the front counter. I was the only customer in the restaurant so I sat at the counter. I placed my order and began reading the newspaper.

On page three there was an article titled, "Two men found murdered in building in Harlem connected to Russian mob." It went on to say that information from an informant linked these men to Andre Zgersky. Zgersky is still missing. The article continued, "The police are certain that further discussions with Mr. Zgersky will provide the information needed to solve the murders of these two men and Mr. Eugene Ransom." Where is old Andre? I like it that he is getting the blame for our murders. What is one or two more murder charges?

I finished my meal and walked home. It was three p.m. as I approached my place.

I decided to call Mr. Wilson and let him know I might have to spend six hundred dollars to rent storage space. I dialed the telephone number he had provided. A woman answered and said, "This is Ms. Wolf speaking."

"This is Phil Storm is Mr. Wilson available?'

"One moment please."

Then I heard Mr. Wilson say, "Hello, Mr. Storm what can I do for you today?" I asked him if Ms. Turner had discussed my findings with him. He said, "Yes." I told him about my visit to the Warehouse Complex in New Jersey and the possibility of having to lease some space so I could have a valid reason for being in the area. I advised him of the rental cost. He said, "If needed Mr. Storm lease the space. He then asked if he needed to provide the rental fees today." I said, "No." We ended our call.

I made some coffee and sat down. I decided to return to the Warehouse Leasing Office tomorrow and lease the warehouse space in building 49. I took some pain medicine and stretched out across my bed.

The next morning I arrived at the office at seven fifty-five. Jamie was already there and the coffee was ready. We exchanged greetings. I poured my coffee and told her that later in the morning I would be returning to New Jersey. I explained why.

Once I had finished my coffee I picked up my coat and walked to my car. My first stop was the bank to withdraw the six hundred dollars for the lease fee. Then on to New Jersey. The roads had frozen dry over night. So traffic was moving normally.

I arrived at the leasing office at eleven thirty a. m. I walked into the leasing office and noticed that the young man from yesterday was not there.

I saw a lady and asked her where he was. She indicated that he was not in the office today and asked if she could assist me. I informed her that I wanted to lease some space in Warehouse Building Number 39.

She said, "Just a minute," and walked off. When she returned she looked confused.

"Sir, it appears that Building Number 39 is totally full. Are you sure it was Building Number 39?"

"Well there was room in it yesterday?"

The lady laid down a file and said, "This building is currently leased by the Exquisite Furniture Company."

Then it hit me, I was looking at space in Building Number 49. But here is what I need lying before me. I said, "Madam, before you put this file up would you check Building Number 49 for space?" She walked off.

I picked up a pencil and began writing. "The Exquisite Furniture Company, Tegucigalpa, Honduras." Then under the address information of the Exquisite Furniture Company was the name of the lease-holder. The name was Daniel Sundman. There was a Manhattan address. I wrote down the address. What a great mistake I made. I stumbled into a gold mine.

When the lady returned I said, "Madam, I am so sorry. It was Building Number 49."

"Well I was very confused." Then she confirmed that there was one 6,000 square foot section available in Building Number 49.

"I'll take it." She gave me a lease agreement to complete.

Once I had completed the paperwork I handed her the six hundred dollars. She asked, "Sir, do you need someone to show you around the building?"

I said, "No, just give me the key. If I have any questions I will get in touch with you." She handed me the keys and thanked me for my business. I thanked her and asked if I could use their telephone. She showed me to the telephone.

I called Jamie. When she came on the line I said, "I want you do some legwork for me. Take the name Daniel Sundman at this address in Manhattan and see what information you can retrieve. I will be back in the office later this afternoon." I ended the call.

With the lessee information plus the name and address of the Furniture company I was making headway with the case. I drove to the Warehouse Complex. As I approached Building Number 39 delivery truck number five was unloading. I took my note pad out of the glove compartment and noted the day and time of the truck's visit to Building Number 39.

As I entered Building Number 49 I could see that 6,000 square feet was a lot of storage space and the gang using Building Number 39 was using the whole 25,000 square feet. That would hold a lot of furniture. I walked across the road and tried to open the backdoor of Building Number 39. It was locked. I then approached the door on the near side of the building and it was also locked. These men are careful.

I decided to return to Manhattan and determine what information Jamie had uncovered on Mr. Sundman.

On my return trip to the office I stopped for lunch. My mouth was feeling a lot better. I thought when I finished my soup I would try a piece of pie, especially if they had chocolate, lemon or pumpkin. I could leave the crust. Lunch was very good and so was the two pieces of chocolate pie.

It was two thirty p.m. when I entered the office. It was good to see Jamie's smile. It looked normal. She asked me, "Would you like for me to make some coffee?"

"Sure. Then come tell me about Mr. Sundman."

When Jamie entered my office she said, "I have been able to determine that Daniel Sundman is an Attorney. He has a reputation for being one of the best attorneys in the City on international law. His specialty is in import/export law.

"He prepares many contracts between International Companies and the United States government. These contracts ensure that when companies ship merchandise into the United States they have complied with all United States import laws.

I said, "Jamie, I am very impressed. This is great. How did you do it so fast?"

"Once I discovered he was an attorney I called Alvin's friend at the newspaper and he was familiar with the name. He said Mr. Sundman has a lot of personal dealings with the New York City Port Authority.

Because of his involvement with international businesses and his advising the Port Authority of new international businesses shipping merchandise into the New York port it makes their merchandise entry and unloading more timely."

I told Jamie that Mr. Sundman was the name on the lease for the storage space in the New Jersey Warehouse. "Jamie, I have one more item I want you to check for me. See what you can find out about this company. I handed her the note where I had written down the name of Exquisite Furniture Company, Tegucigalpa, Honduras. Maybe you can contact the long distance operator and get a telephone number for the company. Then make it a part of our file.

As I swirled in my chair I began reviewing all of the pieces of the case. A New York City Attorney is the leaseholder of warehouse space for a company with the mailing address in Honduras. Why is this attorney involved with renting storage space? What is in the storage area besides furniture? Who hired the men I see unloading and reloading the furniture at Building 39?

As I sat and thought about Mr. Sundman I would bet my fee that this attorney is involved in criminal activity. Who does that sound like? The Scumbag, (King) Leo Filpatrick! It seems like a very clumsy way to acquire high quality furniture.

I thought what is driving this furniture exchange? Is it a plot to ruin Mr. Wilson?

If there is any merit to this line of thought this furniture switch could send financial damage throughout the ColeMark Corporation. But the question remains, why? There has to be something else in play.

Is the answer about the imitation furniture or the individuals exchanging it? I decided to call Donna Turner and determine how far along the furniture replacement is.

She indicated the furniture replacement was fifty percent complete.

I asked her what floors have the imitation furniture. "The first twenty floors are complete. Why is that important?"

"I am going to check into the Hotel tonight and I want to be sure I am assigned a room with the imitation furniture. I am still trying to determine if the crime is the furniture exchange for the resale value of the quality furniture, or if a more subtle crime is being committed."

When I arrived at the Hotel I asked for a room on one of the lower floors. My request was honored. I was assigned room 702. I took my suitcase to my room and then decided to see what was being served in the Hotel restaurant.

As I scanned the Hotel menu I noticed they were serving meatloaf. I thought meatloaf should be easy to chew so I ordered it. It was delicious. I am finally able to eat solid food again.

With dinner completed I returned to my room to begin my examination of the furniture. I began my search with the small sofa. I removed the cushion. Even with sore ribs the sofa could be lifted with ease. I found nothing unusual. I moved to the bed. The bed's footboard was easy to lift. It seemed to be made out of a lighter weight metal that what I lifted in the Executive Showroom. It was the type of headboard and footboard that had metal caps on the top of the bedposts. You could lift the caps off. So I removed the caps and looked inside. The bedposts were hollow and empty.

I turned the end tables upside down and looked under them. Again nothing. I took the drawers out of the chest of drawers and looked in the chest. Again nothing. There wasn't anything else to look in. I put the bed back together and lay across it.

I sat there thinking where do I go from here? I came to the conclusion I had to gain access to the contents of Warehouse Building 39. I will do that Monday. I dozed off.

When I woke up Saturday morning I had a feeling of loss. It took a moment to remember where I was. I noticed my room had a radio. So, I found some music and began preparing for the day.

It was eight thirty a.m. when I arrived at home. I checked the mail and found a note from the Emergency Room Doctor indicating it was time to remove the stitches in my mouth. I'll work that in the first part of next week. Saturday and Sunday were relaxing days. It was very cold with snow flurries.

26

Monday morning was a cold gray day. The temperature was near zero and the wind was gusting. The groan my car made when I hit the ignition made me wonder if it is going to start. Thankfully it did.

I arrived at the office at seven thirty-five a.m. Once the coffee began perking I sat down and documented all of the money I had spent over the last two weeks. I would have Jamie forward this information to Miss Emerald. Since Mr. Wilson didn't pay any of his fees in advance I needed to be able to submit an accurate expense report to Alvin.

Jamie entered the office at eight a.m. on the nose. Her nose was bright red. We greeted each other and I placed the completed paperwork on her desk. I informed her that I was returning to New Jersey later in the morning.

I gave Jamie the letter from my doctor and asked her to make me an appointment for Tuesday or Wednesday. She asked, "What is this appointment for?" Just like a woman; must know the details.

"It is time for the stitches in my mouth to be removed."

With a smile on my face I reached for my coat and walked to my car. It will be a cold drive today.

I entered the Warehouse Complex and parked in front of Building Number 49. I walked across the road and tried to open the back door of Building 39. It was locked. I walked to the door to my right and to my left. They were both locked. I decided to try the front door.

The front door was a solid metal door. I opened it gently and stepped inside. There wasn't anyone in the office area. I entered. Then I opened the side door that lead to the warehouse floor.

With that door open I could hear men talking. The noise was coming from my right. I eased out of the door until four men were in sight. They were sitting on boxes eating. I looked to my left and determined if I walked with my back against the wall I could walk to the front of the warehouse without being seen. Once there I could hide behind boxes as I moved to the opposite side of the warehouse.

Once on the other side I began looking at the boxes. These boxes contained the furniture from Mr. Wilson's store. Each box had Broyhill Furniture's name on it. Then I saw a piece of paper taped to the boxes. It read; "For pick up by Turner Freight Line." So, Mr. Wilson's furniture is being moved somewhere by Turner Freight Lines? I needed to have Jamie look into Turner Freight Lines.

I moved from the front to the back of the warehouse and then I crossed to the other side. The furniture on this side had labels that read, "Exquisite Furniture" with a Tegucigalpa, Honduras address. The "To" address read "Fast Jersey Storage Co." with the Warehouse Complex address, Weehawken, New Jersey.

While I was checking the labels I saw three men entering the warehouse from the office area. Two of the men wore suits and the other one had on coveralls. The four warehouse workers approached them and they began talking. I could not hear their conversation.

After a few minutes the four warehouse workers began uncrating the furniture from Honduras. Since I was on that side of the warehouse I had to move to the very rear of the building. After a few minutes the workers quit uncrating boxes and returned to the front of the warehouse.

In a few minutes the man in the coveralls approached the uncrated furniture. He had an empty sack in one hand and a small tool in the other hand. The tool was a straight piece of metal about six inches long with a slight curve on one end. He began taking the covers off of the headboards. Then with the cover off he placed his tool inside the opening. He worked the tool around and around. Then he pulled it up toward himself. On the end of the tool was a bag about twelve inches long. He placed that bag into his large sack. He continued the same procedure with each headboard and footboard that had been uncrated. His sack was getting full of these smaller bags. As he approached the last two headboards I froze. The man in the overalls was Walter Ragsdale. I knew at that moment that Filpatrick was involved. I couldn't understand why they did not open all of the crates of furniture. I knew once Ragsdale and the other two men left the warehouse I would see what was in those bags. Ragsdale took the large sack to the two men.

Then Ragsdale picked up another empty sack and a box cutter. He then walked back to the open furniture. He reached out and took a sofa cushion and cut across it. Then he reached into the cushion and removed several items shaped like bricks. He put the bricks in his sack.

He continued until he had removed all of the bricks from the uncrated sofa cushions. He then took that sack to the men in suits.

One of the men in the suits talked with the four workmen for several minutes then Ragsdale and the two men left the warehouse.

Once the three men were gone the four workers began picking up the cushions that had been cut open. Then they began cutting several large boxes open. Those boxes were full of cushions. They replaced the damaged cushions with new ones. I had to see what was in the furniture. I began pulling on one end of a crate that contained a headboard. I pulled the headboard out of the box. I removed the cap and put my fingers inside but I could not reach the bag. I turned the headboard upside down and gently hit it against the floor.

After the third try I was able to reach the bag and remove it. It was full of gems of every size and color. If I wasn't an honest man I would take a few of these and disappear. I did take one gem of each color to show Alvin. Then I replaced the bag and gently placed the crate back together.

I heard the loading dock doors open. I walked closer to the front of the warehouse. It was the truck from Wilson's warehouse. I have to attempt to slip into the office because once Mr. Wilson's furniture is unloaded the furniture they will reload is in front of me.

As the workers brought the first furniture into the warehouse I positioned myself to make a leap for the office door. I knew it would hurt but I had to move. As they returned to the loading dock I made my move. I was successful.

Once in the office I hoped that no one would enter the office until the delivery truck left. I listened as the loading continued. Then all was quiet and I could hear the truck engine start. Then I heard the loading dock doors beginning to close. I opened the front door and returned to my car.

Once in my car I removed the stones I had placed in my pocket. They were beautiful. So it appears that Wilson's furniture is being re-sold once delivered to a new location by Turner Freight Lines. I now know that Filpatrick is involved.

I returned to the office at four p.m. After greeting Jamie I walked into my office and called Alvin. He wasn't available. I asked Mary to have him return my call or meet me at Tennyson's after five thirty.

When I had completed my call I asked Jamie to find the address and telephone number of Turner Freight Lines.

Jamie buzzed me. When I picked up the telephone she indicated that the Company is located in Manhattan." I asked her to call the company and determine who is in charge.

In a few minutes Jamie buzzed me and told me Mr. Morse Turner is the owner. "Is there anything else you need to know about Mr. Turner?"

"Would you see if you could find a home address for him?"

"I'm on it."

I began reviewing the newspaper again. Jamie walked into my office and handed me a piece of paper with the home address and telephone number of Morse Turner. It was in the same area where Donna told me she lived. Could this be Donna's father?

By five thirty p.m. Alvin had not returned my telephone call. I decided to drive to Tennyson's before going to dinner.

When I arrived at Tennyson's the regulars were all in their places. I sat at the bar and ordered a drink. As I sat drinking I thought, "What is my next move?" I need to protect my client as much as possible. That includes preventing Turner Freight Lines from removing his furniture from the warehouse and stopping any more imitation furniture from being taken to the Hotel. Since I am not a cop I don't need to worry about the contraband.

After a short stop at Tennyson's it was on to dinner then home.

Before going to bed I changed my alarm. I wanted to be in the office by seven a.m. to call Alvin.

It was seven ten a.m. when I arrived at the office. I laid my newspaper on my desk and started the coffee. While it was perking I dialed Alvin's number. On the third ring I heard, "Alvin Wilson speaking."

"Good morning Alvin this is Phil. I want to provide you an update on our case. Yesterday I hit a triple.

I was able to get inside of the New Jersey warehouse yesterday. I found that Wilson's furniture is still in the warehouse but it is to be rerouted via Turner Freight Line in Manhattan. I do not know when Turner Freight is to pick up the furniture or where they are to deliver it.

"I was able to determine what this exchange of furniture is all about. The furniture from Honduras if full of un-mounted gems and some packets in the form of bricks. I do not know what the bricks are but I would guess they are drugs. The bricks are inside the sofa cushions.

"I also determined that Filpatrick's organization is involved. Some men came to the warehouse yesterday and removed the contraband from some of the furniture while I was hiding in the warehouse. I know the man that was removing the contraband. I have used him to gain access into Filpatrick's illegal businesses."

I took a minute to inhale.

Alvin said, "It sounds like you had a very busy day."

"I did."

"Where do we go from here?"

"I think it's time to update Mr. Wilson and get his input."

"You're right. I will call him today and schedule the meeting. Once I have the time and date of the meeting I will contact you."

I returned to reading the paper but I could not stay focused on it. All I could think about was how Filpatrick's men were going to get away with their crime.

My thoughts were interrupted when I saw my everyday beauty come through the door. She took her coat off and walked into my office. Her wonderful smile made my day. I could tell she had something to say.

I said, "Jamie, what's on your mind?"

She began laughing. "Last night I was with some girlfriends. One of the girls brought a friend that I didn't know. When I was introduced to her she asked me where I worked. I told her I worked for a private detective."

She looked at me and said, "You work for a shamus? Phil, did you know you were a shamus?"

"I've heard the expression. A police officer called Abe a shamus once." So Jamie has a new word. "If you call me a shamus it better be Mr. Shamus." She laughed her way back to her desk.

I placed my call to Mr. Wilson. He was not available but the lady that answered his telephone said she would have him return my call.

Jamie returned to my office, "I forgot to tell you but you have a doctor's appointment tomorrow at nine a. m." I thanked her and she returned to her desk.

By nine a.m. I had read the newspaper twice.

As I sat at my desk nearly asleep my intercom buzzed. Jamie said, "It's Mr. Wilson."

"Good Morning." He returned the greeting.

"Alvin and I want to schedule a meeting to provide you an update on the case and to get your thoughts on the next move."

"Can you meet me at six p.m. this evening at the 42nd Street Men's Club?"

"Yes. We will see you then."

On my return trip from the coffeepot I asked Jamie to call Alvin and advise him we have a meeting with Mr. Wilson at six p.m. this evening at the 42nd Street Men's Club.

As I returned to my desk I began thinking about Turner Freight Lines. I removed the business card that Donna Turner had given me. On the back she had written her home telephone number. I buzzed Jamie and asked her to come into my office. When she entered I said, "Take this business card and see what home address is listed for this name and number?" Jamie returned to her desk.

In a few minutes she buzzed me and said, "Phil, the name on the card isn't in the directory but the telephone number is. It is listed under the name, Morse Turner."

So Donna's father is involved. I hope his Company's involvement is perfectly honest.

Now with the meeting of the minds set for six p.m. I was out of work for the day. I opened the newspaper and turned to the section that listed movies. I looked down the list of movies. One of the movie theatres in the Bronx was showing a Humphrey Bogart movie by the name *Conflict*. I walked out to Jamie's desk and said, "I will be out of the office for awhile but I will return before five p.m." I put on my coat and left.

I was back in the office by four o'clock. Jamie was still reading her book. I said, "I'll be here until five p.m. why don't you take off early?"

"Thanks."

She cleaned out the coffeepot and washed my cup. Then she put her coat on and left.

I arrived at the 42nd Street Men's Club at five forty-five p.m. There was a man sitting behind a desk in the lobby. I approached him and said, "I have a meeting with Mr. Terrence Wilson here at six p.m." He stood and escorted me to a waiting area. I will return for you when Mr. Wilson arrives. Then I remembered Alvin. There will be another man by the name of Alvin Wilson joining us also. The man thanked me and walked off. He had no sooner left until he returned with Alvin.

At six p.m. the man returned and asked us to follow him. He escorted us into another room where Mr. Wilson was awaiting. We exchanged greetings.

I started the meeting by telling Mr. Wilson I have been able to determine that the imitation furniture is coming from a company in Honduras. This company is using the furniture to smuggle in contraband.

They are placing un-mounted gems in the bedposts and some type of contraband in the sofa cushions. That contraband is probably drugs. The furniture is being delivered from the New York City harbor directly to the New Jersey warehouse where the contraband is being removed. Then that furniture is exchanged and delivered to your client.

I was able to enter the warehouse. I found your furniture there with a hand written label on each piece indicating that this furniture is to be picked up by Turner Freight Lines.

I have not contacted Turner Freight to determine when they are scheduled to remove your furniture or where they are to deliver it. Mr. Wilson interrupted me by saying, "I will handle Turner Freight."

I continued, "Your deliverymen drive your furniture directly to the New Jersey warehouse. So the employee that schedules deliveries is in on the exchange. We can close the case by removing your furniture from the New Jersey warehouse and terminating your two deliverymen and their supervisor."

Mr. Wilson looked frustrated. He said, "Will we have any trouble removing my furniture?"

"Yes. The reason I say that is there are four warehouse workers that will call their boss as soon as we begin removing your furniture. If there were just a few pieces of furniture, which we could remove in one trip that would eliminate the trouble. The four workers are not the problem it is their employer, Leo Filpatrick."

Mr. Wilson sat in his chair silently for several minutes. You could see his mind working. You could tell by his expression that he knew Filpatrick. He said, "If you can develop a plan to retrieve my furniture I will take care of my internal employees and we will close this case."

I said, "Your furniture covers about 12,000 square feet. I have no idea how many truckloads that would be or the amount of time it would take to move it?"

Mr. Wilson said, "Even if I provided all of my trucks it would take more than one trip. Plus I have no space to store that much furniture."

"Mr. Wilson, you have 6,000 square feet of storage space just behind the warehouse where your furniture is currently stored. If there were forklifts and drivers available we could remove your furniture from Warehouse Building 39 and place it in the space I have leased in Building 49. Could this be accomplished in one day?"

"Sure that is doable."

"The furniture would have to be stacked two high. Would that be a problem?"

"No."

"Do you think this is an option?"

"Yes."

"If we could procure enough forklifts in advance we could store them in our warehouse space. Then we could begin removing and re-stacking your furniture the following day."

"I can procure forklifts and drivers."

"Sir they should not be your employees."

"I realize that. I know a company that will provide the men and equipment.

"You confirm a day that the equipment can be moved to our ware-house and I will be there to unlock it. Then the day we move it I will determine a way to entertain the four workmen. Alvin I will need you that day."

Alvin said, "I will make myself available.

Mr. Wilson said, "The day we schedule the furniture move I will discontinue delivering furniture to the hotel."

"It sounds like a plan. Sir let me know how soon we can move forward. I must tell you Mr. Wilson I really don't know if all of your furniture is still in the warehouse or if Turner Freight has moved some of it."

"I will contact Turner Freight and determine if they have moved any of it."

"Mr. Wilson, when we begin moving your furniture it won't take long before Filpatrick becomes aware of it. That could mean real trouble for you."

"I will be fine. I am not taking any of Filpatrick's contraband. All he will have to do is find another source to sell his furniture through. In New York City it will not be difficult."

"Mr. Wilson, doesn't it bother you that Filpatrick will go unpunished?"

"I need to worry about my business. There will always be a Filpatrick no matter what I do. Phil, I worry about you and Alvin. Filpatrick's workers will see your faces. Unless you kill them they will be able to tell Filpatrick who spoiled his setup."

Crap, I hadn't considered that. I cannot stand another beating.

"Sir I will determine a way to hide my identity but I don't know how to remove my name from leasing document."

"As long as Filpatrick's men do not see where we store the furniture there shouldn't be any reason for them to check with the leasing company. I will make you a deal. I will leave the furniture in storage for sixty days. By that time there shouldn't be any eyes on the Warehouse Complex. What do you think?"

"I like that. Mr. Wilson, what about the employees that will be moving the furniture?"

"These men are day laborers. They couldn't care less why the furniture is being moved from one warehouse to another. They just want a day's pay."

"It sounds like we have a plan. Any comment or questions, Alvin?"

"No."

"Sir, we will wait to hear from you."

"Phil, make sure you are available over the next few days."

"I will."

We ended the meeting.

I asked Alvin if he would like to drop by Tennyson's for a drink. "I'll follow you." Once we had a few drinks we went to dinner. It is enjoyable having a friend to talk with.

27

I awoke feeling well rested. My ribs were feeling much better. Being able to get a good night's sleep makes all the difference.

I knew it was cold outside when I looked out my only window and saw that ice had formed on it. Today is another gray day.

As I stepped outside the strong north wind chilled me all the way to the bone. I drove to the Newsstand and then to the Coffee Shop. It was a little after seven a.m. when I arrived at the office. The old gray dreary day made the office feel cold. I started the coffee. I decided to leave my coat on until the room warmed.

I settled into my chair and began reading the paper. As I turned to the society page there was Mrs. Robinson's picture. So she is still out and about doing her good deeds.

My telephone ringing made me jerk. The jerk sent a cold chill all through me. Mr. Wilson was on the telephone. He said, "Good Morning." Then he informed me that he had stopped the hotel deliveries for the next five days.

He also indicated he had contacted the "Daily Equipment Rental." They will have forklifts available tomorrow and they will deliver them. They will also provide the drivers. "Phil is that satisfactory?"

I replied, "It is quicker than I expected but yes it is acceptable."

"Here is the telephone number of the Rental store. You will need to contact the store and provide them the address of the warehouse and the delivery time. We will need to provide the Company twenty-four hour notice regarding the employees. I told Mr. Wilson I would handle the details. We ended our call.

So we will have the equipment arrive tomorrow. Delivering the equipment should not raise any concerns or questions. I do need to think about how I am going to entertain the four workmen the following day. They will have to be removed from the warehouse complex before any of the furniture moving can begin.

Jamie had arrived while I was talking with Mr. Wilson. On my way to fill my coffee cup we exchanged Good Mornings and I updated her on my schedule.

I contacted the Rental Company. Mr. Wilson had told me to speak to the owner, Charles Seat. After the normal conversation with a receptionist Mr. Seat came on the line. We established the time for his company to deliver the forklifts and the employees.

My next concern is determining how to remove the four warehouse workers from the warehouse. Then once removed what will I do with them? I decided to rent a large truck and lock the workers in the back of it.

Next how do I keep the warehouse workers from identifying me? I opened the yellow pages to the heading "Costumes." I can rent a mask that covers my entire head. That will hide my identity. The mask and my gun would get their attention. Then once locked in the truck where will I take them? I have time to determine that.

It was time for me to leave for my doctor's appointment. I put on my coat, waved at Jamie and made my way to the doctor's office.

The doctor's appointment didn't take long. He told me that the healing was going well. He wanted to leave the stitches in my head for another week. He removed the stitches from my mouth.

When I arrived at the Costume Shop I was amazed at the number of costumes. I selected the plainest mask they had. I didn't want anything creepy just one that would hide my identity.

On my return drive to the office I realized I didn't know what time the warehouse workers in Building 39 reported to work. I need to determine that. I will drive to the Warehouse Complex early tomorrow morning. I will park where I can see Building 39 without raising suspicion.

As I walked into the office Jamie informed me that Alvin had called. He wants to meet you at Tennyson's tonight at six thirty.

That is good; it will provide me time to discuss my plan with him. I enjoy working with Alvin and I hope it will continue. It feels good having another brain to bounce ideas off of.

I entered Tennyson's at five thirty p.m. I realized it was an hour before Alvin was to arrive but I needed a drink. I reminded myself that I had to wake up early tomorrow morning so I needed to go easy on the drinks.

At six fifteen Alvin came through the door. I couldn't believe it. This was one of those nights that the owner of Tennyson's was re-citing his poetry.

All of the locals were into his reading. They seemed to hang on each word. Alvin came over and asked, "What's going on?" I told him about the owner. He laughed. After a few silly moments the owner and his poetry were silent.

I reviewed my plan with Alvin. We had a couple of drinks then we departed Tennyson's to have dinner.

Once we finished eating we went our separate ways.

Once at home I set the alarm at four thirty a.m. I decided that five thirty a.m. would be early enough to arrive at the Warehouse Complex.

Man my alarm clock is loud. The world is so dark at four thirty a.m. After my shower I drove to the Coffee Shop. I knew the Newsstand would not have the morning papers until six a.m. My stomach wasn't ready for food. I drank a cup of coffee and asked the waitress for a to-go cup. It was so cold outside.

As I returned to my car I noticed it was beginning to snow. As it fell on my windshield it was more like very fine sleet. I hoped it wouldn't stick to the roadways. I arrived at the Warehouse Complex at five twenty a.m.

I looked around the complex trying to decide on a parking place that would allow me to see Building 39 without being noticed. I saw a truck parked in front of Building 37. By parking next to it I wouldn't be noticeable as the workers approached Building 39.

My coffee was gone. All I had to do was sit and listen to my knees chatter together. It was cold.

At five fifty-five a.m. a car pulled up. Four men stepped out of the car. They entered the warehouse. That is all I need to know. Now it is time to find a restaurant and have breakfast.

After a good breakfast and a gallon of coffee it was time to call Mr. Seat. I informed him I was at the warehouse and he could begin the delivery of the forklifts. I returned to the Warehouse Complex and parked in front of Building 49. Once in the office I noticed a heater. In a few minutes the office was warm.

After awhile there was a knock on the outside door. I opened it and found three men looking at me. I asked them in and introduced myself. One of the men indicated he was the driver and the other two men were his helpers. I gave the driver the key to the warehouse and asked if he would be driving the workers tomorrow. He said, "Yes." I told him to keep the key and I would retrieve it tomorrow. I turned the heater off and returned to the office.

When I arrived I asked Jamie to call Mary. I needed to talk with Alvin. In just a minute Jamie buzzed me. She said, "Alvin is on the line." I provided him an update of tomorrow's schedule. When I ended that telephone conversation I updated Jamie on tomorrows plan or at least as much as she needed to know. Then I left the office.

I drove to the Rental Store and rented the truck I would need tomorrow.

I drove the truck to Tennyson's; I needed a drink. While driving this big boy I found myself getting a little sick at my stomach. To be honest I was worried. I had never taken men prisoners before let alone keep them captive for hours. What if they take off when I point a gun at them? Then what do I do? I didn't want to think about that because I would have to stop them.

While sitting in Tennyson's I did begin to calm down. I knew it was the alcohol. Alvin came walking in. I said, "I am surprised to see you."

He ordered a drink and said, "I wanted to discuss tomorrow in person."

"Are you nervous about tomorrow?"

"Yes, I am always nervous about days like tomorrow. Things can go wrong which will make us do things we don't want to do."

"That makes two of us. It's nice to have company." After a few drinks we drove to dinner.

Once at home I couldn't push tomorrow out of my mind. I poured myself a strong drink. The next thing I remembered was the alarm going off. I looked at the clock. It was four thirty a.m. I was still fully dressed.

I undressed and stepped into the shower. After dressing I drove to the Coffee Shop. Coffee sounded good but breakfast didn't. I just wanted this day over.

As I drove away from the Coffee Shop I was noticeably shaking. I felt the gun in my coat pocket. When I arrived at the Warehouse Complex I parked beside the same truck I had parked beside yesterday. It was five thirty a.m. The excitement was about to begin. Crap! Maybe I need a new line of work.

28

At five fifty five a.m. a car pulled up in front of Building 39. Four men stepped out of it and entered the warehouse. Here I go.

I backed my truck up to the loading dock door and stepped out. I unlocked the back doors of the truck and swung them open. At that moment there wasn't anything in sight but a cold dark morning. I placed the mask over my head and entered the warehouse.

The four warehouse workers were sitting on boxes talking. I made my appearance, mask on and gun drawn. All four of the men stood. I said, "Get in single file and walk toward me." Without a word they lined up. The man in the front of the line said, "What is going on here?"

"There will be time for that later. I walked them outside and into the truck. I said, "If you sit down and be good you will live to see tomorrow." I then locked the rear doors and drove away. It was six a.m.

I hoped Alvin and the forklift drivers would be on time. They were to arrive at the Warehouse at six fifteen a.m.

I exited the Warehouse Complex and pulled onto the highway. The morning traffic was very heavy. After a few miles I exited the highway and drove through a business complex. Then I returned to the highway and drove back to the Warehouse Complex. As I was approaching Building 49 I could see that the men were at work. I pulled up and parked in front of Building 49.

I exited my truck. Alvin was in the office. He said, "The furniture moving is going faster that I had anticipated. I would say they will be finished in three to four hours. Why don't you just leave your four workers where they are? They can't get out."

"Okay. I'll go out and turn the truck's engine off."

When I returned to the truck I asked, "You men in there, can you hear me?"

I heard, "Ya! We can hear you."

"We are going to be parked here for awhile. Just stay where you are and be quiet. You are being watched."

I returned to the office area. Alvin said, "Come look at our progress?" We walked out into the warehouse. The workers were doing a very good job. We returned to the office.

After awhile Alvin said, "Phil, maybe I am wrong about leaving the men parked in front. I'm afraid they can hear the forklifts and they may determine they are in the warehouse complex. We don't want to provide them any help in determining where they are."

"Okay. I'll give them a ride." I returned to the truck and drove off.

I entered the highway and drove for thirty miles. I then left the highway and pulled into a truck stop parking lot. I went inside for a coffee to go. I kept watching the time. The minutes were going so slow. I left the truck stop and returned to the Warehouse Complex. When I pulled into the Complex I could see that the first of the forklifts was being loaded. I stopped the truck and watched.

Once the truck loaded with forklifts drove away I pulled up in front of Warehouse Building 49. I went in. Alvin met me. He said, "The Rental Store is sending two trucks on their return trip. That will allow them to load the remaining forklifts and men. Then Phil, this will be over."

I said, "Alvin, that is music to my ears. I'm going to drive my passengers into the City and then return to the warehouse. I will see you then. You are going to ride with me on the return trip aren't you?"

"Yes." I returned to the truck.

As I was driving into the City I realized that this day hasn't been as bad as I thought it would be.

The weather was still cold. The sky was colorless. As I approached the Warehouse Complex I could see that the loading dock doors on Building 49 were closed and all was quiet. I entered the office. Alvin was standing there. He said, "Phil, let's give your guests another short ride and then we can return them to their warehouse."

"That is music to my ears." We walked out of the warehouse and drove off. In about twenty minutes we began the return trip to the warehouse.

As we approached Building 39 my stomach began to roll. There were three cars in front of Building 39. The loading dock doors were open and there were several men in the empty side of the warehouse. I looked at Alvin and said, "What now?" He said, "Just exit the Complex."

"Alvin, there is a Truck Stop a few miles from here. Do you think we can drop them off there?"

Without a word Alvin picked up a piece of rope that was lying in the floorboard between his feet. The rope was at least fifteen feet long. He said, "Phil, pull into the truck stop." I pulled in.

"Just a minute. I want to find the restrooms. I thought what a time for a break."

He returned to the truck and said, "Phil, the restrooms are on the outer wall of the truck stop. I am going to put on your mask and march the men into the restroom. Once in there I will tie their hands and then bring the rope through the door and tie it to the outside doorknob. It will take them several minutes to untie themselves. By that time we will be gone.

"Sir, you are a genius."

So Alvin placed the mask over his head and marched the four men into the restroom. In a few minutes he returned to the truck and said, "Let's get out of here."

We drove in silence. When we looked at each other we knew our day was finished. I couldn't help but think about the men standing on the loading dock of Building 39. I am sure Filpatrick has been notified by now. I don't think he will let someone walk away with the front he is using to move his contraband without a fight. He will know Wilson is involved. Wilson didn't seem worried about Filpatrick.

I drove to the Rental Store to drop off the truck and pay the rental fee. Once that was complete I asked Alvin, "Where to?"

"Let's get a drink and talk about what else you and I can do together. It will be nice having a partner."

"Alvin, I agree with that. Is Tennyson's okay?"

"Yes that's fine."

I smiled. Tomorrow is a new day, hopefully a new case and a new partner. The World does seem to be at peace tonight.

The next morning I woke up with a smile. I was on top of the world. I started the coffee and stepped into the shower. I couldn't imagine anything but a good day.

I filled my coffee cup and continued to prepare for the day. With the day before me I began my daily routine; with the newspaper in hand it was on to breakfast. Yesterday is history. I had never been so stressed in my life. I can't explain how I hurt. My stomach muscles were so hard that my sore ribs began to vibrate. My head pounded and there were times my eyes would not focus. But today is a new day and I feel relaxed.

While I waited for my breakfast I began reading the newspaper. There weren't any articles of interest, which was good. I didn't want anything to impact my day.

After breakfast I decided that this PI needs a change of scenery. I have money so I am going to plan a vacation.

I want to go to Florida or some Caribbean Island. I would close the office, give Jamie some paid time off and enjoy myself for a few days. I wish I could take her with me but I didn't think that would work.

I arrived at the office at seven thirty-five a.m. I started the coffee and walked into my office I will contact a travel agent to assist me in planning my vacation. I was still in dreamland when Jamie came walking through the office door.

She walked into my office and asked me about yesterday? I hadn't told her much about the Wilson case. All she knew about yesterday was that I would be out of the office all day. I told her the day went well. She indicated that her day was quiet.

As we were talking the telephone began to ring. Jamie walked to her desk to answer it. She buzzed me and said, "It's Miss Donna Turner."

I picked up the receiver and said, "Good morning Donna."

"Phil, our Midtown warehouse is on fire."

"The warehouse is burning now?"

"Yes. Mr. Wilson has gone to the warehouse. He thinks this is in retaliation of yesterday. He wants to talk with you. Can you drive to our warehouse?"

"Yes Donna, I will leave immediately."

Once I ended the call I walked to Jamie's desk and told her I had to leave the office. I briefly explained why.

As I entered Manhattan I could see the fire. I had to park several blocks away and walk to the warehouse. It took me fifteen minutes to find a police officer that would allow me into the area where Mr. Wilson was.

When I approached Mr. Wilson he was talking with another man. He looked my way and raised his hand, as to say just a minute.

When he ended his conversation with the man he turned to me and said, "You and Alvin did a fine job yesterday but it appears that Filpatrick is one up today." I was a bit surprised by his comment. I remembered the comment he made a few days earlier; "I need to worry about my business. There will always be a Filpatrick no matter what I do."

So now Filpatrick has gone too far and retribution is the business of the day. I asked Mr. Wilson, "What can I do sir?"

"I want you to drive to the New Jersey warehouse and determine if the imitation furniture is still there. Once you make that determination call me and I will give you more instructions. If Alvin is available take him with you. I will explain later."

"Is there anything else I need to know?"

"No."

I left the warehouse and located a telephone. Once Alvin answered the telephone I explained my morning. We agreed to meet at a restaurant that was on the way to the New Jersey warehouse.

I was drinking coffee when Alvin arrived. I finished my coffee and we began our drove to the warehouse complex.

Mr. Wilson's orders were very clear. All we need to accomplish is determine that the furniture is still in the Warehouse 39. As we approached the warehouse we could see two cars in front of it.

One of the cars was the workers car. I wasn't sure about the other car. Since I was in the warehouse when Ragsdale and his two friends arrived I did not see the car they arrived in.

I asked Alvin if he would enter the warehouse. I told him if I enter the warehouse and Ragsdale is in there he will recognize me. Alvin indicated he had no problem entering the warehouse.

I parked on the far end of Building 39. Alvin stepped out of the car and began walking toward the warehouse. All of a sudden he returned to the car. I asked, "What is going on?"

"There are three trucks and one car pulling up to the loading dock door."

"We need to find a telephone and call Mr. Wilson."

We drove to the restaurant where I had eaten breakfast two days earlier and called Mr. Wilson. When he answered the telephone I told him what we had found.

He told me that he has some men on the way and they will take charge of the warehouse situation.

"Phil, you and Alvin have accomplished great things this week but these men will end this situation. You and Alvin can return to the City. The burning of my warehouse guaranteed Mr. Filpatrick that he will lose his contraband, his furniture and a few of his men. Then and only then will we be even." At that time Mr. Wilson ended our call.

I turned to Alvin and said, "I'll explain as we return to the Warehouse Complex."

"I conveyed Mr. Wilson's comments to Alvin. Alvin looked at me and said, "There doesn't seem to be any difference between the good and the bad once the situation reaches a certain point. Neither Wilson or Filpatrick will win the war but they each may win a battle or two."

I told Alvin we were going to see this job through to the end even if Mr. Wilson told me to return to the City.

When we entered the Warehouse Complex I parked across from Building 39's loading dock. We could see three cars and three trucks in front of Building 39. One of the trucks had backed up to the loading dock door. No one was in sight.

Then three more cars drove up. The lead car parked directly in front of the truck backed up to the loading dock. The second and third cars parked behind the other parked cars. That prevented the cars from being able to leave. Then four men stepped out of each of the cars. All of them were armed.

They entered the building.

In just seconds we began hearing gunfire. After several minutes the gunfire ended.

I looked at Alvin and said, "I'm going in the building." Alvin stepped out of the car also.

We walked up to the loading dock door. I began banging on it. The door began to open slightly and I could see a man with a rifle.

I said, "This man and I are working for Mr. Wilson. We are the ones that made him aware that his furniture was in this building."

"What do you want?"

"I want to see this case to the end."

The man said, "Come in. There isn't much to see. We are removing the contraband. All of Filpatick's men are dead." I began looking at the dead men and there he was. Ole Walter Ragsdale. I don't imagine he ever drew very many winning hands.

Seeing Ragsdale dead made me remember Johnson. He wanted me to provide him the outcome of the Robinson/Coleman case. I will call him tomorrow and provide him the same conclusion given to Mr. Coleman. I will not tell him of Mary's dirty little secret. That will stay with me.

I turned to Alvin and said, "I'm ready to return to the City, are you?"

"Yes I'm ready." We returned to our car. As we began our drive into the City we talked about working together on future cases. It was good to have a seasoned investigator as a partner and a friend.

Once I dropped Alvin off my mind drifted back to planning the vacation that would take me away from the business, the City, the trash that litters the backrooms of our society, and their dirty little secrets.